W9-BZJ-244

RED PALMS

RED PALMS

CARA HAYCAK

WENDY
LAMB
BOOKS

Published by
Wendy Lamb Books
an imprint of
Random House Children's Books
a division of Random House, Inc.
New York

Wendy Lamb Books is a trademark of Random House, Inc.

"Your Breast Is Enough" from *Twenty Love Poems and a Song of Despair* by Pablo
Neruda, translated by W. S. Merwin, copyright © 1969 by W. S. Merwin. Used by
permission of Viking Penguin, a division of Penguin Group (USA) Inc.

Visit us on the Web! www.randomhouse.com/teens
Educators and librarians, for a variety of teaching tools, visit us at
www.randomhouse.com/teachers

Library of Congress Cataloging-in-Publication Data
Haycak, Cara.
Red palms / Cara Haycak.
p. cm.
Summary: When fourteen-year-old Benita's wealthy family goes bankrupt as a result of
the Depression, they go from their luxurious life in Guayaquil, Ecuador, to a primitive
island, with the wild scheme of starting a coconut plantation.
ISBN 0-385-74648-2 (trade) — ISBN 0-385-90883-0 (lib. bdg.) [1. Island life—
Ecuador—Fiction. 2. Farm life—Ecuador—Fiction. 3. Indians of South America—
Ecuador—Fiction. 4. Ecuador—History—1895–1944—Fiction.] I. Title.
PZ7 .H3138785Red 2004
[Fic]—dc22
2003026104

Printed in the United States of America

November 2004

10 9 8 7 6 5 4 3 2 1

BVG

For my mother, Maria Azucena,
WHO GAVE ME EVERYTHING

PART 1

PRIVILEGED
BAGGAGE

CHAPTER

1

My fourteenth birthday was the most important day of my life. Not because of the party. We didn't have enough money for one. And not because it meant I was no longer a child. On that special day my father announced to my family that he'd sold our beautiful house on the Malecón Simon Bolivar in Guayaquil, the city in Ecuador where we lived, and we were moving to an island called Paíta.

He gathered us in the parlor, me and my mother and three younger brothers. Papa wasn't a man who knew how to smile, and the grin that cracked his face was evidence that what he was telling us was making him completely miserable.

"Do we have to go?" I asked Papa.

Mama answered for him. "Your father has lost his business, Benita, and we have no money left and no choice."

"But what will we do on an island? I mean, how will we live?" I asked.

"Well, that's the good news," my father said, and he looked

at each one of us. "I have a plan to make us rich. With the money we'll make on the sale of this house, I'm going to start a coconut plantation."

"So . . . you're going to sell coconuts for a living?" I asked.

"No, no. Just the oil. That's what the big American corporations want. They put it in all their products—soaps, detergents, creams."

Next he told us that Paíta was a three-hour boat ride from Guayaquil. The middle of nowhere.

"I can see farms from the window of my classroom," I said. "Why should we go so far away?"

"Because I've been generously given a parcel of land there to tend. Ten acres plus a house."

"Who would give this to you?"

"My mother," said Mama.

"Grandmother Tita?" She hated my father, and I couldn't imagine that she'd give him anything good.

José, who was twelve, and the oldest of my three brothers, asked, "Who lives on Paíta?"

Papa told him, "Fishermen."

"Are there other children there?" asked Alfonse, who was only eight.

"Probably," Papa said.

Manuel, who would soon turn eleven, asked, "Will I like living on the island?"

"That's up to you." And that was the last thing Papa would say about it.

Before bad luck hit us like a tidal wave, my father had owned a business exporting handmade French lace all over the world—even all the way to America. The women there loved it so much they used it to decorate the backs and arms of their chairs and sofas. In Ecuador, women used my father's lace sparingly—to accent the wrists and necks of their best clothing. But every woman who saw my father's lace wanted it, and that made us very wealthy. Papa bought the grand house we were now leaving. I had clothes and hats and shoes and gold jewelry, my brothers had toys and bicycles and Mama had as many servants as she needed, as well as paintings, rugs and silver to match any of the finest homes in the city.

According to all the newspapers and the radio, the Great Depression of 1929 was what had brought on our bad luck. As my father explained it, everyone became poor at once, not just where we lived, but in America too, and there was no one left to buy his lace—not when they were struggling to put food on the table.

I learned a new word then. Bankrupt. This became the subject of every dinnertime conversation in our house, but never once did I hear my parents say it had happened to us. But less than a year later, we began losing things. The chambermaid who washed our laundry and made our beds was the first to go, then the two who cleaned the floors and polished all the silver. A few weeks later Papa said, "Silver always gets a fair price," when he took a piece from the breakfront to market. Not too long after that, most of the silver was gone and we didn't need anyone to care for it anyway.

In a few short months many of my school friends' families lost everything too. And even some of our neighbors on the wealthy Malecón had let out their rooms to help with expenses, turning their mansions into tenements. Overnight, torn sheets and stained underwear were flying out their windows to dry. Strange people shouted at each other in the street as if they were performing in an opera, and they didn't seem to care what time of the day or night it was.

"That won't be our fate," my father declared during supper

4

one night. "We will not be a part of this unstoppable degradation of our society."

But I never thought that meant we'd move away. I couldn't tell him so, but I thought we were making a huge mistake. Even though we had no money anymore, we still had one of the nicest houses in the city. I was going to miss it. Everything in the house was touched by a special beauty that was just like a magic trick, always taking me by surprise. I knew every flowering mildew stain in the plaster. I loved where the tile floor was worn smooth, like river rock. In our courtyard, the palm trees reached to the sky, and in the morning we woke to the sweet songs of brightly colored birds that perched upon those wide green leaves. My favorite room was the library, with its tall windows and heavy wooden cabinets that held my father's rare book collections. And most of all, I loved spending time there with him. He would read to me, or I to him, and we would completely lose track of time.

The day after Papa's Paíta announcement, we started packing, right in the middle of a terrible heat wave. Even though it was only late April, already the cobblestone streets outside our windows cooked up a bad smell—a mix of rotten vegetables left unsold after market day, dirty cooking oil tossed out into the gutter, cat pee. Mama kept the front door closed so that the stink wouldn't enter our courtyard, but it didn't help. I said, "Mama, why don't we take out a bucket of water and wash down our sidewalk?"

"And let the neighbors know we've become scullery maids? I'd rather die." To keep the smell at bay, she shuttered up the entire house. The hot air turned still and thick—it hung around like an unwanted guest, impossible to ignore.

It was my job to label all our ugly moving crates. I had a huge rubber stamp with my family's name on it and a spongy pad soaked in red ink. I stamped the top, front and sides of each one. My palms were stained red for days, but every one of the crates bore our name like a banner: MARIAH.

We spent hours arguing over what to bring to Paíta.

My brothers packed their train set, but Mama took it out to make more room for their clothes. When they complained to Papa, he told them, "You won't be able to play with it. There's no electricity where we're going, boys." That news was so shocking that they gave up fighting for their most precious toy.

"How will we see at night?" asked Alfonse. He'd been born cross-eyed, so his eyesight was very bad even in the daytime.

"We'll use oil lamps and candles," Papa said.

"How will we listen to the radio?" asked Manuel. Every night we listened to the Voice of the Andes, a religious station Papa favored. None of us cared much for it, but we liked hearing a voice coming out of a box.

"We'll get a radio that runs on batteries," said Papa.

José, who was serious and responsible, asked, "How will we keep our food from going bad without an icebox?"

"We won't need to store food; we'll gather it fresh every day."

"What do you mean, Papa?"

"We'll eat the things that grow on trees, and vegetables right out of the ground. And there are chickens and pigs on the island. You won't starve, son."

My father was able to put my brothers at ease. But the more Mama heard about island life, the less she seemed willing to accept it. Papa told her not to bother packing our fancy china or the silver tea service that had been in her family for generations. She replied, "Josef, how can you ask me to completely forsake the life to which I've grown accustomed?" and she packed all our fine things—even those odd-looking finger prongs we used to pierce asparagus at the table. But when Papa asked her to pack his expensive collection of Cuban cigars and the humidor, Mama said, "There's no more room in the crates for luxury items." Papa put a dozen cigars in his luggage and left the rest.

One day I found Mama in the library, mumbling to herself, dragging Papa's most prized volumes off their shelves and dropping them on the floor.

"Why don't you let me pack the books?" I asked.

"I'm almost done with it now."

I looked into the half-full crate. "And where's my *Encyclopaedia Britannica?*"

"I've picked out the ones I know your father wants." She was digging into the crate. "See? These are his favorites . . . Dumas and Tolstoy. And all the texts concerning plant biology. Plus this one on the chemical processing of root plants."

"I don't see my books here."

"You don't need them, not where we're going."

"You're wrong. I do need them."

"They won't be thrown out. Grandmother will keep them safe for when we get back."

"When will that be?"

Mama sighed. "I don't know, Benita."

"What do you mean? Papa said in a year or two!"

"Listen to me now. . . . I'm not packing any more of these stones to throw into the ocean. We're going to sink the boat with all these books."

Mama didn't care for books. Not because she couldn't read; she came from a privileged background, and it included being educated at the convent of Santa Maria. Her feelings about reading had to do with her father, and they went way back to before I was born. My grandfather came from a wealthy Ecuadorian family that bought land and grew tobacco. He made his mark on the world by starting up a newspaper called *El Universo* that was published throughout South America. He valued the written word so much, he risked his entire fortune on it. Mama told me that her father had once said, "Real knowledge lies on the written page." But in Mama's opinion, her father hadn't understood a thing about real life—and his values were all twisted up.

When he died just after I was born, he left his estate to his widow, my grandmother Tita, but to his only daughter, my mother, he left nothing—all because she'd married my father.

There were lots of reasons my grandfather didn't like my papa. My father came from Lebanon, so he was "a blasted refugee foreigner," even though Papa was no poor immigrant. It was true he'd come to Ecuador as a young man with nothing to his name, to escape serving in the army in his home country, but he'd made his fortune long before he'd met my mother. Papa was also fifteen years older than my mother, who was only seventeen when they married. Their age difference wasn't unusual; there were many happy marriages of this sort. The problem was that my grandfather had hardly met Papa before he was informed that a wedding would take place. Mama was pregnant with me, and that meant the blasted foreigner was going to be his son-in-law.

I knew this story very well by now. Mama and her father didn't speak after that, and her relationship with my grandmother was strained as well—for Tita made it clear she would honor her dead husband's wishes regarding the withholding of Mama's inheritance. So my mother put herself completely into the care of my father. Until we lost all our money, she'd never regretted that she had.

Whenever Mama told me about her father, I felt sorry for her. The stories always reminded me how lucky I was to have Papa, who made me feel as if my happiness was the most important thing to him.

Packing up the books, Mama said, "Reading books is like living in a fantasy. You need to be more practical. When you grow up and have a household of your own to run, you'll understand what I mean."

Oh, she makes me so mad! Those encyclopedias were the only things I owned that I truly cared about.

"Look here. There's plenty of room in this crate," I said.

"Oh, Benita! Give me some peace. If you want to be helpful, why don't you start making dinner?"

"With what? We packed all the pots!" I yelled, but I was shaking with fear that I might not get to take my books along.

"What's all the fuss about?" Papa stood in the doorway. I was surprised to see him. He let Mama make all the decisions about how to run the house, and he never got in the middle of an argument.

"Mama won't let me take my encyclopedias. I don't want any of my clothes or shoes or anything else. But I can't live without these!"

"Agh! Such a dramatic child. We've all had to make sacrifices. Josef, you know we can't take everything, and we agreed to bring just one crate from the library and—"

"And my books should go too, not just Papa's!"

He stepped into the library and put his hand on my shoulder. Instantly, I felt calm. "Pilar, I can pack the books with Benita," he said. "We'll figure out what should be done here."

I wanted to jump up and hug my papa. I could always count on him.

Mama threw up her hands. "Have it your way," she said as she left the room.

Papa turned to me. "You know how difficult this move has been for your mother. We must help her as much as we can." He poured himself a glass of port wine, took a long sip and then reached into the crate. "Let's see now. . . . I'll keep this book on plant biology, but all these chemical science books can stay. Now we have room for about six of your encyclopedia volumes."

"Thank you, Papa!"

"What else has she got in here?" He lifted out several books at once. They were a matched set, all with red leather covers and gold lettering on the spines. I knew Papa had brought these books from his home in Lebanon. They were older than he was, and the only things he had saved from his old world.

"Oh, these are the timeless classics. And you're old enough now to be reading these on your own. The shame is there's not room for them all in the crate. We'll have to choose carefully."

Papa put a book in my hands. *The Works of Alexandre Dumas*," I read. "He's French?"

"Exactly. He wrote great tales of brave men who struggle in difficult circumstances on foreign soil. It could be a source of inspiration for us in our upcoming adventures."

I smiled. "Maybe they were meant more as tales of warning. You know, when the moral of the story is you're better off to never leave home."

"My dear girl. That's no way to think. Leaving home can be a great advantage, opening up whole new worlds of opportunity. I left my own when I wasn't much older than you are now. I'd hate to think what my life would have been if I hadn't taken that risk."

"Maybe you would still have your fortune."

10

"But I wouldn't have met your mother, and you wouldn't have been born. I would rather lose ten fortunes than never have had you."

"But, Papa . . . are you saying that you have no regrets? I mean, you can't be happy about what's happened to us."

He sighed deeply and took another sip from his glass. "What good are regrets? Most of the world is in the grip of the same tragedy. There's no escaping it anywhere."

Papa's mood darkened, and I didn't like to see him like that. "Which story should we read?" I said.

"You choose."

I opened the red leather cover gently. The spine had already been cracked. It was soft and supple, and I knew this book had been well read by Papa and by his father before him. Its pages were impossibly thin, like tissue paper. The book felt like a living thing to me, needing tender care. I looked at the table of contents. A story called "D'Artagnan, the Gascon" caught my eye.

"D'Artagnan? Is that some sort of funny name?" I asked.

"Not for a musketeer . . ." Papa gave me a sideways look to see if I was catching on.

"Oh! So this is the story of *The Three Musketeers?*"

"It's a part of it, and a marvelous tale. Read that one."

While Papa sipped quietly from his glass, I turned to the first page of the story and began. "*M. de Troisville, captain of the Musketeers, as his family was yet called in Gascony, or M. de Treville, as he called himself in Paris, had actually begun life without being worth a sou.*"

I stopped reading. "A sou is a French coin, right? And so this captain fellow had none?"

"Yes. But it didn't matter one bit. Read on. You'll see."

"Maybe this book is too hard for me."

"Don't give up so fast. Do you realize you're reading at a superior level for a girl of your age?"

"My teacher says I'm the best reader in my class."

My school year ran from May through December. Everyone stayed home during the rainy season, but I wouldn't be going back at all when the rain ended. As I sat on the floor of my father's library, I could perfectly picture the big green blackboard at the front of my old classroom, the row of wooden desks and my seat in the first row on the right-hand side. I remembered the smell of chalk dust, the shelves of textbooks and the faces of my classmates, to whom I'd said goodbye at the end of the year.

A terrible thought dawned on me. "Papa, is there a school on Paíta?"

He looked me straight in the eye. "No. I'm afraid there isn't."

This was the worst news yet. "How am I going to study? You always said I could go to college, but I'll never get there if I don't stay in school."

"How about if I were to teach you?"

"I love to read with you, but it's not the same as school. We study world history, math and French."

"I can help you with all those subjects."

"No, Papa, this is terrible!"

He got up from his chair and wrapped me in his arms. "I know and I'm sorry. But I have an idea. I'll bring over a tutor for you and your brothers once we get settled. You'll learn even more than all your old classmates."

"You'd do that?"

"Would that make you happy?"

I tried to picture sitting out on the beach with a teacher dressed in his suit coat and freshly pressed tie. Would he write my lessons in the sand? It was an absurd idea. But I couldn't hurt Papa's feelings. He was trying his best to give me what I needed.

"I guess so. Do you promise, Papa?"

Papa hugged me tight. "You have my word. Don't worry about it for one minute more."

It was late already, and I was very tired from all the packing. The words on the page were getting fainter in the dim light. After my tenth yawn in a row, Papa said, "You should go to bed. I'll finish up in here."

"And my encyclopedia books . . ."

"I swear you'll see each and every one on Paíta. A to Z."

I kissed him good night. Before I left, I turned to see him sitting in the light of the lamp with an empty glass in his hand, adrift among the nearly bare shelves of his library, his precious books spread around the floor.

I went upstairs and got right into bed. Many hours later, when it was pitch-black and moonless, I woke in the dark, startled to find Papa sitting on the edge of my bed. He shook my shoulder roughly and whispered, "Benita, get up now. . . . Talk to me. . . ." He pressed his forehead to mine, and for the first time, I knew what too much alcohol on the breath smelled like.

"Will you, will you . . ." He was choking on his words.

"What's wrong, Papa?"

"I need you to promise something. Promise me you'll try to be happy. I cannot bear the thought of causing you any more grief than I already have."

"Of course I'll try to be happy."

Suddenly Papa was kissing me all over my face, burning my skin with his rough, wet beard.

"That's my girl," he said. "Let's pray together."

I knelt beside him as I had many nights before, but I did not close my eyes. I kept them open and glued to my father's face. He was trembling as he spoke. "Lord have mercy on me and my family. We have suffered a great loss and cannot stand much more. Return us to the prosperity which was so harshly taken from us." We both said, "Amen," and he left my room on tiptoe.

I lay staring into the dark. What stuck in my mind was that Papa had never, ever needed anything from me before. And I had a bad feeling that the promise I'd made—to try to be happy on Paíta—would be very hard to keep.

CHAPTER

2

Our friends and neighbors insisted on giving us a proper send-off. It would be a real celebration with delicious food and festive music.

We were all dreading it.

The party would be one big ugly reminder of the kind of life that was slipping through our fingers—that once was ours.

It was an afternoon affair, held late on a Sunday, when all the husbands would be home from work, although Papa was always home now that he had no job. Our neighbors the Herrera family were to host. They lived next door to us on the Malecón. I wore the pleated blue wool skirt that was the bottom half of my school uniform with a clean linen blouse. My mother got dressed up in a beaded chemise and satin shoes.

We gathered in the vestibule of our house, and Mama did a quick check on all of us, straightening Papa's tie, tugging down on the hem of my skirt. "You're growing like a bean, Benita. Luckily we won't have to buy you a new school uniform next year."

We stepped out onto the Malecón, busy with all sorts of people enjoying their day off. Mama took Papa's arm, and my brothers and I followed behind in proper form. Like ours, the Herreras' house had a grand entrance framed by stone pillars. Black wrought-iron terraces decorated the windows above and provided views of the park and beyond, to the Guayas River. Through the front door was a large central courtyard just like ours, except theirs had been decorated for our party; four long tables were covered in linen and china and crystal, and a huge banner that said GOOD LUCK IN YOUR NEW LIFE! hung overhead.

We heard the happy voices of people in the parlor.

"Time to face the music," Mama said.

"It won't be that bad." Papa took her arm.

Señor Herrera, a retired ship's captain, was still a rich man. All the oil lamps were lit even though it was the middle of the day. They made the house glow. Mama noticed too and seemed to bask for a moment in their warmth. Large oil paintings hung on the stone walls. A portrait of the Madonna hung at the farthest end, granting her blessings over the household.

Señor Herrera shouted, "Here they are! The guests of honor!" All of a sudden we were surrounded by our friends.

Someone shouted, "Speech, speech!" and Papa said, "What can I say to such an outpouring of warmth and affection? We are so grateful to you all."

"Your family must be so excited," Señor Herrera said, "to be setting out on this new course."

Papa didn't give any of us a chance to answer. "It's all they can talk about."

"We'd love to hear about your life there. Will you be able to send letters?" asked Señora Herrera.

"We'll have to arrange for mail service, but I don't know how to do that yet."

"Oh! You'll be so out of touch," said the señora.

"I'm afraid that's how it will have to be for now."

Our priest asked, "Is there anyplace to attend service on the island, Josef? Or to receive communion?"

Papa looked down at the ground, and I knew he was ashamed to answer. "No, Father, there is no house of worship that I am aware of, and this pains me deeply. But we'll return to the mainland every few months. This will have to be sufficient for the nourishment of our souls for now."

"Jesus understands your difficulties, I am sure," the priest said.

"But tell us of your plans," said Señor Torres. "And all about your new business."

Papa took a deep breath. "I'm getting into farming. The time is ripe for it. I'll produce coconuts on a grand scale, and we'll be selling the copra to big corporations, like the Colgate-Palmolive-Peet Company."

The crowd *oohed* and *ahhed*. Señora Torres said, "Very ambitious."

Mama said, "Yes, well, when you've lost everything, it seems the time has come to dream big."

Someone in the crowd gasped, and Papa put his arm around Mama, but he didn't seem able to say another word. The silence that followed was uncomfortable. Papa had always followed my mother's lead when it came to Guayaquil society, a world she'd introduced him to. Now she'd abandoned him while still standing by his side. My poor papa seemed lost.

Thankfully Señor Ziade spoke up. "I tried to bring Señor Mariah into the railroad business. But he'd have none of it. Wants to be his own boss. I understand that, of course." Señor

Ziade built the railroad that ran between Guayaquil and Quito, and now that it was finished, people would pay forever to use it. But this was the first I'd heard of him offering my father a job. *Did Papa turn him down? How could he?*

"I'm accustomed to running my own business," Papa said quietly. "I wouldn't fit into yours, señor."

Señora Ziade said, "My father made his money in cacao. But he got out just in time. There's too much left to chance when it comes to farming. The weather. The prices. The problem of getting dependable labor."

"You have to admit," Señor Ziade added, "it's a bit backward, going into farming now, when the industrial revolution is finally making its way to our shores." He was about to make his usual speech about how it was important to be "forward thinking."

"One good thing about farming as a profession . . . ," Papa said, "I'll never be out of a job, because everyone needs basic things like food and soap, no matter how poor the economy."

Señor Herrera interrupted. "Everyone! Please come out to the courtyard." A mariachi band started playing, and things became festive again. My parents were seated at the head of the table in the middle of the room while my brothers took their places at the boys' table and I found my seat with the girls.

I knew most of them from parties just like the one we were at now, and they bored me with their talk of nothing important, but three girls who I liked were there. Francesca, Christina and Olga were all two years older than me, but they treated me like their favorite little sister. They each kissed me hello on both cheeks, and then Olga said, "Sit here, Benita. I've saved you a seat next to me." Her three younger sisters sat down at the other end of the table.

Olga was Señor Ziade's oldest daughter. We grew up playing together. I liked her so much. She had long wavy brown hair and enormous blue eyes ringed with thick black eyelashes. She was a beauty, but she was also the nicest girl I'd ever known, who never said a bad word about anyone. I was so happy she'd picked me to sit next to her.

Olga's cream-colored dress was cut in the latest style, with thick shoulder pads that made her look as if she were in charge of herself, just like that American movie star that men usually fought over on-screen. The other girls were dressed in the same way, but they didn't look nearly as perfect.

The girls sat up with their backs straight and folded their hands in their laps, as I knew they'd been taught to do in etiquette class. I'd been too young to go. Now I doubted I'd have to go at all.

"How are you?" Olga asked.

Everyone at the table was listening with eager ears, but "I feel like I'm dying" didn't seem like proper party talk. "We're all ready to go," I said as brightly as I could.

"We're going to miss you," said Olga.

Francesca said, "And we think you're so brave."

Christina was nodding in agreement.

"You do? Why?"

Francesca stumbled for an answer. "Um . . . well, because . . . you'll be so far from home and . . ."

Christina said, "She means that we would dread having to live in a place like—"

Olga interrupted them both. "It takes a lot of strength to make such a big change. And you haven't complained. Not once, Benita," she said. "We all admire your courage."

I looked at my plate. I didn't feel strong at all, and I was only pretending having to move wasn't a big horrible shock. But I guess how I really felt must have been obvious to everyone. I knew they were waiting for me to say something.

"Well, I trust my father to do what's best for us."

Olga's younger sister Rosa said, "I heard Mama say they practice voodoo on that island."

"Be quiet. You don't even know what voodoo is," Olga said. "Ignore her, Benita."

"I know what it is," Rosa snapped. "Black magic. Witchcraft. Mama said the people who live on Paíta worship the sun and the moon and sacrifice animals and . . ."

"Oh! That's horrible!" Francesca looked ready to cry.

"That's enough, Rosa!"

I realized I'd been holding my breath the whole time they were arguing. Olga turned to me and whispered in my ear so no one could hear, "Don't let her upset you. Mama thinks anyone who doesn't wear a hat when they go outdoors is a heathen. I'm sure the people who live on Paíta are no different than the *indios* who live on the farms outside the city."

I hoped she was right.

The waiters had gathered to start serving the first course. Señor Herrera rang a little bell and stood to address us all. "To commemorate this special occasion, we've arranged to have a portrait taken. So before everyone ruins their lovely outfits with the happy meal we're about to be served, let's put on our best faces for our dear friends, the Mariahs."

A photographer entered and began to set up his equipment in the doorway to the courtyard. There was lots of murmuring, and chairs scraped the floor as everyone got into place to face the camera, a huge wooden box on a three-legged stand, with a large black cloth attached to the back of it like a hood.

The photographer ducked under the cloth to compose his picture. "Hold that pose now, please."

Everyone in the room went completely still. We all knew it took several long seconds for the picture to be set against the glass inside the box; moving even one inch would create a blur in the final image. But Olga quickly put her arm around my shoulder, and my smile got even bigger. It was the only happy moment I'd had all day. Maybe even all year. When the blinding flash went off, I knew that picture would always prove that Olga and I were best friends. It was a great feeling.

Then the meal began. There were huge bowls of guacamole and tabouli salad. Spicy chili and peppers stuffed with Gorgonzola cheese, empanadas filled with ground pork. There were several Middle Eastern dishes to please my father, as well as paella, a dish of yellow rice with gulf shrimp and spicy chicken. Finally a huge roasted pig was brought to my parents' table atop a wheeled cart.

The chef came out to carve, and he took the apple out of the pig's mouth, split it and put one half on my mother's plate and the other on Papa's. Mama was laughing and Papa had his arm around her, and I could tell how much they enjoyed being the center of attention. It made me smile just to see them forget their worries for a while.

Somehow we managed to get through the desserts—fruit tarts and chocolates. Quieter music was played then, a wooden flute that barely rose over the sound of clinking cups and forks. I looked around the room, and it was so busy that I wondered how I would be able to keep it in my memory. I lifted my hands up to my ears. The party went quiet and I could finally see what was really happening. All the noise that the laughing faces were making was the sound of goodbye.

I felt very sad, and I excused myself and went to sit with my parents, but all the men in the room were beginning to rise and go off into the library to smoke their cigars. As Papa stood to go with them, I reached for his hand. He looked woozy and a little tired. "Did you have a nice time, Benita?"

"Yes, Papa. It's been a wonderful party."

Papa patted my head. "I'm so glad," he said, and then he drifted away with the others.

As soon as the men were gone, the women gathered closer to Mama, moving into seats that were empty, their concerned faces closing in on us.

"Dear Pilar, how can you stand for this?" said one of the women. "Are you really going to live on that island?"

Another lady asked, "Why on earth don't you return to your relatives in Quito? I'm certain they would take you in."

Mama cast a quick and nervous glance at me. "Don't think I haven't thought of it," Mama said to the ladies. "If not for myself, then certainly for the sake of the children. I want nothing more than for Benita to marry well, and for her brothers to grow up as quickly as possible. I pray that when they are men, they will be able to provide for us properly."

As if they'd been called to arms, my brothers showed up at our table. But they were simply getting restless and asked Mama if they could go out and play. Mama cast a glance at me. "Go watch out for them, will you, Benita? Let me enjoy these last minutes with my friends."

"Yes, Mama." I stood up from the table.

I followed my brothers out of the courtyard. Once outside, they took off, and I saw them running down the ramp that led to the lower-level dock. I went along at my own pace, but kept them in my sight.

My baby brothers. It was impossible to imagine them as men capable of doing anything useful, much less earning a living for the family. Alfonse was a sickly boy who cried a lot. José did have a good heart, but whenever our younger brother

Manuel was around, he acted like a street ruffian who didn't care whether he got into trouble. Manuel was the worst of all three. He bitterly fought for any kind of attention he could get. Mama made it my responsibility to watch over all three of them and keep them out of trouble—a task I failed at every day. Now they were running and shouting, behaving as they damn well pleased. And here I was, stuck watching them do whatever they wanted.

I turned to look at all the activity in the park. Things had changed a lot since the start of the Depression. Men sat on the benches begging for money from anyone who walked by. No one came to pick up the garbage anymore. All day long men and boys came to pull fish for their dinner from the water that was the shade of an oil slick, lapping thickly at the wall holding it back. In front of our house a food stand had opened, a wooden shack surrounded by stools that were never empty. Men hunched over their meals, eating hand to mouth and with barely a breath between bites. The two women who ran the food stand wore tight-fitting clothes and bright lipstick in the middle of the day. They had a lot of energy, and they bantered with the men and with each other. I envied them.

I often wished I could be a part of the life that was happening in the park, even though Papa referred to it as "lower class." Instead I had to be always standing apart and watching, because it was a separate world from my own. That it was happening right at my doorstep made no difference.

All of a sudden I remembered my brothers. Alfonse was lying on his stomach on the dock with one arm trailing in the muddy water. José and Manuel were shoving him out to the edge, threatening to throw him in. He was clinging to the rough boards, trying to make himself heavy as stone, and shouting at them, "I'm going to tell on you!"

Will they ever grow up? If they threw him in, Mama would punish me for letting them ruin his clothes. I bounded down the gangplank, yelling as if I had good news. "Guess what I heard, boys! Bet you can't guess!"

They froze like figures in a painting. I had their attention for that one second before they'd decide they didn't have to listen to me. "We're not leaving."

All three started shouting at the same time, "What? Huh? How?"

"That's what I heard."

"Who told you that?" said Manuel.

"Mama said. She sent me to get you."

"I don't believe it," said José.

"Yeah, I don't either," said Alfonse.

I reached down and lifted Alfonse by his lapels. "You'll just have to find out for yourself then, won't you? It's time to go. Now move it. All of you."

I spun Alfonse around and shoved him toward the gangplank. When he tried to push me back, I whispered in his ear, "I just saved you from a good dunking. So you be good, or I'll feed you back to your big brothers."

"We're not staying in Guayaquil, are we?" His little cross-eyed face was suddenly drained of hope.

"Of course not, dummy," I said, pushing him along. "But let's keep that our little secret."

Back at the Herrera house, Mama made a fuss when she saw that Alfonse's shirtsleeve had gotten dirty, but we heard an angry shout coming from the library, and she got very quiet. It was my father's voice.

"No one can predict the future, gentlemen!"

My mother stood up from her chair, and I followed as she

went toward the room with the men. She moved so slowly that her clothing barely swayed in the breeze.

"All I know is that to live in fear is to die a thousand deaths." Papa was still shouting. "I will not give in to that!"

No one spoke. Then Señor Ziade said gently, like a man trying to calm a child, "You've twisted our words. We only meant to say that you shouldn't make any big decisions based on fear. Not that you yourself are fearful."

"I will make a success of this business venture. I guarantee it."

"Josef, I believe the time has come for us to go," Mama said from the doorway.

Papa stubbed out his cigar. "How right you are." He stood up then and joined us outside the library. Turning back to the men, he said, "I am beyond fear, and I hope you never understand what that feels like. Good night."

My parents said nothing on the way home. Papa seemed to be in a trance, and as soon as we entered the house, he went straight up the stairs without saying good night.

"Alfonse, give your shirt to Benita," Mama said. "It's time for your bed, boys. We have to get up very early in the morning."

Mama led me into the kitchen, handing me a brush. "It shouldn't take you long to get this dirt off his shirt."

Before she could leave the room, I said, "Can I ask you something, Mama?"

"What is it?"

"Why didn't Papa take a job with Señor Ziade on the railroad?"

"It wasn't a generous offer, and wouldn't have saved us. We can't live on a ticket taker's salary."

"Did you really think about going back to live in Quito with your family?"

Mama was staring into space as she answered. "I did think about it. And I did write to your grandmother to ask if we could go live with her."

"What did she answer?"

"She sent a telegram. It said, 'You've made your bed and now you'll have to lie in it.' Do you know what that means?"

"It means no, doesn't it?"

"That's right, but it also means she doesn't care what happens to us."

"Then why did she give us that land on Paíta?"

Mama laughed, but not in a happy way. "I think she felt it was a proper punishment. As if we haven't suffered enough. Please don't ask me any more questions tonight, Benita."

After she left, I scrubbed at Alfonse's dirty shirt. I thought about the party and the fact that I should never have packed up my encyclopedias so soon. I needed to look up that word "voodoo" to find out what it meant and whether I had anything to worry about on Paíta. Now the only thing I could do was wait and see for myself.

CHAPTER

3

Early on moving day the pale morning light seeped through the cracks in my window shutters, and I heard Mama moving through the house, pouring water into her washbasin, splashing it around. A few moments later she came into my room. "Benita, are you up? Wear the dress Tita gave you for Easter."

I put on the white linen dress that was two years old, a little girl's frock with silly pink flowers embroidered on the collar. When I reached around to try to zip up the back, I could hear a seam tear in the armpit. Soon it wouldn't fit at all and that would be just fine with me.

Two pony carts had pulled up to the curb outside the house, and Papa stood in the entrance hall giving out orders to the driver boys loading all our belongings. They were nearly as young as my brothers.

Mama was quietly watching from the base of the stairs. I crept down and tapped her on the shoulder. "Mama, can you help zip up my dress?"

One of the cart boys stopped what he was doing, looked at me and smiled. I smiled right back.

"Go into the kitchen, Benita." Mama gave me a shove and followed close behind.

I walked into the ghost kitchen, taking in the dark outlines of cooking utensils that once hung on the wall, the bare and dented counters. The only thing we'd left behind was a sticky fly strip that hung down from the lamp over the chopping table. It swayed stiffly in the hot breeze.

"You should know better, Benita." My mother gave me a queer look, as if she were seeing inside me or even beyond me, but not seeing the real me. "You're too old to act like a child, coming down to the entrance half naked. You're a young lady now. You have to act like one."

Mama was a small woman and slender as a bone. As I stood in front of her, I realized we were now eye to eye. I'd be taller than she was soon.

"I just needed you to zip up my dress," I said, and turned to present my back to her.

"Did you hear me?" It wasn't really a question.

I sighed heavily. "I don't feel like a young lady, Mama. Do young ladies get shipped off to some ridiculous island because their parents have no money? Do young ladies wear dresses made for them when they were twelve years old? Do young ladies have to do whatever they are told just because they're young ladies? If that's the case, then I don't want to be a young lady, thank you very much."

Mama spun me around fast and held me by the shoulders. "Yes. Yes they do. We all do what we're told. Now, I don't want to hear any more complaints from you. I am sick of it." She zipped me up quickly and left the room.

I was so mad I could have torn out my hair. *Just do what*

you're told. Why was no one in my family willing to admit we were making a mistake? If only I could stay here by myself. I'd make my own living like those busy women in the food shack. In our old kitchen I could cook dinners for the peddlers in the park, for the priests at the mission, for the man in the moon— I didn't care who. I'd take in wash. I'd shine shoes. Anything was better than going to Paíta. I just knew it.

"We're all set. Let's go!" Papa shouted out. At the sound of his voice, I remembered my promise. *Try to be happy.*

"Benita?"

From the entrance hall I saw that Mama was in the front seat of the cart. My brothers were in their tight woolen suits and big red bow ties, pushing each other around on one of the cart's painted benches, fighting for the best seat.

Papa smiled when he saw me, and he held up his arm for me to take. He looked like the perfect gentleman in his freshly pressed linen suit. We walked outside together, locking the door behind us, and he gave me a hand getting into the cart. "We're ready now," he said to the young driver, who cracked his whip on the back of the naggy pony, and we pulled away from home.

I took a look back one last time and noticed that we had forgotten something: the brass sign on the front gate that said MARIAH. Once, it had meant that we belonged there. Now it was only the name of a big vacant house.

★ ★ ★

The rising sun cast a rosy glow over the fishermen's boats beached on the tar-stained strip of sand below the main dock of the Guayas River. Papa went down to the water's edge to find our captain, leaving me and Mama to watch over our freight scattered across the wooden planking.

When I'd first heard about our voyage, I'd pictured a broad

white vessel, its chrome railings polished to sparkle in the sun. These boats were filthy fishermen's skiffs, just big enough to carry all the nets and a good-sized haul.

Papa returned with a hungry-looking, hunched-over old man who wore a sailor's cap with a black patent leather brim. The white fabric of his cap was stained gray, his skin looked like leather and he had a habit of poking his tongue into the empty space where his two front teeth should have been.

"This is Captain Pepito," Papa said. "His boat is below, down near the end of the row."

"How are we going to get all our things over there?" Mama sounded alarmed.

"Yes, how?" The captain took a walk around our crates. "You have much too much baggage. I can't carry all this. And the people too," he said, as if *we* weren't the people he was supposed to transport.

"Now look here," Papa said. "You knew very well that I have a family of six and one cartload of household supplies to make the trip as well. That was our contract and you agreed to it."

"I'm very sorry. You have too much here. More than I thought could fit in a cart. This job will take me several trips. Maybe I will have to make the last trip in the dark."

"I'll give you an extra hundred for each trip you have to make. You're the one who agreed to this job in the first place. We'll find another boat if you won't take us."

Captain Pepito looked as if he wanted to hit my father in the knees, but said, "You follow me, people," walking away down the gangplank toward the beach.

Mama turned to Papa in alarm. "But our things!"

"Pepito will bring them in the next load," Papa told her. "Let's go, children. It's time to get on the boat."

"Yes, Papa," we chimed, and followed him. When we got down below, Papa turned to see Mama standing there above us, still furious.

"Leave it all, Pilar!" my father bellowed, and my mother, who'd probably never heard my father raise his voice to her, quickly grabbed two pieces of hand luggage and rushed after us, her white skirts raising dust as she ran.

Captain Pepito led us down the beach to a boat. Painted on the front was a shark face with rows of pointy teeth, and the outboard motor was held in place with rope. There was only one seat, a plank stretched across the rear. "Lady sits in the back. Careful of the motor, now. Father goes in the front and children in the middle."

Once he had us loaded in, Captain Pepito and another fisherman shoved our boat toward the surf. They huffed and grunted as the heavy boat dragged against the sand, but as soon as it touched the water, it lifted up easily.

"Say goodbye, family," the captain said to us. He tugged on the motor's cord. The engine sputtered and shot some burning gray smoke into the air. Mama leaned away from the exhaust. I was crouched down in the belly of the boat holding my skirt up around my knees to keep it from trailing in the fishy water that swayed back and forth. Then a wave crested over the side and splashed me in the face. My brothers laughed. "Idiots. It's not funny," I snapped.

"There's room up here with me, Benita," Papa said. "Why don't you come forward?"

I crept up toward Papa, and he held out his hands to catch me. I spun around, sat in his lap and stuck out my tongue at the boys, who were now smoldering over my good luck.

As the dingy harbor receded, the brown river water fanned

out and thinned, disappearing into the royal blue of the ocean. Captain Pepito revved the motor, and a shock of ocean breeze struck us, mingled with spray that shot up the sides of the boat. I began to feel good, or hopeful even. It was the fresh air, the speed and nothing to think about but the sky and sea. This was such a relief. I felt Papa inhale very deeply, then release his breath in a rush, and I guessed he was feeling it too.

Mama sat perfectly upright beside the captain in the back of the boat. She was turned away from us, to let the ocean air strike her full in the face. The tail end of the flowered scarf she wore around her head whipped out in back. She was muttering to herself, unaware that she could be heard. "Everyone can just go to hell." Papa turned to face straight ahead. His profile was sad and hard, and I could see the comb marks in his jet-black hair from when he slicked it back that morning, like ridges in rock.

It was a bouncing, wet, cold ride. After what seemed like hours, the sky all around us turned bright white. The ocean got choppier and ocean spray spilled onto us, stinging cold. I tried to think of nothing, to ignore the discomfort, but I saw how my brothers were shivering and huddled together against the pitiless ocean.

"How much farther, Papa?" I asked, but he only patted my leg.

Captain Pepito spoke up. "Look over the port side, children, and you'll see where we're going."

The boys scrambled up and held on to the side of the boat. Sure enough, a thin strip of land hovered above the blue water. I watched it grow and turn into a place that was real—too real—and then we were there, chugging along the shore in our little boat.

Paíta looked as perfect as an island described in a book.

Enormous palm trees swayed in the breeze, with heavy green leaves as big as the arms on a Dutch windmill. There were hundreds of these palm trees, a forest protected from the surf by a white beach, short and steep and uninviting. In the distance a mountaintop was barely visible, shrouded in gray storm clouds moving steadily across the island and toward us.

Everyone got very quiet as we pulled closer to shore. I spotted a sad-looking blue shack up on stilts. It stood on the empty beach, all windblown and weather damaged. The paint was cracking and it had no door. I was relieved to pass it by.

The captain slowed the motor as we approached a half-moon bay, and we drifted toward what appeared to be a tiny village. "Here we are. This is Subidalta."

"I thought we were going to Paíta," I said to Papa. Maybe this wasn't the place we were destined for.

"Yes. Paíta is the island," the captain said. "Subidalta is where the people live, right here."

As we got closer, I saw that the village was nothing more than a bunch of thatched shacks built into the sand. More fishing boats were beached at the water's edge, and standing guard over everything was a steep muddy hill covered with some scrappy-looking vegetation.

When the captain cut the motor and threw the anchor over, I felt my heart sink. Did he mean for us to get off here? Papa asked, "What should we do now, Pepito?"

The boat was bobbing violently, and the gray storm clouds were moving over our heads. The captain studied the shoreline, where the waves were breaking in a hard curl against the beach.

"Can't bring the boat in now. Too rough. Might flip us over."

So we sat there as the bright white sky turned gray and a light rain started up. I began to shiver in my cold wet clothing. I couldn't watch the rosary Captain Pepito wore around his neck swaying back and forth one minute more. It made me dizzy and the saliva in my mouth had turned thick and sweet.

"Papa, I'm getting sick," I said. "When can we get off?"

My brothers gazed up beseechingly at Papa; they looked utterly wretched. Mama was sitting completely still, staring at the bottom of the boat as if she'd just been hit with a blunt object.

Papa said, "We can't remain here any longer. Is there nowhere else to land?"

The captain said something under his breath; then he put his thumb and forefinger into his mouth and produced a whistle loud enough to be heard clear around the island. Mama jumped.

"Don't worry, señora. I don't expect you to swim." He whistled again, and this time several people appeared in the doorways of those huts on the beach. A strong-looking man called to our captain. We could hear him perfectly, despite the rain and distance. "Need help?"

"Need a ride!" Captain Pepito yelled.

"How many people are there?"

"Six!"

The man on the hill looked back toward his hut and then at us again.

The captain shouted, "They'll pay!"

The man walked down the hill to the beach to speak with the other men. A few crossed themselves, and then they waded into the rough ocean together. They came marching through the tossing surf. The man from the hill walked a few feet ahead of everyone else. He stared at us with a menacing look, sizing us up.

As they came closer still, I was surprised to see that he was young. The others were weathered and wrinkled, and he was very handsome, with a perfectly square jaw and straight nose, like a statue. When he came up beside our boat, I saw that his eyes were a light hazel color that looked lit from within. He put his hand on the rim of the hull, next to where I sat, to steady the boat, and spoke to the captain, giving me a chance to study the muscles in his arm. His skin was the color of caramel toffee and his teeth were very white. The ocean swirled around his smooth brown shoulders.

Papa spoke up behind me to interrupt their conversation and I realized, in a daze, that I had not heard one word of what was being said. "Women and children should go first," Papa said with authority. All eyes turned on my father then, but no one moved. When the young man looked in Papa's direction, we locked eyes for a split second. It was easily the most em-barrassing moment of my entire life. I looked away quickly.

Captain Pepito said, "The boys will go first. Then mother. Then you and the girl."

The captain signaled to the men, and three of them held out their arms. The village men were able to pick the boys straight up over the side of the boat and flip them around to sit atop their broad shoulders. Slowly the men began to walk away toward shore, their movements sloppy and uneven.

"The lady will go next," Captain Pepito said, and to my great disappointment I saw that the handsome young man was going to carry Mama.

"NO!" Mama cried. "I will not go this way. I cannot!"

"Easy now, señora. You have nothing to worry about. Raúl won't drop you."

Raúl. What a strong name! He stepped up to get Mama, and she didn't make another peep. It took two of the men to pick

Mama up and place her on his shoulders. Her abundant white cotton skirts must have been heavy with water. But Raúl did not sink under her weight. Instead he jostled her a bit to get her placed better against his neck. He remained expressionless the whole time. Mama took hold of his hand, which he held up to support her. I watched them turn away from us and head for shore and felt as if I'd been left behind on another planet.

The last two men shared Papa's weight between them on their shoulders, and then the captain jumped down into the water, turned around and hoisted me with ease, as if I weighed no more then a sack of potatoes and were not even as important as that.

We all lumbered toward the island. It was quite a spectacle, seeing my entire family perched like privileged baggage on the backs of a tribe of strangers who treated us like a simple bit of work to be done.

I watched the muscles of Raúl's back shift and change shape from carrying Mama's weight. I had no idea that people could have such beautiful forms, that they could look as if they were specially made. Why did I turn away when he looked at me? Next time he glanced my way, I'd smile, or say hello. I had to think of a way to get him to notice me again, or Paíta, from the looks of it, would be nothing more than a very boring and backward place to live.

CHAPTER

4

The storm quit as quickly as it had begun. As soon as the sun peeked over the rim of vanishing clouds, the whole place went hot and sticky, and the water turned turquoise blue and clear as glass.

Our carriers put us down on the beach. Captain Pepito came round and paid the men, introducing Raúl as his son. As soon as Raúl got his money, he turned away without a word.

All the other villagers came closer in packs of three and four, tentatively at first, as if we might lunge or bite. But once a small crowd had gathered, the rest of the village poured out of their huts to have a look. They stared into our faces in a way that expressed curiosity and fear at the same time, studying us as if we were some kind of alien race.

Their attention was unnerving, but I stared right back, trying to smile. I wouldn't have thought that so many lived on Paíta; nearly a hundred people were on the beach by then. Where did they all sleep? There were only ten huts on the whole island, as far as I could tell.

These people were nothing like the *indios* back home. Those people covered themselves with handwoven woolen garments—shawls and ponchos and long skirts. These islanders were practically naked, barefoot and beaded, their faces splashed with red mud paint. The women wore some cotton rags tied at the breast, and the men went shirtless.

One old woman grabbed Mama's hand to get a better look at her gold wedding ring. Mama let her, but when the woman tried to take it off her finger, Mama pulled her hand away. They made some remarks to one another about that, in a language I could not understand. Another lady held a leaf up to the side of her head and then pointed to me, and I realized she was commenting on my flowered hat, but I moved back before she tried to take it off my head. My brothers faced a trio of naked, giggling native boys with round brown bellies.

I snuggled under Papa's arm to hide, trying to make their garbled voices fade away. Papa pulled me in close, then reached into the breast pocket of his jacket to pull out a folded map. "All right, Benita. What we need to do is find the territory on the southwest quadrant, which should be . . ."

"Hello, there! Yo hoy!"

We turned to see a man riding along the shore on a small donkey. A boy trotted beside them, swacking at the donkey's hindquarters with a branch. This man yelled out in Spanish. "*Hola!* Welcome to our island!"

The donkey stopped short all of a sudden, though the boy madly whacked at the beast's backside.

"I am the mayor of Paíta! And we welcome you to our humble island." He kicked away at the donkey's sagging gut but it wouldn't budge. The islanders erupted into laughter.

"He's no mayor," Captain Pepito said to my father. "He's crazy in the head."

Without warning, the donkey bucked and threw this person, whoever he was, backward over his scrappy rump, then ran off, kicking sand into the rider's face for good measure.

The crowd was hysterical now, and the man in the sand laughed too. "Help me up," he said to the boy. "Don't let my people see me like this."

What was most confusing about all of this was trying to figure out why some people spoke Spanish and others did not. It was almost as if two different races lived on the island. The Spanish-speakers, such as the captain, were dressed more like us, although their clothes were dirty and well worn. The mayor wore pants, a shirt with a collar and a straw hat. The island *indios*, or whatever they were, wore hardly anything at all. How these two groups communicated was unclear, but the peasant crowd understood enough to laugh at the mayor's joke. Perhaps it was one he had played before. Maybe they just liked to laugh.

All of a sudden I felt very tired, and I wanted to get where we were going. I was glad these people greeted us with laughter rather than anger, but so far, Paíta only made me want to run away home, to shut the door and never come out again. No wonder the handsome Raúl had left the beach. Maybe he hated all this silly joking just like I did.

I tugged on my father's shirtsleeve. "Are we staying here, Papa?"

"Good question, Benita," Papa said. I was still snuggled close to him and I could feel how fast his heart beat inside his chest. "Tell me, Mayor, because you must know your way around this island . . ." Papa pulled at the accordion folds of his map and attempted to spread it open. "Let go of me now, Benita," he said. Reluctantly I took my arms away from his waist. Papa bent down low and laid the map out on the sand. The crowd gathered around noisily, but I couldn't tell whether they knew they were looking at a likeness of their own island.

"See this body of water here?" Papa said to Captain Pepito and the mayor. He pointed to a small lake on the map. "Can you tell me where it is located? Our land is one kilometer directly to the south."

Captain Pepito bent down to get a closer look. "It doesn't exist now," he said.

"Then why is it here on the map?" Papa asked.

"Because this is where it will be."

"What kind of nonsense is that?"

The captain started to walk away from us, away from the beach. He gestured for Papa to follow, then turned and continued walking.

Papa shook his head and stood, brushing the sand from his trouser legs. He and I went after the captain. We walked beyond the village huts and through the yards out back. Sleeping hammocks hung haphazardly across rooms, dirt floors were strewn with clothing and foodstuffs. Little children, too young to walk, peered out at us pathetically from their dark dens. I caught a whiff of a nasty smell from a boiling pot. I kept my gaze fixed on the back of Papa's shirt. At least we didn't have to live here like this.

On the back side of the village, there was a clearing in the jungle, at the end of a long ravine. The clearing was nearly circular, and the vegetation was matted down. Clumps of cattails grew all along the farthest edge, and at the center the ground was marked by what looked like a mineral stain, almost sea green, that swirled in the same pattern that water makes when it goes down the drain.

"I see now," said Papa.

"See what? See what?" I said.

"This is our lake," Captain Pepito said. "When the ocean tide is high, the seawater shoots up the beach. See how it made that ravine? All the water collects right here."

"It's a saltwater lake, then?" my father asked.

"Yes, good for fishing. Good for a steady supply of food for the months that it is here."

"Fish can't live in the jungle," I said, thinking I'd catch Captain Pepito, for Papa's sake, in what was obviously a lie. His story seemed all made up.

"They ride in on the ocean tide," Pepito answered. "You will see."

"I have seen all I need to see," said Papa, and he turned away then. He seemed disappointed. I followed him back down the beach. We'd left the captain standing at the edge of the dried-up lake.

"What's the matter, Papa?" I asked, afraid of what he might answer.

Papa turned to me. "I was counting on finding a freshwater reservoir here, to irrigate the planting fields. I can't irrigate with salt water. But that's not the only problem."

"It's not?"

"Because if this is the reservoir, then . . . Do you remember that shack on the beach we passed on our way into the village?"

"You mean the one we saw from the boat? How could I forget it? It's so awful."

"That shack sits right on our property."

"Oh well. We can always tear it down."

"If we tear it down, we'll have no place to live."

"What do you mean? What about the house that . . ." As soon as I said this, I realized what Papa was trying to tell me. The house we were planning to live in, the house that my grandmother had supposedly given to us, was that awful blue shack on stilts down the beach. "No!" I cried.

Papa clamped his hand over my mouth. Beads of sweat clung to his forehead and quivered as he spoke. "Not now, Benita. Don't say another word. If your mother hears, she might throw herself into the ocean. I need you to pretend it's all going to be all right. And it will be, you'll see. I promise. The shack will only be temporary. We'll build a real house. As soon as we can. I promise, all right?"

I couldn't answer. Papa had my face in his hands, and he nodded my head for me. He looked and sounded as if he were out of his mind. When he let go, I just kept nodding, even after he turned to walk back toward the rest of the family. I felt as sick to my stomach as when we were on the boat.

The crowd was gone. A few of the little boys had hung around to play with my brothers, hunkered down in the sand taking turns slapping at each other's wrists, a game my brothers had obviously taught them.

Papa clapped his hands. "It's time we were off!" he said, his voice full of false enthusiasm.

"Where are we going now?" Mama had taken a seat on a piece of hand luggage.

"Just down the beach a little way. It's not far to walk. We can make it on foot. Stand up, Pilar. I'll get that bag." Papa pushed her off it and grabbed the handle. "Let's go, kids, let's go," he shouted back over his shoulder.

We marched up the beach single file, with Papa in the lead

of course. Mama had little Alfonse by the hand, to help him walk in the soft sand. A few of the villagers trailed along at a distance, as if they were minding their own business but just happened to be headed in the same direction. It sort of bothered me that they were still with us, but I figured there had to come a time when we would no longer be so strange to them. Surely they'd grow bored of us.

After walking for several minutes, I spotted the blue shack. It wasn't that far from the village. When we'd gotten close enough, Papa stopped us and said, "All right, everyone. We're here."

The hut, leaning sideways on its stilts, stood staring down at us from its lopsided height. It was much worse up close, barren and deserted, and for good reason. There were planks missing from the walls, and a patch of sky showed through the thatched roof. From the looks on their faces, I could tell that Mama and my brothers had realized that everything was about as terrible as it could be. I dropped the bag I was carrying and it hit me in the foot.

Papa went up the stairs first, taking care to step over the gaping hole where the third and fourth ones were missing. He called from the doorway, "Pilar? Boys? Benita?" No one answered and no one moved. He went inside the shack and yelled, "There's plenty of room in here. It's just fine for a temporary shelter. José! Manuel! Bring up the bags." My brothers kicked at the sand as if they were hoping to dig themselves out of there.

"You should come see it from up here. It's not as bad as you think." Papa sat down on the edge of the hut's front porch, a single plank of wood that ran the length of the shaky structure. "You can see the whole ocean. I'll bet that on a clear day you can see all the way to Guayaquil. Just come and have a look. Pilar?"

"What a disgusting mess, Josef."

"You're not going to leave me alone here, are you?"

Mama sighed. "It's a bit late for that now."

Sounding relieved, Papa said, "Then why don't you come inside? We need to eat and get some sleep. In the morning we'll get up early and decide where to build our house. This is only temporary."

"And every temporary step we take goes from bad to worse. Where is it going to end?" she said.

"Right here," Papa answered. "It's ending here. Because everything is going to get better. Trust me. This hut is just for now. Come on up. We just have to bear this for now."

I found that I had been holding my breath during their conversation. My parents had never spoken to each other like that before. Not in front of us.

Finally Mama said to us, "Come along, children," in a resigned-to-living-in-hell voice. "Your father can't run his *plantation* all alone."

So we dragged ourselves into the hut just as it started to get dark. The islanders who had followed us now started to walk away down the beach. Would they go back to their kin and say some kind of voodoo spell to protect them from the crazy intruders—us?

That night we ate a dinner of rice salad that Mama had brought from home and fresh mango picked from a tree just behind the shack. Afterward, I wrote in my journal about the trip and how terrible things were on Paíta, how mad I was about where we wound up and how weird the people were. I also wrote about the handsome one, Raúl, but I did not write about him in a way that anyone reading my diary might know that I was interested in him. All I wrote was that one strong man carried Mama all the way to shore, and that maybe he would be a nice person. In my mind, of course, I composed a completely different description of him.

Late that night, we sat on the rickety front porch and watched the moonlight play on the swaying ocean. There was nothing else to do. My brothers started to fall asleep there, Alfonse with his head in Mama's lap. My father leaned back against the hut studying the water intensely as if looking for clues. I could have fallen asleep myself, the sounds of the waves gently lapping at the beach were so peaceful. Back in the jungle behind the shack, an orchestra of crickets kept their own time, chirping away at one another.

But the lovely monotonous noises were interrupted by the sound of a boat's motor, growling in the distance and getting louder by the minute. I could tell by the little blue light pegged to its bow that the boat was traveling toward us.

"That must be Pepito," Papa said, jumping up. He kept his gaze riveted to the water.

All of a sudden I felt glad the boat was coming. Strange that I hadn't thought about our belongings even once, because we had no light except the moon, and no bedding except for two hammocks hanging from the walls of the hut. Now I wanted my nightgown and my hairbrush. I wanted a pair of socks because I was sick of the bugs biting at my ankles, and I wanted my hand mirror to see whether I looked any different after this strange day.

Soon the little boat was beached in front of our shack. "I'm sorry. I'm sorry it took so long," Captain Pepito said. He and Papa carried our things one crate at a time, across the sand, up the steps and into the hut.

I fell asleep watching them and woke up in the middle of the night to find that I had been placed in one of the hammocks. I was sweating in the bedding. I lay there half asleep, fanning my nightgown around my legs to cool off, vaguely aware that something was moving around in the thatch of the roof. A rodent was sneaking around up there. I had almost fallen asleep again, when the sound of persistent rustling gave way with a snap, and the gentle night air was punctuated by a piercing cry.

"What was it, Papa?" I cried.

"I don't know, darling. Go to sleep. You're safe," he said.

We lay awake for a while after that, all of us. I heard the same terrible sound again, but this time it wasn't hard to guess what it was: the snap of a predator's jaws closing around its prey, and a small animal screaming for help. There were snakes in the thatch and they were having a busy night. I didn't fall asleep until daylight came because that night took forever to end.

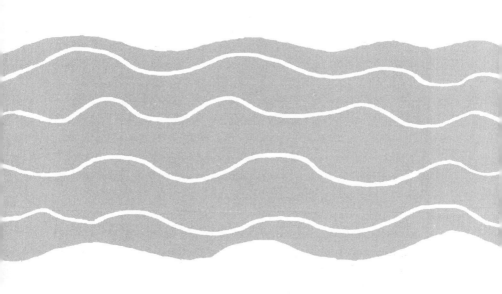

PART 2

ISLAND LIFE

CHAPTER

5

On that first day, when I finally got up from my hammock around noon, the sunlight was beating through the cracks in the hut's wooden planking. I searched through my things and found my toothbrush easily enough, but then all I could do was stand in the middle of our one-room shack wondering what to do with it as the sweat ran down from my armpits. At home I'd have a pitcher with clean water to use in a basin on my dresser. But here there was no sink with a tap I could turn to get water. And more importantly, where was the bathroom in a place like this? Yesterday I'd had to squat behind a tree. I was hoping that today we'd find a proper toilet of some sort.

I went out of the shack and onto the front porch, where I found Mama sitting in the sun. She was still in her traveling clothes, but she'd taken her hair down from the bun she always wore to run a comb slowly through her tangled black locks. I could see my brothers swimming in the ocean not far from our shack, their brown heads bobbing in the surf.

"Where's Papa?"

"He went in search of water," Mama said without looking up. "He's been gone quite a while."

"Well, I don't need to brush my teeth right away, but I do need to do my business."

My mother pointed at the sea. "Your father and your brothers relieved themselves while taking a swim."

"Did you do that too, Mama?"

"That's a private matter and I'd rather not discuss it." She wiped away the sweat on her brow with a long white cotton sleeve that was stained from the voyage.

"It might be nice to swim," I said.

"The ocean doesn't hold any appeal for me, but do as you like. "

As I stood on the porch, wondering what to do, Papa came trudging up the beach. Two buckets dragged at his arms. He placed them on the front porch.

Mama peered into one bucket, crinkling up her nose. "Is this river water? Are we to wash ourselves with it?"

"It's fresh, Pilar. There's a spring not far from here."

"Thank goodness."

"Where did you get the buckets?" I asked.

"They belong to Pepito. Get dressed now, Benita," Papa said. "I want to show you where to get water until I build a cistern for the new house."

"I have to go for a swim first. You know why."

"Yes, of course. Go right ahead."

I ran into the house and found my bathing suit. I shouted, "Don't come in here!" but I wasn't going to take a chance of being seen naked by anyone, so I changed beneath my nightgown and then threw it off over my head.

"Be right back!" I yelled to my parents as I jumped off the porch, landing in the sand.

"Don't rush about like that, Benita!" Mama said.

"I think you'd enjoy the water, Pilar. It's quite refreshing," Papa said.

"For a fish," I heard my mother say as I took off at a run.

The tide had taken my brothers down almost halfway to the village, and I had the wide and beckoning beach all to myself. I waded into the ocean up to my waist. The water was warm like a turquoise bath, and it swayed all around, rocking me gently. As I lay back, my hair fanned itself around my shoulders. The sun was already high in the sky, and I liked how it made my skin sparkle beneath the surface of the rippling sea.

If I didn't look at our awful shack up there on the beach, Paíta almost looked like a pretty island—white sand and clear blue water—a great place to have a vacation. I certainly wouldn't mind swimming in the ocean every day. But that brief morning swim was the last time I would think of Paíta as a lovely place to relax in the sea.

Our first day on the island was filled with the kind of chores no one would even think about in Guayaquil. Everything we took for granted back home was done with much effort here. Just getting water to drink and to wash ourselves with took every ounce of strength I had. The only fresh water supply on the island came from a spring located at the bottom of a loose gravel slope a mile from our hut. Papa led our family there first thing.

It was a long walk, and my feet were sweating in my leather oxfords when we finally arrived at the spring, which was nothing more than an iron pump handle poking out of a patch of wet red dirt. Several women from the village surrounded it, chanting in a way that sounded like grunts and coughs. They barely looked at us as we approached.

"What are they saying, Papa?"

"We ask for more water," said a man I didn't know. He was the only man at the spring, and he was just about the oldest person I'd seen on the island, or anywhere else. His skin was thick and dark as a hide. Papa said his name was Joam.

Joam turned directly to Papa. "You took two buckets today."

My father explained that Joam's job was to make sure no one took more than eight buckets of water a day.

"No rain," said Joam. "Big problem."

"What does that mean?" Mama asked Papa.

"It seems there's been a drought, and since this spring is now the only source of fresh water for the village, they want to control how much each family uses."

Mama stiffened, and when she spoke, she was too loud. "This is appalling. We need water to survive, Josef!"

All the women stopped their chanting and turned to look at my mother. Their serene eyes seemed to be a sort of reprimand, and Joam was staring at her with the same look. She flushed at all the attention.

"Please calm yourself, Pilar. We're lucky to be getting water at all, since we're not living in the village."

Mama opened her mouth as if she was about to say something else, but changed her mind. She turned and walked away from us. Papa did not try to stop her or call after her. She managed to look as if she were having a pleasant stroll along the Malecón back home, her movements calm and elegant, her parasol tilted over one shoulder.

"Let's fill those buckets," my father said to José and Manuel as he led them to the pump. The women stepped back. Papa cranked down on the handle three or four times, and a steady stream of water poured out of the spigot. But after a few seconds it stopped flowing and Papa said to my brothers, "You pump it now."

Manuel grabbed the handle while José held the bucket in place. My brother's arm looked so scrawny pushing down on the iron bar. "It'll get easier," Papa said to him, "once you get stronger." Manuel was pumping with all his might then. I didn't think he liked being told he was weak.

When both buckets were full, Papa turned to Joam and said, "We'll be back." The old man gave us a sad nod. "Pick up those buckets, boys," Papa said to my brothers.

They could barely stand up straight, and they sloshed water each time they took a step. "You're going to waste it," Papa said. "Here, carry it in both arms if you can't hold it in your one hand." The boys held the buckets to their chests and they followed us away from the spring.

As soon as we moved away, the women started their chanting again. I turned and saw them close their circle around the pump. "So are they praying to God for water?"

"I honestly don't know," Papa said. "Gathering water will be your job, children. And we'll have to conserve just like everybody else who lives here until I figure out another way to get water."

My brothers couldn't hear what he was saying, however, because they couldn't keep up with us. We had to stop several times along the way just so they could catch their breath.

Later that day, it was my turn to go get water. The chanting women were still there. Obviously they didn't give up easily. I stood and listened to their song for a moment before Joam spoke to me. "You come for more?"

I nodded, and though he gestured for me to go to the pump,

I didn't move because I didn't want to disturb the chanting women. Their voices were urgent, demanding. I found myself hoping they would be heard, for our sake and theirs.

Then Joam spoke to the women. They parted the circle and let me in to work the pump. I filled one bucket but couldn't lift it, so Joam helped me divide that water between the two buckets. I'd have to come back for more later.

On the way back my feet got so sweaty in my leather lace-up shoes that I was slip-sliding in them. I tried going barefoot, but the ground burned the soles of my feet and every pebble and thorn on the island seemed to spring up in my path.

Papa started a list of things we needed from off-island and put new buckets and sandals for all of us at the very top.

From then on, this business of getting water to the hut seemed to take up our entire day. Every time I turned around we needed more water. But despite all the effort my brothers and I put in, there never seemed to be enough to go around. I was thirsty all the time, and the inside of my mouth was as dry as if I'd swallowed a spoonful of dirt. Certainly there wasn't enough to do a proper wash, and soon we resembled the islanders, going around in dirty-looking rags.

The only way to get ourselves truly clean was to dip into the ocean, but I felt crusty as a snail soon after my swim, and I could barely stand the smell of my own body. The rest of my family smelled even worse to me. Mama had brought a bottle of perfume with her, and she'd drop a dab behind our ears whenever we started stinking too much.

During our first few days we mostly ate whatever we found on our land. There were avocado, banana and mango trees. Papa added a ladder to our list of supplies, but in the meantime the boys played at being monkeys. Though they were good at climbing up to pick this fruit, much of what they brought down was spoiled from being on the tree for too long. We ate it raw until Papa managed to build a fire for us, using driftwood and fallen tree limbs he found lying around our hut. We had boiled mashed bananas and avocado soup after that, but although this food was not unpleasant and we ate as much as we wanted, we were always hungry. One night while we were sitting around the fire, roasting pieces of mango that we held to the flame with our fancy silver asparagus prongs, I thought back to our going-away party. I wanted to be filled up by that memory of delicious food, but my stomach only felt emptier, and I couldn't hide the sound of it growling angrily.

"We're surrounded by the sea, Josef," my mother complained when she heard it. "Do you think you might be able to supply us with fish?"

Papa seemed happy she had a suggestion for once. "What a good idea, Pilar. I'll talk to Pepito first thing in the morning."

We woke before the first light, to what sounded like a hundred roosters crowing. In the village Papa and I spotted Pepito and Raúl working in the shade of an open-air lean-to that sheltered two fishing boats. I made sure to smile at Raúl when we got near, but he didn't notice. Neither he nor his father stopped working to talk to us.

"Captain, I've been meaning to ask you," Papa said, "what kind of fish do you usually catch?"

"Depends. Sometimes grouper. Or cod."

"And could you sell some of it to me?"

Pepito said, "I'm willing, sure, but it's not possible. I go to market in the city. I don't bring the catch here, señor."

"Couldn't you save one or two fish from the catch and bring them back with you? I'll pay you, of course."

"I don't come back for several days and your fish won't keep in my boat. But you can fish for yourself. The sea belongs to us all."

"I could fish," Papa said. He seemed to mull this over as if he'd just been told to take a walk on the water. "I've never done that, but I could learn how."

This got their attention. Raúl and Pepito looked at each other, and I could see that they were trying hard not to laugh.

"And we don't have any equipment," Papa said. "That's another problem."

"You can borrow my line and reel," Raúl offered.

"Right. How hard can it be to drop a hook in the surf?" Papa said.

Raúl went up the hill to his hut and came back carrying an elegant store-bought bamboo rod and a small basket with fishing lures and hooks that he showed to my father.

"I'd like to get a rod for myself. Where did you buy it?" Papa asked him.

Raúl nodded toward the top of the hill. "At the island store."

It took me a moment to understand that he was talking about a store on the island. I thought at first that he meant the name of a store somewhere else. . . . Sure, everyone knows the *island store*. It's on such and such a street. . . . I think Papa was in shock just like me, because he didn't say anything at first.

"You bought that here?" Papa asked.

"On *this* island?" I said.

"Yes, Little Girl," Raúl said, looking directly at me with his incredibly beautiful hazel eyes. I was kicking myself for not being nicer to him. "It's up there on the hill. A store with all kinds of things for you and your family to buy."

"In that case," said Papa, "we'll purchase some fishing equipment of our own right now."

"You should take mine," Raúl told him. "They may not have one in the store today."

Raúl and Pepito went back to work then, and Papa and I left them alone. I don't know whether he thought we were out of earshot, but I heard Raúl say to his father, "How long, do you think, before they starve to death?"

And Pepito called out to us, "I will try to bring you some fish, señor. Maybe tonight."

"That would be wonderful," Papa called back. To me he said, "Aren't they nice men, Benita?"

"Yes," I said, making sure not to sound too enthusiastic.

The store was set in the shade of a circle of trees. Built from concrete blocks painted blue, it was more like a storage hut than a shop, but it had a screen door and a bell that rang when we entered. Papa and I stood at the counter and were waited on by a seven-year-old boy whose round stomach stuck out over the elastic waistband of his shorts. A heavyset man swung from a sagging hammock in the corner.

"Are you the proprietor?" my father asked the boy.

"I am Carlos," he answered.

"My son," said the man in the hammock. "And my store. I'm Francisco."

"What can I get for you?" said the boy.

There wasn't much on the shelves. Some boxes of candles. Dried milk sold by the case, bags of rice, cooking oil. And, I was most happy to see, several rolls of toilet tissue.

"We'll take five kilos of that rice," Papa said. "A box of candles and matches too, please."

I whispered in Papa's ear, "I want some toilet paper, please."

"Two rolls of that paper product, boy."

"You like Mexican beer?" asked the man in the hammock. "Tastes good on a very hot day."

Papa's forehead was beaded with sweat. "I'd love some, but we don't have any way to keep it cold."

"It's already cold. Show him, Carlos."

Carlos led us to a back room. There was a large humming metal box and attached to it was a medium-sized ice cooler. Carlos opened the lid on the cooler to let us have a look inside, and we saw a stock of bottled beer and soda pop, tubs of butter and a few dozen eggs. Papa pulled out two bottles of the beer, an orange-flavored soda for me, a handful of eggs and brought these out to the counter.

"That generator runs on gasoline, then?" Papa asked the store owner. To Carlos, he gestured to the bottles of beer. "I'll drink those now." Carlos cracked the necks of the bottles against a metal opener attached to the wall, and Papa drank them down very fast. "Ah, that's good," he said.

Carlos opened my soda, and like Papa, I drank it down in a freezing cold rush. I felt the sugar hit my blood almost immediately. The empty bottle was still cold and ice dribbled all down the sides. I wished I could stick it inside the front of my dress and rub it all over my body.

"I was told you sell fishing rods," Papa said.

Francisco said, "I have to order them. Takes a few weeks."

"Also, I need these other things. Maybe you can help." Papa showed him his list.

"Yes, I can get all this for you but it will cost more than if you go to the mainland and get it yourself."

"I can't leave the island right now. Can't leave my wife."

The store owner climbed out of the hammock with a groan, then took the list from my father, copied it into his book and handed it back. "I'll go next week. But you pay now."

Papa carefully counted out the coins. As we were leaving, he reached out to shake hands with Francisco.

"We're very glad to have found your shop," Papa said. "My name is—"

"Yes, everyone knows about you, Señor Mariah." He didn't shake Papa's hand. "See you soon."

On the way home Papa said, "Just wait till your mother hears. That store is going to make our lives so much easier."

Somehow I didn't think cold beer was going to make much difference to Mama. But I decided to let her tell Papa that herself. Besides, I was busy building up my own hope—that once we got our own rod, maybe I could ask Raúl to teach me how to fish.

CHAPTER

6

Papa got to work building our new house right away. He used money from the sale of our home in Guayaquil to have construction materials brought over from the mainland. His vision for our tropical compound included a grand house that would one day be surrounded by fields of coconut palms stretching as far as the eye could see.

The ten men who'd signed on to help with the building project came one morning to begin work, and Papa took them and Joam, who'd act as his interpreter, on a tour of the supplies stacked at the back of our hut.

"What are these flat pieces of wood?" one of the islanders asked.

Papa picked up a sheet of milled plywood and stood it on its end. "We'll use these for the walls."

When Joam translated this, the crew laughed out loud. "You can't use boards to build a house," they told my father.

"And why not?"

They said that boards were too heavy and that a strong wind could pull such a house apart. Palm thatch was much better because it let the wind through and also dried more quickly after a storm. Then they asked him about the pile of plain two-by-fours lying on the ground. It was nearly two stories tall.

"What will you do with those big wood sticks?"

"That's what we'll use to frame the house. You put the boards on top of the sticks."

Papa took four of the "wood sticks" to show the crew what he had in mind, placing them flat on the ground, end to end in a square. Then he dropped a piece of plywood flat on top.

The islanders were in an uproar, all yelling at once. Joam tried to keep up with their voices. "They want to know how you will tie the boards to the sticks with lianas vine."

"Forget the vines. You're going to nail it all together," Papa said.

Apparently nails were not common on the island either, and Joam didn't even try to translate this for the crew at all. Papa sent everyone home and stood there then, just staring at the sky and muttering, "Goddamn backward *indios* . . . Can't even count on them to do a simple job."

That night Papa asked Mama whether he should hire real builders from off-island, but she said, "We can't afford it. Do as the islanders do, Josef." And so he returned most of the building supplies, got his money back and reconfigured his ideas about the kind of house he'd build.

In the meantime he took us fishing. We set out with Raúl's rod to see whether we could catch our dinner. Down on our beach, near the water's edge, Papa opened up Raúl's tackle box, and we peered inside. It was exciting for me to be going through his things, as if I were learning some secret about him even though I was only looking at a bunch of squiggly rubber lures. "Which one do you think we should use?" Papa asked.

"How about that silvery one?" I suggested. "It looks like a sardine."

Papa picked the one I liked. "I'll bait the hook the first time and then you can each take a turn." He ran the line through an eyehole on the nose of the lure and tied one, two, three knots to hold it in place. "That should do it. Stand back now. I'm going to throw this lure out into the ocean." He took the rod in both hands and swung it around just like a baseball bat. The lure went streaking down the beach, landing in the sand with a thud.

"Let's try that again." Papa cranked the reel's handle to tow the line back to us. He tried a few more times without success, but on the fourth try he landed it in the surf, and my brothers and I cheered.

"Now we've got it," Papa said, but the line went slack as a wave caught up the lure and it rolled back toward shore.

"Blast it!" Papa yelled.

"Can I do it now?" Manuel asked.

We watched Manuel cast out, but he had the same trouble as Papa. And so did José. When I got my turn, I figured out that it was possible to cast farther if you held on to the line with your finger until the very last moment, when the rod was pointed at the ocean, but even I couldn't set the lure out far enough to keep it from trailing back in the waves.

After an hour Papa was ready to give up.

"So we're not having fish for dinner?" Poor Alfonse looked as if that was the saddest thing in the whole world.

"Not tonight."

"Can we fish again tomorrow?" José asked.

My father turned to him. "I have too much work to do.

We'll try again when our rod arrives with Francisco. Return this one to Raúl for me, boys."

I perked up. "I think I should go with them."

"I suppose it's all right. You'll be with your brothers, after all. As long as you're going, bring me a few beers." Papa gave me four coins and then walked away from us very fast, as if he had much more important things to do. But I knew he was probably just going to sit on the porch and smoke a cigarette and look at his drawings of the house he couldn't build.

When we got to the village, we found Raúl working on a fishing boat, smearing some white paste into the woodwork on one side.

"Hello, Raúl," I said, trying to sound casual. My heart was threatening to beat its way out of my chest.

"Yeah, hey." He didn't even look up.

"What are you doing?"

"Patching holes."

I wasn't sure what else to say, but then I noticed the boat had a name. "So . . . who's La Rosita?" I asked.

"She was my mother."

"Was?"

"She died."

"Oh, gosh . . . I didn't know."

Raúl stopped working. "What do you want, Little Girl? Can't you see that I'm busy?"

I hated the way he called me that, because I only felt like a little girl when I was around him.

"Papa asked us to return your fishing rod. Here it is." Then I blurted, "And I'm sorry your mother died."

Raúl stood up and wiped his hands on his shorts. "It was a long time ago. I was ten." He reached for the rod, and as I handed it over I noticed how beads of sweat were rolling down his brown chest and into the waistband of his shorts, which had slipped low onto his hipbones.

"How old are you now?" I asked.

Raúl stared at me as if I were a little crazy. I was beginning to think that maybe he didn't like me. "I'm twenty-one," he said, and before I got a chance to tell him my age, he turned to my brothers. "Any luck with this?" he asked about the rod.

José spoke up. "We didn't catch anything. Every time we threw the lure out, it came right back to us on a wave."

"Do you think it's magic? Throw the lure in and a fish bites? You have to learn how to trick them. Come, I'll show you."

Raúl led us down to the water's edge. My brothers were skipping to keep up with him, like a pack of happy puppies. They looked so much like him—dressed exactly like Raúl in shaggy shorts clinging to their bottoms, their skin dusty and dark like his, wild heads of black hair.

"Who tied this lure?" Raúl asked. "You'll need a knife to get it off." He cut the line and retied it, then handed the rod to José. "Let me see you cast."

José gave it his best shot but sent the lure right into the first wave.

"You have to hold on to it longer," I told him.

Raúl looked surprised. "She's right." He took José's index finger and put it in the right spot. "Don't let go of the line until the rod is straight over the sea. Point it at the sun."

This time José cast the lure properly. It sailed out into the ocean a good thirty feet or so. Raúl patted him on the shoulder. "Very good," he said, and José looked so pleased. "Now, don't just let the lure come back on its own. You've got to reel it in."

José started spinning the reel's handle.

"Too fast," Raúl said. "Do it slowly. Make the lure look like a swimming fish. I'll show you." He took the rod and spun it delicately, observing the line the whole time. "Watch the water. Do you see the lure jumping in the white surf? Looks like a sardine, yes?"

"Hey, that's what you said, Benita!" José said.

"She's a know-it-all," said Manuel.

"Well, then you better listen to her. Right?" said Raúl.

Manuel looked up at Raúl in shock. "I guess so."

"Now keep doing that, José. Cast and reel in. Again and again. You'll catch a nice big fish."

"Say thank you to Raúl," I told them.

"It's no problem," Raúl said. "But I have to finish my work now or La Rosita will spend the day on land again tomorrow. Good luck with your fishing. Best time is early in the morning or when the sun is low at the end of the day. That's when the fish like to eat."

"Don't forget your rod," I reminded him.

"Don't you want it?"

"Papa bought us one, so . . ."

"So you don't need mine anymore? Is that how it is?"

He seemed mad about it. "It's just that Papa asked us to return it to you. That's all."

"Two rods are better than one, but if that's how he wants it . . ." Raúl shrugged and left us.

A week later the supplies Francisco purchased for us arrived. Papa got a shovel that he promptly brought to the back of our property, away from the shack, and he dug a deep hole. He asked the island natives to build a thatched hut around it, and finally we had some privacy to go to the bathroom instead of always having to try to hide behind a rock or a big shrub.

My brothers took their new fishing rod and went out in the

morning and early evening of every day. Though they did catch fish every once in a while, they never hooked anything big enough to put a stop to our hunger.

Meanwhile Papa dug holes all around our land, looking for another spring, but the metal blade came up dry every time.

Papa's other useful purchase was an ax, which made it possible for us to chop wood for a fire, rather than having to forage for it as if we were lost in the woods. My father did most of the chopping. He had the boys practice their swing against the base of a coconut tree.

The tall ladder that arrived made picking fruit from the trees easier, and that became my daily job. I didn't mind. Sometimes I'd climb up the ladder and sit on a high branch for a while, just watching the whole island from my perch. I could see the village of Subidalta, the fishing boats being launched in the morning, the women playing with their children in the surf, the islanders working in their cotton field. The islanders seemed to have a peaceful life on Paíta—unlike my family. Everything was a struggle for us, though we accomplished very little.

In a way, watching the islanders was like being back on the Malecón. The lives of strangers were going on all around me with a pleasant rhythm. I sat there wondering why I couldn't be a part of it. Not then and not now.

But I was happy about the sandals Francisco had brought. He called them huaraches; they were made of a basket weave of narrow leather straps. They protected my soles from the harsh ground, but stretched and moved easily, and they were much cooler than my oxfords. My old school shoes were getting too small for me anyway, and they were only a reminder that all my classmates were back at their desks learning things I might never get to know.

When I'd asked Papa about the tutor, he'd said, "Not yet, Benita. I haven't time to find you a teacher. There's too much to do. Be patient."

I snuck down to the beach that night and threw my school shoes into the surf.

Mama had asked for a broom, and she swept every hour or so, as if she were on a God-given mission to keep the shack clean. Papa and I learned to brush off our feet at the door but she would get angry with my brothers every time they passed through. One time she cuffed Alfonse on the ear when he came into the hut with tar-stained feet. I'd never heard him scream like that, and Mama felt so bad that she held him in her lap for an hour, just rocking him and saying over and over, "Forgive me, forgive me."

Mama's other occupation was making rice. She'd cook up a huge pot twice a day and we filled our bellies with it. We'd eat it fried up with butter and if the boys caught a fish, no matter how small, Mama would make us a fishy rice soup. We were all getting sick to death of rice. One night Papa tried to make a joke about it. He lifted the lid on Mama's pot and said, "Rice again?"

Mama spun around. "How dare you! I've done everything I can with the little that you've provided!"

"Of course you have," Papa said. "I didn't mean that . . ."

"If my cooking isn't good enough for you, why don't you hire a cook? One of those barefoot pathetic *indios*."

"Pilar, I didn't mean to hurt your feelings."

Mama's fury filled up the whole room. "Don't you think I hate it too? And not just the rice. All of it. I hate this hut, I hate this island and I HATE YOU!"

Papa rushed to her side and Mama collapsed in a weeping heap in his arms. "Children, why don't you eat your dinner on the porch tonight?" Papa said.

I served my brothers and we went out and ate our rice by candlelight without saying a word, all of us trying to eavesdrop on our parents. But we didn't hear another sound coming from the shack.

The next morning Papa asked whether I wanted to go with him to buy a chicken. We left at first light and the shrieking roosters announced our arrival in the village. Several men came out of their huts. Papa's presence seemed to cause a bit of panic; I heard them call for Joam. But Papa didn't wait. He spoke to the oldest man in the group.

"We'll take that one," he said, pointing at the red rooster. "We want a few chickens, too."

The islanders were clearly baffled: Why had this strange man woken them up to point at their chickens? "They don't understand you, Papa. We need to find Joam."

"I'll make them understand." Papa reached into his trouser pocket and pulled out a heaping handful of coins. "How much do you want for that rooster?" He pointed at the scrawny thing pecking at the ground, but this time he held out the coins.

Three men shouted at Papa; each of them wanted to be the one to sell the bird. There was some pushing and shoving, and the women came out of their huts to see what was going on. Everyone crowded around. The oldest man in the group shouted something and put an end to their argument. I could see him calculating: How much should he ask for?

Papa held the coins out toward him, saying, "Take what you want."

With great uneasiness, the man took one coin and then two more. When Papa did not object, he took a fourth and a fifth. But as he reached for the sixth, Papa closed up his hand, and the man stepped back. Two chickens were sold to us in the same way.

"See that, Benita? Money is the universal language."

When this business was done, waves of joy swept through the village. There was so much excitement, I realized it must have been the first time they had ever held a coin that they could call their own. The people around us were laughing and dancing in the sand. A coin toss started up, but it turned aggressive, and when Joam arrived, he stopped it, returning the coin to its rightful owner. The older man's wife took it from him then and placed it deep inside her cleavage for safety.

Joam walked us home that day. "Where did the people of Paíta come from?" I asked him.

"The Jivarro have always been here," he told me. "We were born on the island, our parents were born on the island and our grandparents came from Paíta too."

"*Indigenos,*" Papa said. "They're simply the natives of Paíta."

"Were you born on the island, Joam?"

"Yes, but my father was not happy here. He left with my mother and me and found a job on a sugarcane farm in the mountains far away. When he died, my mother brought me back here."

"So you learned Spanish as a child growing up on that farm?"

Joam simply nodded.

"Are you the only Jivarro person who can speak our language?"

"My people know some words, but they never speak it. And the men who fish know some of ours. It is enough."

"Those women who stay at the spring all day and ask for water . . . who are they talking to?"

"There are spirits that watch over this place. They are very old, but powerful."

"And the Jivarro believe those spirits can make it rain?"

"No, the spirits we speak to *are* the rain. But there are many other spirits that give life to the island. The sun is our father. It grows our food. The earth is our home. Our mother."

"Do you understand now, Benita?" my father asked. He sounded annoyed.

"Not really. You pray to the earth? Is that voodoo?" I asked Joam.

"I don't know that word," he said.

"Benita!" My father looked shocked. "That's enough. Who put that idea in your head?"

Back at our hut Papa followed me inside and shut the door. He spoke in a whisper. "What the *indios* believe is sheer blasphemy. It's an insult to God for you to even speak of those things. I don't ever want to hear you talking like that again."

"I'm sorry, Papa. I didn't know."

After he left, I stood there stunned for a moment. How could speaking about what the *indios* believed be wrong? It wasn't as if I believed what they did. I was only asking questions. I'd have to consult my encyclopedia rather than bring it up with Papa again.

I picked up volume J-L and looked up Jivarro, but there was nothing. These people were unknown to the world; they didn't exist outside of Paíta. I also looked up voodoo and found out that Olga's sister had got that wrong. It was a kind of religion practiced on a completely different island that was nowhere near Paíta.

Maybe I'd never understand exactly what these island natives did believe. All I knew was that they'd been very helpful to my family so far.

A few weeks later Papa purchased a scabby-looking goat from another island family, which started us out with our own little farm. Now we had fresh eggs and milk every day. When the islanders heard about the snake problem we had, they came to us in a group, and Joam translated what they said: "Snakes are evil. They cannot be allowed in the house, and not on the roof, either. You must use this poison, and they will leave." We put it into the thatch that very day and those wicked snakes never came back.

When Papa had new drawings finished, he was ready to try building our house again. It took the islanders only a few weeks to construct it. Finally, after three months, we could move out of the shack. Our new house was very much like a huge thatched hut. It was two stories tall, but there wasn't much to the inside; it was mainly one big room with a very high ceiling that had two little windows sticking out of the roof way up there. That was the one element from his original plan that Papa wouldn't give up, because these "dormer windows," as he called them, reminded him of a classic American plantation house.

It would have been very nice if a second floor had been built. As it was, our house had the distinction of being the only one on Paíta with windows nobody could look through.

There was a long porch on the front of the house, and a kitchen area at the back. We had a sink to wash things but no running water, and there was a cooking pit that vented through the roof. We had to supply it with wood. And we had some furniture as well—a dining table and several chairs made from some of the wood Papa had purchased when we first arrived. We placed rough shelves in the kitchen area to store Mama's fancy tableware.

My parents had their own room, and Papa built a bedroom for me so that I wouldn't have to sleep with my brothers. My quiet room with its single window was right next to the kitchen area, and it was so small that I had only a bed of cotton batting on a simple wooden frame and a bookcase made from a couple of pieces of scrap wood. But I liked the room well enough. It caught the morning light, but was cool and dark from the middle of the day into evening. It was all mine with a door I could shut, and I insisted that my room was off-limits to anyone who did not knock first.

The last thing the islanders did was place a figure of a bull, made of red clay, on our roof. They told us that the bull was strong and would protect our house. But Papa said it was "a bunch of mumbo jumbo," and he took it down and threw it into the ocean. I was sorry he did; I thought it was nice of the islanders to give us something, and besides, that bull seemed special. I could see the fingerprints of the person who'd made it embedded in the clay, and it wasn't at all spooky or weird. I wouldn't have minded having it in my room. But I didn't say any of that to Papa.

Our lives didn't change much even though we had this new house. Night would fall and we'd sit around in the growing dark all together. Papa spent his evenings smoking cigarette after cigarette and staring into the distance. Mama would take out her jewelry and look at each piece, as if she needed to make certain it was all still there. My brothers thought it hysterical to make farting sounds. Our radio was useless on Paíta; otherwise there would have been something else to listen to. This was a big frustration for Papa, cut off from the spiritual sustenance of the Voice of the Andes.

I wrote in my diary or read by candlelight. And I replayed every detail of Raúl's fishing lesson in my mind: how nice he was to my brothers, how helpful, how strong his hands looked holding the rod, the way his beautiful eyes focused on the water and how the light was reflected in them. I calculated our age difference too. He was seven years older than me, which was much less than the number of years between Mama and Papa. I let that fact take hold of me. It heated my blood even more than the sun that seemed to burn a hole in the sky every single day.

CHAPTER

7

Constructing the house was easy as hopscotch compared to starting the coconut farm. The first stage in Papa's plan: clear a field large enough to plant two hundred coconut palms. We'd have ten rows with twenty plants in each.

It didn't make any sense to me. Not when there were hundreds of coconut trees on the island already—that army of palms we'd seen lining the shore the day we arrived on Paíta.

"Oh, those palms are too old," Papa said when I asked him why we couldn't use the Paíta palms to get rich. "They're past their prime."

"But they've got coconuts growing on them."

"From my studies I have learned that the oil produced by a single coconut starts to diminish when the tree is ten years old. Those trees you're referring to are probably twenty years old at the very least. Do they produce coconuts? Yes, but those coconuts are of no use to us."

"But we could harvest the old trees. You're simply saying they won't produce as much, right, Papa?"

Papa had to think for a moment. "Yes, yes, I suppose so. But my research shows that they'd produce so *little* that we might as well weave baskets for a living. Trust me on this. I did my homework, child. We need younger trees to make money here. Understand?"

I was starting to annoy Papa, so I shut up.

We needed to level three acres of overgrown jungle. All of us—Papa, me and the boys and the same islanders who built our house—had machetes in our hands twelve hours a day. Mama had been excused from the job. Papa said she wasn't feeling well, and when I went to look in on her, she was lying in bed with a wet handkerchief over her eyes and moaning softly. Her hair was loose, flowing over the pillow like a patch of dark seaweed, a crazy mess.

"Are you all right?"

"It's my head," she said weakly. "It's pounding. But don't worry about me."

As soon as I left her room, the moaning stopped.

Once I got to work, I realized that having a headache would be better than doing this sweaty job. The mosquitoes were terrible. I had bleeding bite marks all over my body. By the end of the second day, the bites on my ankles got infected and my legs were all puffy and numb.

When Papa noticed, he got worried, but I said, "It's okay, Papa. It doesn't hurt. When I touch them, they don't even seem like my legs."

"That's not good. I want you to go rest in the house. We'll finish up here."

My brothers stood there as if they'd just been slapped. "How come she gets to quit?" Manuel yelled, hysterical. The sweat was running into his eyes, making him squint. "I don't want to do this anymore either!" he screamed.

74

Papa strode over to Manuel and caught him by the ear, picking him nearly straight up off the ground. He shouted in Manuel's face, "I'll make you sleep in this field if you ever talk like that again!" Manuel was fighting back tears. I got out of there quickly, before Papa changed his mind and called me back. He yelled at Manuel, "Get to work, now. Don't be such a girl. Put some muscle into it!"

The next morning my legs were still numb, but as I watched my brothers pick up their machetes and head out the door, I felt guilty. I changed my mind when I went out into the field with lunch. Even the tough-skinned islanders looked pale from the heat. They collapsed to the ground when I handed them their napkins full of fried banana, and they practically inhaled the food. Then they just sat there, exhausted, staring out at nothing in particular until Papa gave the word that it was time to go back to work. It was horrible to see them so beaten down. But I couldn't build Papa's plantation for him. I told myself that at least these people were earning some money, unlike my brothers.

Not very long after we'd cleared the field, the coconut plants arrived. From the porch of our new house, we saw the cargo ship come in. It was huge, with a black metal hull, and everyone on the island went down to the village beach to watch it pull in.

The large ship dropped anchor a little way out in deep water, even farther out than we had been on the day we arrived on Paíta. Then a much smaller boat was slowly lowered from the deck into the surf. The ship's cargo bay door slid open to reveal a couple of large wooden crates sitting at the threshold. Two of these crates were picked up by a crane that extended over the ship's deck, and they were placed precisely into the smaller boat waiting on the water.

Many of the islanders watched, forming a circle around us as the smaller boat motored toward shore. They seemed as eager as we were to get the delivery. The boat came in only thirty feet from shore, and then it stopped. It wasn't as small as I'd initially thought; it was a seaworthy ship with an upper and lower deck. A man came out from the cabin at the top.

"Who here is Josef Mariah?" he yelled to us onshore.

Papa took a few steps into the ocean toward the boat. "I am Mariah."

"This is the port of Subidalta?"

"Yes, it is," my father shouted.

"Where is the dock?"

"There is no dock."

The boatman cursed under his breath. "How are we to unload this cargo, señor?"

"Can't you come in any closer to shore?"

"Not unless we want to live here. We'd beach the boat."

Papa stood in the water with his hands on his hips, staring at the boat and his precious cargo just out of reach. "How many crates have you got for us?"

"Four total. These two and two more on board."

"Let me think for a moment." He waded toward shore and faced the crowd of islanders. They looked back at him, full of doubt.

"Please translate for me, Joam." Papa addressed the crowd. "People. We need to bring what is in those boxes to the farm."

When Joam translated, several of them walked away without a word.

Papa continued. "If the fishing boats were here, I would not ask you to help. I would ask the fishermen instead. But they are gone for the day. If we do not bring in the seeds for planting, the coconut farm will not be built."

The islanders still on the beach began to murmur among themselves.

Why would any of them care? I wondered.

"If we do not plant the field, I cannot promise you work every year of your life, not now or in the future. Any hope we had for prosperity when the farm produces coconuts will be gone."

Joam translated this, and there were groans from the crowd. Papa did not turn to look at us. He waited for the islanders to respond. I had no idea how dependent he was on these people, that he had promised them a permanent livelihood, or any of the success we might enjoy. I could tell Mama was surprised too. But worst of all, Papa had made a promise that he couldn't keep, and now they knew it. They talked angrily among themselves, and I stepped back, wishing I could run. What if they tried to kill us?

I got the shock of my life when Joam translated their answer for Papa. "They say, 'You need our help, and we will help!' "

"That's the spirit!" Papa shouted with joy. "You won't be sorry." He ran up and shook each person's hand, and they were all laughing together then. I felt that they were laughing at him a little bit, and that Papa knew it and he didn't mind because everything had worked out.

"Come, come," Papa said. "Let's get busy!"

He walked into the sea and gestured for the islanders to follow him. "Come along," he said to me and Mama and the boys, and we walked into the water along with everybody else. I could hardly believe that Papa had turned things around so quickly.

He spoke to the boatman. "We need you to unload the cargo for us. Right here. You'll have to put it down into the water."

"You'll lose half of it, señor. You want to watch it float away in the current?"

"Well, it's mine to lose, isn't it?" Papa said.

"Are you nuts?" said the boatman.

Papa threw his head back and laughed as if he *had* gone mad. "That's it!" he shouted. "I've gone stark, raving loco! Now unload that cargo!"

The boatman disappeared into the boat's cabin and came back out with a crowbar. He started hacking into the top of the cargo crates.

I must have been looking at Papa with all the panic of that crazy day on my face, because he came splashing through the ocean and scooped me into his arms. "Don't you worry, Benita. Everything is going to be just fine. I have an idea of how we should do this." He was shaking with excitement. "Joam, ask someone to bring all the fishing nets they can find. Let's go! Quickly now." He put me down and clapped his hands, and two of the islanders bounded out of the water to do as Joam had said.

They came back with three small nets. "Perfect," Papa said. "I want you to unroll them. We need a person standing every two feet. Spread out now, people." Joam spoke, and the villagers moved into place.

"Try to drop the cargo into the nets, please," Papa shouted up to the boatman.

Three men began hurling coconuts into our fishing nets. We had the three nets filled up almost immediately.

As I stood holding my section of the net, I realized that I was looking at a bunch of raw nuts. I thought we'd be planting little sprouts—the beginnings of coconut trees.

"How much is left in that crate?" Papa asked the boatman.

"Only a quarter empty now."

"We're going to have to take these to shore." Before the boatman had a chance to respond, Papa started walking slowly toward the beach with the cargo, pulling the tribe of islanders along with him. "We'll dump this load on the beach and come back for the rest. We should be able to do it in a couple of trips."

"This is going to take all day!" the boatman yelled.

"Just ignore him," my father said to all of us.

Late in the afternoon we stood looking at those coconuts on the beach, all two hundred. The pile was bigger than any of the huts.

"How are we going to move them to the planting field, Papa?" I asked.

"Like this," Papa said as he bent over and started to load his arms with big brown nuts. We all worked into the night, carrying coconuts back toward the grove clearing, nearly a mile from the beach. We stumbled back and forth in the sand, in the dark, passing each other like weary ghosts until there were no more of those stupid coconuts left to move. We were so tired we didn't even bother with dinner. I fell onto my bed in my sweaty clothes and slept a black, dreamless sleep.

Papa woke up before any of us, and we found him in the field, marking where he wanted each coconut to be planted with sticks. The islanders met us there and began to break ground under Papa's close supervision. Papa did not ask his family to help. We stood around and watched. The islanders looked more tired than I had ever seen them. Papa was too excited to notice, or care, how anyone else was feeling. He marched back and forth up the rows, like a wartime sergeant surveying the field of battle. If he was unhappy with the placement of a coconut, he made the islander dig it up, fill the hole and start over.

During the lunch break I sat down next to Papa. "I thought you would start the farm with little plants."

"I chose to sow coconuts instead, because they're more hardy and travel more easily than tender young shoots. They're cheaper, too. I wouldn't have been able to buy as many plants and the grove would have been much smaller than it needs to be to earn a profit. I'm glad you're taking an interest."

"How long before they grow to be trees?"

"Before you know it," Papa said, and stood to address the islanders. "Time to get back to work, people."

They worked quickly and by midday the grove was finished. Everyone gathered at the entrance to the grove at quitting time and spoke quietly to one another and to Joam. They seemed to discuss something important, and many angry looks were coming our way.

"I think you should thank everyone, Papa," I said.

"Of course, you're right." My family walked to where the islanders stood together.

Joam said, "Mariah. Now you have your field. Our work is done. We will not come back here again."

"Don't give up now. This is only the beginning of wonderful, profitable operation."

Joam stopped him. "Not for us. We want no more to do with this place of yours."

We shared a look then, my mother and brothers and I. "But . . . but why?" Papa stammered.

"Too much trouble." He said something to the islanders, and they all put down their shovels and left the grove. They seemed stunned, too tired to laugh or make jokes as I had often seen them do when the workday was done in their cotton field.

We turned back to look at the grove. It was one big patch of red dirt, raw and aching. "Just you wait," Papa said, and we followed him back to our overgrown hut.

PART 3

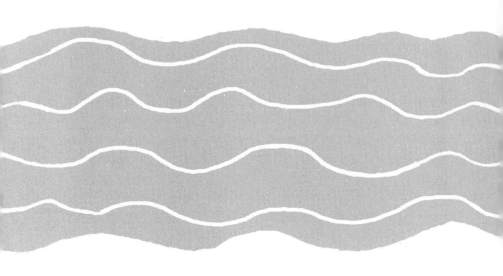

ENCOUNTERS

CHAPTER

8

So we waited for the coconuts. And waited. Months went by, but nothing happened in the grove. In the meantime everything changed for us. I had the feeling that time was rolling over my family like the ocean waves that crashed on the beach—washing away the people we once were, making our lives completely unrecognizable from what they were before.

Every day Mama would ask, "Josef, what are we going to do if the coconuts don't grow?"

"They will. Just give them time."

"And what we will live on until then?"

"We're doing fine. What are you worried about?"

"We are not fine!" she shouted. "You planted most of our money in the ground. My God, what will we do when it's all gone?"

"Now, now, Pilar. You're just upsetting yourself."

I didn't want to get hysterical like Mama, but I had the same question for Papa. Even though he seemed to be ignoring her, he must have been worried too.

The islanders kept away from our part of the island after the plantation project, as though they'd decided we should remain strangers. But Papa needed them too much to allow that.

He headed over to their cotton field one morning and I decided to go along because I didn't have anything else I wanted to do. We just sat on the hill for a while watching the natives work. Their cotton field wasn't very large, maybe ten feet by twenty, and it was nothing more than a dry, dusty patch of ground. But the plants looked healthy despite the lack of fresh water on the island.

Raúl was bent low over the rows, which brought out the big muscles of his broad brown back. Like the others, he moved with a mechanical rhythm as he picked the white tufts from the jaws of the plants and stuffed them into baskets.

"They'll have about two bales' worth, when they're finished," Papa said. "They produce a crop just big enough to give them what they need to spin and make that rough cloth that the women and children wear. Or they turn it into rope and make hammocks."

I just nodded. I didn't care anything about the cotton.

"If they had planted a few weeks earlier," Papa continued, "they could have taken it to the big market in Guayaquil at the first of the month. Now they'll have to wait." He was studying the field and barely breathing.

"Do they take it to market, Papa? I thought you just said they used it up themselves."

"Yes, that's right. They use it up. They waste it. But I'm going to change that." Papa stood up and headed down the hill. I followed him to where Joam was working. The translator stood slowly; I could tell he didn't want to speak to Papa. "Tell the islanders I want to buy their cotton."

"What for?" Joam pointed at me. "Your children have clothes to wear."

"It's not for me. I'm going to sell it."

I'd been watching Raúl this whole time. Like the rest of the people working in the field, he'd been ignoring my father. But now he came right over. I had to step back to get out of his way. "This cotton is not for sale," he said.

Papa started talking much faster to Raúl. "Listen, if you let me buy this crop, I'll take it to market in Guayaquil. I'll sell it there and split the profits with you people. Half to me and half to you. You'll make money enough to buy hammocks to last you ten years."

Raúl laughed then, and the people nudged at him, as if to say, "What does the crazy man want now?" Joam translated my father's speech for the crowd, and when he'd finished, every single islander was staring at my father with disbelief.

But I could see that Raúl was intrigued, even though he tried to hide it. "What makes you so sure you can sell it all?"

"I know all the dealers in the market because I used to sell them lace. They'll purchase your cotton because we can price it lower than everyone else does. And do you know why? Because other sellers don't grow it themselves. They must buy it from a source like yourselves, and then they raise the price so they can make a small profit when they sell it to the dealer."

I could see that Raúl understood exactly what Papa was talking about. "The market is not something you can control," he said. "You can't guarantee you'll sell it."

"I *will* sell all of it, and you'll have more money than you could ever dream of. And if I don't, I'll return all your cotton. You have nothing to lose."

"We will think about this," Raúl said, and everyone went back to work.

The very next day Raúl and his father came walking up the beach toward our house. I took a quick look around and saw how my brothers' soiled clothes were heaped in the main room and dirty pots littered the cooking area. Quickly I gathered everything up and went to store it in my parents' room. Mama was lying in bed. I dropped the pots beside her. "What's gotten into you?" she said.

"We have company!" I shouted, and went back to the living room to sweep as fast as I could.

Mama came out of her room and looked out the front windows. Raúl and his father were already at the porch, and Papa was inviting them inside. I stashed the broom and ran my hands through my hair. "I'm sure Pepito will be very impressed." Mama gave my cheek a pinch. I swatted her hand away.

They didn't stay more than a minute. Raúl told Papa they'd sell him the cotton.

"I didn't know Raúl was in charge of the cotton field," my mother said after they left.

"He won't be for long," Papa said. A week later he took the cotton to Guayaquil. He sold it all, returning to the island with a pocketful of cash, as he'd promised.

Papa took over the cotton production after that. He had the islanders plant three more fields with the money they'd earned from the first sale, increasing the crop. According to Papa, the islanders were happy because they liked having brand-new hammocks to sleep in and clothes to wear, and because of that they were working for him. Just as it had the day the coconuts arrived, everything worked out exactly as Papa wanted it to.

This was all very fortunate for us because it didn't look as though the coconut plantation was going to provide us with income anytime soon. Four months after we planted the coconuts, they did sprout, but the pale green leafy stalks that rose out of the red Paíta dirt withered in the searing heat within a week.

Behind Papa's back, my brothers and I referred to the field as "the disaster zone." It was their job to try to keep the plantation grounds moist. Once a week, all our water went to the farm, and each tree got a half inch of water from a bucket. It wasn't nearly enough.

I'd bring my brothers their lunch when the scorching sun was high in the sky, its touch like fire. One day when I spotted José and Manuel on the path ahead of me, carrying water, I ran to catch up to them, jumping from one shady spot to another. Burning hot dirt caught between my foot and sandal. We entered the grove together and I watched as they emptied their buckets.

"Four more done." Manuel threw his bucket down.

I held up their mangos. "Want to rest a minute?"

We slumped down together against the perimeter fence. "How much more do you have to do today?" I asked.

Manuel shrugged. "What difference does it make to you?"

José whacked our little brother across the chest. "Don't be a brat."

Manuel reached out to smack José on the back of the head.

"Can you stop fighting just for one minute?" I said.

"We're not even half done watering," José said.

We sat silently. Then Manuel spoke up. "Papa made some big mistakes when he planted this grove."

José sighed heavily.

"Not again with this, Manuel," I said.

"It's too far from the spring for one thing."

"It's as close as we could get," José said.

"Not close enough."

The boys spat the chewy mango pulp on the ground at our feet.

"So how do normal farmers water their fields? I'll bet they don't use buckets," Manuel said.

"Papa says that they irrigate," I said. "They build ditches to collect the water and then they pump it to their fields."

"So why don't we do that?"

"Because, you idiot, Papa said there's not enough water to pump," José said.

Manuel started to tap his foot back and forth in the sandy soil. "You're the idiot, José. You think if you agree with everything Papa says, he'll favor you," he said. "But he doesn't give a damn about us. Except to make sure we do all the stupid work."

José said, "You only say disgusting things, Manuel. I'm sick of it."

"Calm down, you two," I said.

"SHUT UP!" Manuel stood and kicked sand at us.

"You stupid jerk!" José yelled.

"Grow up, José. He's just acting like that to upset you," I said.

Manuel scampered away across the field. His voice cracked as he screamed, "Even the mangos taste like shit!" José stood up and ran after him. They tore out of the field like angry jackals ready to pull each other apart.

As I headed back to the house to finish up the chores Mama had given me, I found Alfonse sitting beside one of the porch supports. He was digging at it with his fingernails and popping tiny chunks of wood into his mouth, which he spat across the yard.

"Cut that out," I said.

"I'm not doing anything," he said, and flipped onto his back like a rag doll as I passed by, throwing an arm up to cover his face and hide from me.

I didn't like having so much work, but the truth was, aside from chores there wasn't much else to do. That was a big problem for Alfonse. Mama had decided that her little cross-eyed boy needn't do any housework, so he spent his unhappy days doing destructive things such as torturing insects, crushing them slowly with a rock, or tearing down our house bit by bit.

I placed a ladder against the trunk of the mango tree growing in our backyard. I worked my way up, clipping the dead branches, placing the fruit into a basket dangling from my arm. High up the ladder, I spotted Alfonse coming around the corner.

"Be-ni-ta!" he called out to me.

"Yes?" I sang out, imitating him.

He came and sat directly below the ladder, calling my name over and over. His hand shook the rungs.

"Don't touch the ladder! You'll make me fall."

"Benita, Benita!"

"Do you want a mango?" I said, pretending to be his kindly, caring sister.

"Yes!"

I plucked the most overripe fruit I could find and dropped it on his head. My aim was good. The pulpy fruit exploded, washing down the sides of his head and face. Alfonse screamed and burst into tears. I climbed down and ran into the house with my full basket and dropped it on the kitchen table. I meant to bolt for the beach before Mama could discover why her precious boy was crying, but he ran into her room, and I heard his wails getting even louder.

"Benita!" Mama called. "Come here."

She was still in her nightgown although it was noon. My brother clung to her with his face smothered against her chest.

Mama kissed him on the forehead. "You run along. I have to talk to your sister now."

Alfonse stuck out his tongue at me. Then with a sniffle or two, he got up out of her lap and left me alone with her.

"I need a favor, Benita," Mama said. "Would you fix my hair for me today? I'm so tired I don't think I can raise my arms to do it." She sat down on the little wooden stool in front of her mirror. "What would I do without you?" she said, handing me her brush.

She'd never asked me to help her like this before, but for some reason it felt like a bad idea. It wasn't a chore I wanted to do every day. But how could I say no? As I ran the brush through her long dark hair, Mama stared at me in the mirror.

"You're getting to be a very beautiful woman, Benita. Did you know that?"

"I guess."

"When I was your age I wanted so many things. But I didn't know what was most important in life. Not at all."

I sighed. "Like what, Mama?"

"Being practical. Taking care of your family."

I didn't answer.

"Don't you agree?"

"All I can think about, Mama, is getting off this island and going back to the life I was meant to have."

Mama took the brush from me. "You'd be a lot better off if

you stopped fighting against your fate. Don't spend time wishing for something you can't change. And if you can't do that, don't take your unhappiness out on your brothers."

I met her eyes in the reflection of the mirror. "Mama, I'm tired of living on Paíta. Aren't you?"

"Just look at me. I'm on the verge of a nervous collapse."

I twisted her hair up and clipped it at the top of her head.

"Ouch! That's too tight."

I redid it for her. While Mama admired her hairdo, she said, "I'm depending on you, Benita. You're the oldest and you have a responsibility to take care of your family. Don't make me remind you of that again."

Talking to Mama was making me more tired than all the chores I had to do. I couldn't even fight back.

"I think we should wash the sheets today," she said.

I stripped her bed, then went out and put a pot to boil on the fire. When it was ready I poured it into the deep metal drum we used as a washtub, and I scrubbed my parents' sheets against a corrugated metal washboard until my arms felt as if they'd drop off. I hung the sheets on the line and walked out to the beach to have a rest.

I don't know how long I sat there watching the surf come in and go out, but it was long enough to think about all the things I hated about Paíta. My hands were always dirty from work. I missed going to school. I missed my friends. I wished there was someone on the island I could really talk to.

And when I heard Papa calling to me from the porch— "Benita, time for your lesson. Are you coming?"—I remembered how bored I was with our tutoring sessions. Papa and I sat down to read or practice my French together for a half hour every afternoon. We read the same books over and over, and we practiced the language in the same way every time.

Papa drilled me on my tenses, and I realized we had to stick to formal methods because he didn't really speak the language well enough to converse with me. At first I wondered how he had managed to do business with the French lace makers; then I realized he probably had an interpreter over there, just as he did on Paíta.

"I'm coming, Papa," I called back, though I felt too tired to move.

I stood up and found Papa waiting for me on the front porch. He had a cigarette lit and an open bottle of beer by his side. All his books on agriculture were spread around the table. On the top was one titled *Farming Practices in Times of Drought*. I knew he was deep in study, trying to find a way to bring the grove to life despite the lack of water. This is what he did with his days. Sometimes he got desperate and took the shovel out to dig "one more time," trying to find another spring. There were holes all around the grove.

I took my seat across from him. "I don't want to read today," I said. "I just want to talk. Is that okay?"

"Yes, of course. What should we talk about?"

"Papa, what do you miss about living in Guayaquil? Tell me anything. It doesn't matter."

"What do I miss? Absolutely nothing. Those last months were very difficult."

"They were for me, too." I had a moment of hope just then that perhaps Papa would admit how hard everything had been.

He continued. "But it's all worked out as I'd hoped. I'm running my own business once again. The cotton farm provides for us well enough. Everything is as it should be."

"Yeah, right, it's a dream come true."

"Benita, you have no idea how close we were to utter poverty back in Guayaquil."

"I don't think living here is any better. There's nothing here that I want, or need, or dream of for myself. And my chance to go to college . . ."

"Benita, a dream is a good thing to have, as long as it doesn't spoil the life you are actually living."

"That's a terrible philosophy. I hate it."

"Well, I'm sorry, but that's probably the most important lesson I can teach you."

"That's why I should have a tutor. As you promised."

"I'm warning you, Benita. The way you're talking back is pushing me to the edge of my patience. Besides, I've told you that we can't afford to hire a teacher just yet. That's how it is. But I can bring some new books for you to read. Isn't that a good idea?"

I decided to change the subject. "Papa, do you remember when you asked me to try to be happy?"

Papa silently took a drag on his cigarette.

"It was the night before we came here," I reminded him.

"Of course I want you to be happy. What a silly question."

Mama called me to prepare dinner. Papa said nothing more, so I went into the kitchen. While I fried up a chicken we'd bought from the islanders that morning, Mama started cutting vegetables.

I could tell Papa didn't remember our last night back home. My happiness was no longer important to him. Not one bit. And that was absolutely the worst thing that had changed since we'd moved to Paíta.

The man I once thought was my father—he didn't exist anymore.

CHAPTER

9

Hanging around the plantation any more than I had to felt like a prison sentence so I started to spend more time away.

There weren't many places to go. I had once liked to play in the ocean, and my brothers had taught me how to ride the roughest waves. I was a good swimmer, but something happened that I couldn't get over.

I went out to swim on a day when the waves were huge, but I knew that at the very bottom of every churning wave there is always calm water, so that wasn't what frightened me. I waded in up to my knees, getting ready to dive deep beneath one that was rearing up. As it was about to crest, before it fell forward into a frenzied roll toward the beach, I leaned over to dive in and saw the sharp snout of a shark. It was riding that towering wave, its narrow eyes locked onto me. I was its target.

There was no time to run or swim away or scream. And before I could even think, I saw that shark gaze past me and I read in its eyes that it knew it was going to beach itself when the wave broke. The shark pivoted in one smooth and effortless move; it just turned and disappeared back into the sea.

But the wave shoveled and pummeled and pushed me like so much flotsam back toward the beach. I tumbled underwater for what felt like several minutes, the lack of air a crushing force inside my chest. When the wave finished with me, it threw me up onto the beach. Gasping and exhausted, I crawled out of the surf and sat down away from the water, covered in wet sand.

There was the whole ocean, the beach and the sun and sky to look at, but all I could see was that shark's face. I told myself it was only doing what was natural—I was food and nothing more—but it was a cold, mean spirit I'd seen bearing down on me, whose sole purpose at that moment was my death. I sat there on the beach, drying out, and I understood that there were bad things in the world. I knew that now for sure.

After that day I didn't go to the beach when I wanted to get away from my family. I went into the jungle behind our house. But I discovered I wasn't the only one who walked around back there. Many well-worn narrow trails seemed to cross the jungle floor in a strange way. Some meandered, going nowhere. Another one went back and forth across a small open patch of ground—it looked like sets of waves coming in toward the beach. One trail came around full circle to end near where it started.

At first I thought that the island pigs and goats that wandered loose must have made these trails, but I found man-made things that told a different story. I spotted a tiny mat woven from palm leaves. One day I picked up a small bunch of pink and blue flowers that someone had gathered together, then left behind.

And after a few days of searching around, I found a huge black stone at the end of one of the trails. The top of the rock had been carved flat like a tabletop, and a few burnt palm leaves covered the surface. I knew immediately what the stone was used for. It had to be an altar. Here was my proof finally. The islanders did practice some kind of weird ritual, and they did it right where I was now standing.

A wave of fear hit me, nearly as strong as the day I'd almost drowned. There are bad things in the world. I remembered my father's warning about the islander's beliefs—*"It's an insult to God"*—and I knew I must get out of there.

But I was in the grip of an invisible force that made me want to know more. I searched all around the altar. Back in Guayaquil, Olga's sister Rosa had said that the islanders were known to sacrifice animals, but there wasn't a drop of blood anywhere. Instead I found a powdery green substance sprinkled in the center of the altar. I dipped my finger into it, then smelled some kind of peppery spice.

My heart beat fast. I didn't think I was actually being watched, yet the feeling was there all the same. Maybe there were island spirits in this place, or maybe I just didn't belong here. It was time to go, but as soon as I turned away, I heard a familiar sound: female voices chanting, getting louder. The women must be making their way out to the rock.

I dropped to the jungle floor and crawled on my belly to hide beneath a bush. Seconds later they came walking past me in a straight line, one right after the other. They were dressed up with flowers in their hair, their arms and legs smeared with a fresh coat of red clay that made them seem so alike I couldn't tell one woman from the other. There were ten of them, the same age, the same height, the same voice chanting to the jungle.

The first woman carried a bundle of loose palm leaves, and she covered the top of the rock with them. The woman behind her stepped forward with a woven palm mat in her outstretched arms and placed it on the rock. When all the other women had gathered around, the leader lit the leaves with a match.

Their chanting got much softer while the smoke filled the air. This didn't seem at all like an evil ritual, but more like a moment of true communion between the women and the spirits they believed were listening to them. Still, I thought it was best to stay hidden, even though I wasn't so scared anymore and could even take in a normal breath.

When the fire had burnt down, they left one by one, still chanting. When they were far enough away, I stepped up to the altar to see the burnt remains of some fruit and a small bunch of flowers.

Their voices were getting fainter, so I decided to follow them at a distance, hiding behind trees. They were on the trail that was shaped like ocean waves, and they walked across it, a train of women in formation, chanting the same words over and over again. While I watched, I felt myself falling into a kind of trance. Back and forth they went, slowly and carefully placing one foot and then the other as they traversed this course. From where I sat it looked like an ocean of women, crisscrossing in front of and behind one another, swimming in and out of each other's way. Then they stopped, with a loud cry that woke me out of my reverie. Then they hugged one another and started to make their way out of the jungle.

I didn't want to turn around and go home. Nothing back there would be as interesting. I let them get a good head start, and then I followed.

Even though I never went to the village on my own, I started to walk more purposefully, practically marching, determined to make a strong impression on anyone I might meet.

There was no reason I couldn't fit in on Paíta if I tried. I was almost convinced of it when I arrived at the foothill of the sleepy little town.

It was the hottest part of the day, and standing there alone I realized that everyone would be inside their huts by now, sensibly keeping out of the boiling sun. Waves of visible heat stood between me and the first row of huts.

I was feeling a bit light-headed and I moved forward only because it seemed hotter to stand still. The village had the lure of a ghost town, empty and safe, as if it were mine to explore. Walking between the huts, I studied the little bits of native life I found: footprints in the hard, baked sand, scraps of vegetable material with a rotting stench that I had to step around. Then I overheard a twitter of laughter coming from the hill above me, and I moved toward the pleasant sound, arriving at a hut with no door.

Inside, a group of women sat around in a circle, maybe the same women I'd seen in the jungle. Several were braiding palm leaves, making more of the mats like the one on the altar. A pot was on the fire and I could smell the peppery scent that I'd smelled before, but more pungent. Something about the scene made me want to be a part of it. I stood there nearly a minute before they spotted me, near to swooning in their doorway. They stopped working then, and all eyes were on me.

A young woman stood up and came forward with a baby in her arms. She was probably only a few years older than me, her brown hair the same color as her eyes. I smiled at her. She did not smile back. She circled me, speaking in gibberish the whole time. Her eyes had narrowed to dark slits, and she reminded me of that shark.

"How old is your baby?" I said, trying to sound as friendly as I could.

98

"Ow eeth u BA bee!" she grunted as she bugged out her eyes at me.

"Is it a boy or a girl?"

Her mouth curled into a mean, toothy smile. "Ow eeth u BA bee!" she cried, and the other women in the hut laughed.

I realized then we were playing a game, the one in which your opponent repeats everything you say just to be annoying. The women seemed to be studying me to see whether I understood that I was being teased. Though I had stopped talking, the woman continued to dodge in and out, getting closer with every pass. "Ow eeth u BA bee!" she shrieked. I couldn't tell whether she was just trying to communicate or trying to be funny, or whether she hated the sight of me.

Shifting her babe onto her hip, she grabbed for my wrist with her free hand. I didn't wait to find out what she wanted. I slipped from her grip and ran from the hut. The women's high-pitched laughter trailed after me. I heard it in my head even after I arrived back home and was safe in my room.

I crashed down on my bed and buried my face in a pillow. I cried and cried, enormous silent sobs, all my anger and loneliness pouring out. I would never feel safe or belong in any way to this place, and I would never have any friends on Paíta. It was impossible.

After a while my tears wore themselves out, and I didn't feel as if I had any more hurt left inside of me. I decided I'd never tell anyone in my family about what had happened, and I'd never go out into the jungle or attempt to make contact with the natives again.

I spent the rest of the afternoon alone in my room with my encyclopedias. I'd created a ritual that always made me feel better. I called it Where Do You Want to Go?, and I chanted those words over and over while I ran my fingers along the spines of my leather-bound books—A-C, D-F. I knew that if I could stay focused on those words, I would be magically guided to pick the right book, the one that would be my perfect escape.

That afternoon I stopped at volume O-Q, sensing that the thing I was meant to discover was right there. The closed book had the weight and density of stone in my arms as I carried it back to bed. I wiped away the last of my tears and let my fingers travel the book's glossy pages, passing by entries that did not make me want to stop and read. Opera. Orangutan. Pancreas.

Then I landed in Paris, the capital of France. I felt all the tension leaving my body as I studied a beautiful map of the entire city as seen from the sky, and black-and-white photographs. The Eiffel Tower, Notre Dame. There was a photograph of a fashion model in a silky black evening gown that I stared at until I heard Mama calling.

"Benita, did you bring the cooking water for dinner tonight?"

"I forgot to, Mama," I called out. "Sorry!"

My mother came into my room. "What are you doing? Have you been crying? Oh, those books again! Didn't I tell you? You'll make yourself miserable reading all the time. Better get going."

I shut my encyclopedia gently and put it back on the shelf.

Paris was waiting for me. I would get there someday. As soon as I could.

CHAPTER

10

My family had our mail delivered to us at a postbox on the mainland. Papa gave Pepito a key to it, and the fisherman brought us whatever he found in there once a week or so. Papa got back issues of the newspaper and some bank notices that he ignored. Mama wrote away for creams and lotions to hydrate her parched skin. My brothers didn't write very well, so they didn't send letters. I wrote to a few friends at first, but I didn't like getting their letters because once again I was only reminded of things I was missing out on.

But one day the Ziade family wrote to ask when might be the best time to visit. They wanted good weather, and Señor Ziade asked my father to show him some properties for sale. He was thinking of building a summer place on Paíta.

I was thrilled. "I think they should come at the beginning of April. That way they can be here for my fifteenth birthday," I said. "Do you think they'll really move here?"

"Oh, yes. Come to Paíta! What a lovely resort it is!" Mama said.

Papa ignored Mama's tone. "I could sell them some of our land. A bit of beach and the east quadrant. We'll never use it."

"You're dreaming, Josef. They're never going to buy land here."

I didn't understand why Mama was being so sour. News of their visit was the best thing that had happened in months. But my mood shifted when I saw that they had also sent along a copy of the photograph taken at our going-away party. We looked very little like the people we were back then. My brothers were much scruffier. My mother had lost so much weight that she was haggard, and my father had a lot more gray hair. As for me, I had grown much taller and looked like some kind of wild beast now, compared to all the other young ladies in the photo.

In early April the Ziades arrived on a big shiny yacht they'd hired. We watched as their crew lowered a smaller boat with a big motor into the bobbing surf and a driver brought them to the island. The light boat bounced up and down on the waves, and the Ziade girls screamed with laughter.

The girls and Señora Ziade were all dressed for a day at the beach. They wore wide-brimmed straw hats in bright colors. Olga's was hot pink and her lipstick matched. She had grown a lot since I'd seen her last. Her flowered dress flowed around her hips and legs as if it were made of liquid. I felt an instant pang of jealousy just looking at her. But I refused to dislike Olga. Anyone would look dumpy standing next to her; there was nothing to be done about that.

Mama managed to flip into hostess mode. She kissed the adults on both cheeks and hugged all the girls. "How wonderful to see you," she said. "Olga, you've gotten so big. You look lovely. How was your trip over? Benita, say hello to the girls. We're so happy to have you here. Let us show you around."

She did not give anyone time to comment on us or how we looked, thank goodness, but instead took Señora Ziade by the arm and walked her toward our house.

Señora Ziade turned back to address the driver. "Boatman? You'll bring the coolers?"

"Yes, ma'am."

"Pilar, we didn't want to be a burden on you, and so we brought lunch with us. A nice treat. No need to cook, yes? We can have a lovely tropical picnic at your house."

"Oh, that wasn't necessary, but how considerate of you!" Mama said. I knew she was being false. Mama had agonized over what she could possibly serve the Ziades, worrying that nothing would be good enough.

Papa called, "I'm going to take Ramir to see the grove first!"

Mama waved a hand to let him know she'd heard him, but she didn't turn around. The boys ran off after Papa, so just we girls continued toward the house. When we got close I whispered to Olga, "Don't expect too much." She turned, looked down at me and smiled gently. Olga hadn't said a word yet, and it made me wonder whether we were still friends.

Our modest home seemed to take Señora Ziade's breath away. She just stood in our one big room and spun around slowly, taking in the whole nothingness of it. "How perfectly simple," she finally said to Mama. "It must be a relief to have so little to clean."

"Yes, of course. Still, there always seems to be plenty to do," Mama responded.

"Want to see my room?" I asked Olga.

She nodded, and we left our mothers to do their stiff little dance.

Olga came into my room and plopped herself down on the bed. "Ay! I am so glad to be off that boat. I was nauseous for two hours, the whole way here. But God forbid I should throw up. Mama would have a conniption. The captain told me to stare out at the farthest part of the horizon. That worked well enough. I managed to hold it in."

"Well then, I guess you can't go back on that amazing boat. Maybe you'll just have to stay here with us. Forever."

"I don't think I could live here, Benita. This place looks awful."

"You have no idea."

And that was that. We were instantly friends again. I told her everything. It came pouring out of me. Everything that had gone wrong, everything we lacked, how the only thing holding my family together was our shared misery. I did not exaggerate. I didn't need to.

"I'll never forget what you said to me at your going-away party. It was so sad," Olga told me. "Do you remember when you said that you trusted your papa to do the right thing for your family?"

I remembered. "Did I say that?" I lied, and thought about the fact that I *had* said that and everything really *was* his fault.

Olga kept on talking. "Do you want me to ask Mama if you can come to live with us? That's one way you could get out of here. Not that everything is great in Guayaquil. I just haven't told you about it yet."

"It can't be worse than this," I said.

Right then Rosa knocked on the door. "Mama says come to lunch. Now."

"Yes, yes, we're coming."

"Did you bring a bathing suit?" I asked Olga. "I can take you to a beautiful beach later."

"I like that idea. Let's go humor our crazy parents for a while. Then we can do what we want afterwards."

As it turned out, lunch was a terrific treat. Mama had moved our dining table onto the porch ("They'll enjoy dining alfresco.") and decked it out in our fine linen and silver and all the porcelain place settings. We gorged ourselves on the fantastic food the Ziades had brought—olives, four different types of cheese and seviche, a delicious salad of shrimp and calamari that their chef had prepared. Papa grilled a whole sea bass and the Ziades made a big fuss over it. They said it was the best fish they'd ever had. The adults had red wine, got silly, told stories, and it was very much like old times. Just laughing and being loud at the table, swaying into each other, with smiles leaping off our faces.

Toward the end of the meal, Señor Ziade said to Papa, "I like this place, Josef. It is so . . . What is the word? So comfortable. And the ocean is the bluest I have ever seen. Do you think it's possible to find a suitable vacation property here?"

Señora Ziade spoke up in a sharp tone. "Ramir, I don't think we should discuss this now." She turned to Mama and said, "Men can be such bores, no? Here we are having a lovely time, and he wants to talk about real estate prices. Ramir, please, let's just have an enjoyable visit."

"All right. Fine, then." Señor Ziade looked very confused. "I just thought since . . ."

"Dessert, anyone?" Señora Ziade said, cutting him off again. "We have a lovely chocolate cake, a special treat for the birthday girl."

"Yum!" I screamed, and threw my hands in the air, exaggerating my happiness only a little.

"Benita! Watch your manners, please," Mama said to me. "You must thank Señora Ziade for thinking of you." To our guests she said, "Well, that's just another example of what the primitive life has done to us."

Papa stood, and everyone joined in singing "Happy Birthday" to me. I sat quietly and waited for my piece of cake. It arrived on a flowered paper plate and had a yellow frosting rose on top of a smooth chocolate crust. I stared at that rose, torn between wanting to save it and devour it in a single bite. When I could no longer bear to hold back, I scooped it onto my spoon and let it melt down all around my tongue. Then I ate the cake very slowly, and when that was finished I just sat there remembering the taste. I looked at Olga. She'd been watching me, waiting for me to finish. She hadn't touched her piece of cake at all and sat with her hands folded primly in her lap.

"May we be excused, Mama?" I said. "Olga and I want to go to the beach."

"Yes, you may be excused," Mama said. "But don't go in the water right away. You'll get a cramp."

"Yes, Mama." I knew she didn't really care. She was only saying that because the Ziades were with us.

Olga and I changed in my room. She let me borrow one of her bathing suits, a black one-piece. It fit me perfectly and I ran my hands along the sides of my waist, pleased with the way the smooth fabric clung to me. I couldn't have been happier, until I looked at Olga. She was totally dazzling in a shimmering gold swimsuit.

"Look at you!" Olga exclaimed. "I want you to keep that suit. Say you will."

"Okay," I said weakly, "but you look incredible. I don't even want to leave the room now."

"Oh! Don't say that. I mean, it's very sweet of you to say that I'm pretty. But the thing about how I look is I can't take credit for it. It just happened, like a lucky accident." She put her arm around my shoulder and led me to the dirty mirror that hung above my bookshelves. "Stop looking at me now. Look at yourself, why don't you? You look beautiful, too. Your face is like a painting of a Tahitian girl, your skin is so brown, and you have great long legs. You see what I mean, right?"

"Yeah, I guess so." I did have some physical assets to be happy about. I just wasn't as lucky as Olga.

"Here, beauty," she said. "We have these two matching cover-ups to wear."

"You're the nicest person ever," I said to Olga, and I meant it. "Let's go."

I planned to take Olga to the prettiest beach on our side of the island. Just past the village, it was a little horseshoe-shaped patch of white sand enclosed by a high cliff that dropped straight down to the water on one side. The protection of the cliff made the water crystal clear, and there were thousands of perfectly shaped shells to collect.

On the way I asked, "Wouldn't it be great if your father bought a place here? Then we could see each other all the time."

Olga spoke in a sad voice. "We'll never buy land here. Mama won't let it happen."

"But it seems like your father wants to come here. When my papa wants something, it always happens."

"Well, it's different in my family. Mama is the boss, and she wants us to summer in Salinas. That's where she thinks we'll find a suitable husband for me. Not in Guayaquil. She says all the best families have homes on the beach there."

"You're getting married? But you're only seventeen."

"I'll be eighteen in two months, and that's how old Mama was when she met my father."

"I hadn't thought of that. Well, Salinas doesn't sound so bad. You'll be on the beach having fun."

"Ugh. It's no fun at all. All the girls my age belong to this dumb social club. We get together once a week. I have to get all dressed up for it, and all we do is sit around planning parties for some silly charity. But nobody really cares. The parties are only an excuse to interact with the boys' club, so we can all mingle together under the watch of our chaperones. It's the most boring thing in the world."

"I wouldn't mind being in a social club. I haven't even got one friend here."

"These people aren't friends of mine. I don't like any of them and wouldn't trust them to hold a dime for me. The girls only want the wealthiest boys to pay attention to them, and they hate me because all the boys want to talk to me first. I can't stand the boys, either. They have nothing to say, and you have to be polite and make conversation with them anyway. They think they're great because their parents have money. They're nothing but pampered, spoiled little mama's boys. Yuck. I can get really sad thinking about it."

"Why don't you tell your mother you won't go anymore?"

"Because that would be even worse. Getting married is the only way I'm ever going to get away from her. Who knows? Maybe I'll get lucky and find someone to fall in love with. I hope so, or else what's all my so-called beauty worth anyway, if I just wind up married to some rich fool?"

"I'm sorry you're so unhappy, Olga."

"Thanks, Benita. But let's not talk about this anymore. It's too depressing."

We walked past the village, but did not bother to stop. "There's the big city," I said.

"Anything worth seeing there?" Olga asked.

"You could take a look at how the natives cook, eat and live in the dirt."

A group of island women were sitting around a fire. They turned to watch us as we went by. "Just passing through, ladies,"

Olga said, waving to them like a beauty queen in a parade, her hand high in the air. We walked on, giggling as they frowned at us. I didn't look back, but I knew they followed us with their eyes. I almost told Olga about the weird ritual I'd witnessed in the jungle, but then decided I'd better not. After what Rosa had said about voodoo, it might scare her. Besides, I didn't think I could explain it very well because I didn't understand it myself.

The cliff beach was perfect that day. The tide had gone out in the morning, leaving behind little clear pools of water filled up with ocean life—barnacles and hermit crabs and sea anemones. Orange starfish bigger than our hands were scattered on the shore.

"This is fantastic! I can't believe this beach!" Olga exclaimed.

"The natives call it Cotochachi."

"Is that one of their gods or something?"

"No. It's just what they call the cliff behind us. It means high place. Simple enough, right?"

"If you say so, long legs."

"I do, oh perfect one," I replied.

It was a windy day, so we laid down our towels in the sheltered area directly beneath the tall cliff. I noticed a man fishing up there, but I couldn't recognize him because the wind blew sand up around us and blurred my vision.

We stayed quiet, just listening to the distant sound of the waves hitting the beach, the wind whipping the tips of our hair. I fell into something like a pleasant trance, but at the same time I was highly aware of every sound and sensation all around me. I only got this feeling sitting quietly at the beach. The seashore could make you forget everything about your real life.

"Who's that?" Olga asked out of the blue.

"Who? Where?"

"That man up there. On top of the cliff."

I twisted around and looked up. Raúl was fishing right over our heads, casting out deep into the water beyond the beach, where some deep coral grew.

I felt the usual pang of shock at seeing him. "That's Raúl."

"Do you know him?"

"Not really."

"Why don't you say hello?"

That sounded like a good idea to me. "Hey, Raúl," I shouted up the cliff at him. "Hi!" I waved, and he reluctantly waved back at me, with his usual lack of interest.

"Gosh, he's really handsome," Olga said.

All of a sudden I realized that Olga was interested in Raúl, possibly as interested in him as I was. She sat up partway, leaning back onto her elbows, and took a good long look at him. "Do you think he'd come over here? You say you know him, right?"

"Well, we're not friends or anything." The last thing in the world I wanted was for Raúl to get a better look at Olga. I'd have no chance with him after that. "He's older than us."

"I can see that. And you said there was nothing interesting to do on Paíta."

Olga seemed like a completely different girl, acting all kittenish. "Is he looking at us?" She had her back turned to him and faced me, one curvy hip sticking up suggestively out of the sand. I took another glance toward Raúl, just in time to see him turn away to face the other direction.

"I think he was, but not now," I said.

"I'll fix that," Olga said.

"Don't!" I said, more loudly than I intended.

"Why not?"

Olga didn't wait for my answer. I sat there helplessly on my towel while she meandered down to the water's edge. She put on quite a performance. She flipped her long brown hair dramatically off her face so that it flew back over her shoulder. Then she reclined on a long, flat rock, swirling a finger back and forth in a pool that lay by her hip. She looked like a mermaid on holiday from the blue ocean.

I turned to see if Raúl was as entranced with her as I expected he would be. I had to know if he liked her. Because if he did, then I would hate him forever. Plain and simple.

He was looking at her, all right, but in a funny way. His face was all screwed up, his brows knit into a frown and his mouth set into a thin, hard line. I watched him reel in his line. Then he moved away to a different part of the cliff, and I couldn't see him anymore.

When Olga realized she'd lost him, she came back. "Where'd he go?"

"I don't know. He's a funny one. Kind of keeps to himself most of the time." I was trying not to sound as happy as I felt. Raúl didn't give a damn about Olga; he seemed to be mad she was there.

"So, what do you know about him?"

"Oh, not that much. Only that he was born here, and his father is a fisherman."

Olga pouted out her lower lip. "Boring! What else?"

"I heard that his mother died when he was ten."

"Aha! So you do know more about him. Why won't you tell me? All of a sudden you're keeping secrets again."

I looked Olga straight in the face. "You're not really interested in him, are you? I mean, he's just an islander."

"No, it's only that I thought it would be fun to be with a good-looking fellow when Mama wasn't around. I never get to do that back home. Someone is always watching me. That's one advantage you have here. So . . . tell me about him."

I thought about Raúl for a moment. I saw him around the island, maybe once a week or so. A sighting would light my desire for him into a burning obsession every time, and sleep couldn't even erase him from my mind.

"Well . . . the truth is . . . I have a huge crush on him." To say it out loud finally felt like a ten-ton weight coming off my shoulders.

"Benita! Why didn't you tell me? I wouldn't have done all that if I'd known."

"I tried to stop you. But, no, you had to go prancing down the beach," I teased. "Oh, Raúl! Look at ME!"

Olga gave me a playful slap on the arm. "You mean girl! Benita, I feel terrible. Now you think I was trying to steal your boyfriend."

"He's not my boyfriend. He barely knows I exist."

"Have you ever had a conversation with him?"

"No, I couldn't do that."

"Why not?"

"I don't want him to know I'm interested."

"So you plan to love him from afar for the rest of your life?"

"No. I'm waiting for him to make the first move."

"Wow, it is primitive here." I laughed when she said that. "Benita, he'll make the first move, but you have to encourage him. Trust me, these are things I know about. I could write a book on the mating rituals of the human species."

I didn't say anything just then, but it dawned on me that maybe Olga didn't believe in love at all. She just knew how to play at it, as if it were a game laid out on a board and once you knew the rules it was easy to win. "We're just different," I said to her. "What works for you wouldn't work for me."

"Maybe you're right. You'll find your own way."

I couldn't help thinking that my way, whatever it was, wouldn't work on the island. "It's very different here. I don't think anyone goes on dates, for example."

"Well, he sure is cute, Benita."

I laughed. "Tell me something I don't know."

We went for a swim, and not long after that, we stood up, shook our towels clean of sand and then walked back. The sun was just touching down on the horizon, turning the water gold. When we got home, we saw that Olga's family had gathered on the beach and that the small motorboat was ready to take her three sisters back to the yacht.

"There you are," Señora Ziade said to Olga. "We had no idea where you'd gotten to."

Olga smiled at me. "Benita took me to the most beautiful beach."

"Where's everyone going?" I said. "I thought you were going to stay overnight."

"We decided to sleep on the boat," Señora Ziade said. "There's more room, and we all think it would be for the best."

"Tomorrow we could go fishing," I said to Olga. "That would be fun."

Papa came over and put his arm around my shoulders. "The Ziades are headed home tomorrow morning." I had the feeling that something unpleasant had happened while we were gone. "Ramir needs to get back to work." Papa gave my shoulders a squeeze and I didn't say anything more.

Olga said, "We can write to each other, Benita. Okay?"

I nodded. My only friend was leaving. Tears stung my eyes. "That would be good," I mumbled.

Olga stepped forward to give me a kiss goodbye, and she whispered in my ear, "You must promise to tell me everything that happens with Raúl."

I smiled at her. "And you'll write back when you find Mr. Wonderful."

Olga used her most deeply grown-up voice. "Of course I will, darling." Then she sounded like herself again. "I'll miss you, Benita. It really was a wonderful day."

Señora Ziade got into the boat, and Olga stepped in daintily, taking the hand of the boatman, as if she were being helped into an old-fashioned carriage. She put on as much of a performance for her mother as she had for Raúl that afternoon. I remembered what she had told me earlier, about how hard her life was back in Guayaquil. When I thought about all the roles people expected her to play, I finally understood why such a lucky girl would say she was unhappy.

My family stayed on the beach to watch the sunset as the Ziade boat headed away from us into the big reddened sky.

"That was exhausting," Mama said to Papa.

"I don't know what makes them think they have the right to tell us how to live," Papa answered.

"Money," Mama said. "They have it and we don't, and that's how it is."

"Well, I didn't appreciate their attitude one bit. Ramir took me aside in the grove to say he was worried about us. Said our situation is worse than he thought it would be. That the grove might be diseased and the kids look no better than street beggars. That I ought to return and find myself some real work to do. Can you believe his nerve?"

"I hope they never come back here," Mama said.

"That's for sure," said Papa.

Standing there watching the Ziades leave, I realized that my parents were united in their desire to forget the life we knew back in Guayaquil. And that meant we would be staying on Paíta for a very, very long time.

CHAPTER

11

My crush on Raúl never went away. But for a long time I couldn't get close to him, despite all my efforts to do what Olga had suggested, to let him know I was interested.

Then one day Manuel got sick with some kind of stomach bug. He certainly couldn't go out to water the field with José, so Papa asked in the village if anyone could help and Raúl took the job. I was surprised because usually he went out fishing with Pepito, or he worked in the cotton field. Like all the other islanders, he avoided the coconut farm as if it carried some kind of disease.

I spent most of the day hanging off the fence at the grove's edge just watching him work. Every half hour I'd ask him if he wanted anything to eat. Mango, banana, fresh coffee, Raúl?

My brother quickly figured out what was going on, and he'd say, "I'll have a banana, Little Girl," and I'd have to go get him one, or look like a fool for asking in the first place.

Raúl always politely declined but after about the fifth time I asked, he said to me sternly, "Don't you have work to do, Little Girl?"

"Well, sure. But that doesn't mean I can't talk to you."

Raúl laughed. "I guess nothing's going to stop you. Is it?"

"Probably not."

"Your sister is very fresh," Raúl said to José, but I knew he was only teasing.

José just shrugged. He didn't seem interested now that Raúl was paying attention to me.

I visited the field one more time that day, when Papa went to pay Raúl. I knew Papa had been drinking. I'd seen him have a beer for breakfast, and when I found him on the porch to tell him Raúl and José were done working, there were three more bottles stacked up on the table. He was in a very good mood.

We walked together to the edge of the field, and Papa stood proudly looking it over, as if what he saw were a flourishing farm in full bloom, instead of just a huge patch of spindly sprouts. "Someday this plantation will belong to you, Benita," he said. "And you will thank me when that day arrives. Though I may not be around to hear it."

Raúl and José had put down their buckets and met us at the fence. They both seemed to be listening closely to Papa. I felt sorry for poor José, getting cut out of his inheritance, for whatever it was worth. I turned to look at Papa because I could hardly believe what he was saying, but he just stood there with a huge grin on his face, imagining my happy fate and that of his plantation intertwined. The very thought made me want to scream.

"It may not look like much now. But just give it time," Papa added.

Finally Raúl spoke up. "You should water early in the morning. In the middle of the day, the heat absorbs the water before it has a chance to feed the roots."

"Do you think so?" Papa said.

"Yes. Get up at six before the sun is up and start watering then. And the plants need even more water than you give them now."

"And what shall we use to wash ourselves with, if it all goes to feed the farm?"

"You must make a sacrifice if you want the trees to grow."

Papa counted out a few coins and held them out to Raúl. "You'd better not be expecting any more for giving me your advice. I'm not about to pay for that."

Raúl looked at the money in his palm. "We agreed to sixty sucre. You owe me ten more."

Papa looked startled. "I don't think so. We said fifty."

"Pay me what you promised, Mariah." Raúl glared, and I wanted to shake the coins out of Papa's hand before something bad happened.

"This is nonsense. Here. Take what you want." Papa thrust a ten piece at Raúl.

Raúl said nothing more, but what he was thinking was perfectly clear. When he left, I wanted to run after him—to tell him something that would make him not hate us. But I had no idea what that might be.

Back at the house, Mama was waiting for us. "How was it having a big strong man to work with today?" she asked my brother.

"We got done in half the time," José said. "But Benita was happier than me to have Raúl in the field."

Mama laughed, and I yelled at José, "You be quiet!"

"That's enough of that nonsense," Papa reprimanded my

brother. "He won't be coming back here. He didn't stick to our bargain. Wanted more money at the last minute."

"What did you do, Josef?" Mama asked, annoyed.

"I paid him, of course. Who needs that kind of trouble?"

"As you should. He works hard. Pay that man whatever he wants."

"I won't be taken advantage of."

"Are you crazy? No one else on the island wants to work on the farm. Your sons can barely keep up with all the work. And you do nothing!"

"I . . . I . . . I have plenty to do to make sure the islanders tend the cotton. . . . I supervise the entire farming enterprise. And there's my research—"

"Yes, you sit and you read. For all the good it does."

Papa seemed to have swallowed his tongue all of a sudden. I was shocked, too. It was the first time I'd heard Mama stand up against Papa in a stone's age.

"We need Raúl, you fool," she said. "Tomorrow I'm going to give him a basket of fresh eggs, as a special thank-you for helping us. And I don't want to hear another word about it." Mama turned to me. "I think *you* should bring the eggs to Raúl. You don't mind, do you, Benita?"

I tried not to sound happy. "Fine with me."

In the morning I collected an even dozen from our chickens. The egg basket was very heavy and I had to be careful not to jostle it too much or the shells would break. I was very hot and sweaty by the time I got to Raúl's hut, and I knocked on the door harder than I meant to. It creaked open slowly as Raúl checked to see who was there. When he realized it was me, he lowered his head in this scary way, looking me dead in the eye as if he were as angry with me as he was with my father. I told him the eggs were from my parents, and he simply nodded.

"I'm so sorry about yesterday, Raúl. Papa wasn't feeling well, or he wouldn't have treated you that way."

He smiled just a little when I said that, and only for a moment. "Thank you, Little Girl." Then he took the basket from me. I moved away a bit and watched as he shut the door quietly between us.

Walking home, I thought about what I had seen of the inside of his one-room house. There were two wooden platforms with straw mattresses for sleeping, one for Raúl and one for his father, with only a plain table between them. The room was dark, and I guessed that he didn't own very much else. Raúl was so quiet and serious. I wanted to know everything he thought about, and whether he ever, maybe once or twice, had a thought about me.

After that day things changed between us. He'd tease me whenever I saw him, saying I was going to grow up to be too short to pick my father's coconuts. When I teased him back, I got to see his smile and his beautiful white teeth, all his gloom gone with a single grin.

I knew that the villagers took a morning break at noon, sitting out of the sun in the shade of trees that ringed the cotton field on the east slope. If I timed it just right, I could do my water run just before that, and then, with two full buckets to carry, I had good reason to sit with them on my way home because I would be tired from carrying the water. They always looked at me funny when I did this, and no one talked to me but no one bothered me either. "Just resting for a bit," I would say, and plop down next to Raúl.

But one day when I got to the rest spot, I couldn't find Raúl. All the other villagers seemed to be scattered about, sitting on rocks or the bare earth. I looked out into the field and spotted Raúl speaking to a group of men. They looked concerned and stared at the ground where Raúl was pointing out something near their feet. I walked on, to the far edge of the shady resting area, and sat down by myself. Soon Raúl gestured to the men, and they followed him out of the field. To my surprise, instead of going to sit with the other people, Raúl came and sat down next to me.

"Is something the matter with the cotton?" I asked.

"Yes, we found a pest in the field."

"That's terrible. Did you tell Papa?"

"What for? We'll do what we did last time. Put out snails. They eat the pest. It will work if there aren't too many of them."

Raúl took a small wrapped bundle out of the bottom of his basket, a lunch of fried plantain. He ate with gusto, his fingers getting thick with grease.

"You're hungry today. Working too hard?" I wanted to hit myself for sounding so perky.

"No, I love to pick the cotton."

"But it seems like very hard work to me. I mean, you make it look pretty easy but your hands are all cut up."

"Ah, my hands are tough. They heal. No, there is nothing so good as farming the land. To turn up the soil, to put the seed into the ground and to watch it grow. If you work hard, the earth keeps its promise with a rich crop. I would much rather be farming than fishing. Any day."

"Wow, I wish Papa could know farming as you do. For him the promise got broken somehow."

"No. Your father does not know what he's doing. He waters at the wrong time of the day and not enough. But he won't listen to my advice. He's too stubborn."

I felt my face turn hot. "Are you saying it's his fault that the plantation won't grow? I know that Papa isn't well liked by the *indios* on Paíta . . ."

Raúl cut me off. "Little Girl, I know you learned that word from your father, but you should not call the people *indios*. It is a bad word."

"It is?"

"They are not dumb Indians, and neither am I. When you insult them, you insult me."

"But you are different from them." Raúl was looking at me harshly and I started stammering. "I . . . I mean . . . Aren't you? Your father is Spanish, right?"

"No. I was born here. My father came here to fish and met my mother. She was from Paíta and so am I."

"But you don't live as they do, sleeping in hammocks, braiding palm into baskets. They put paint on their faces!"

"We are the same. They do for me and I do for them. We work together. That is all that matters. They are good people. Don't you know that by now?"

"If they're so good, why do they have that spooky ceremony in the jungle? Papa says it's evil to worship like that."

"Is that so?"

"Yes! And I saw it. The women go out there and burn things and then walk around, going nowhere, just singing to themselves."

Raúl was laughing now. "They do it every day. Did you know that?"

"They do?"

"And do you know what they say when they sing?"

I shook my head.

"That they are grateful to the spirits that watch over the island for taking care of every living thing here. They thank the spirits for giving the island life. Do you think that's spooky?"

"I guess not. Is this what you believe too?"

"Yes, I believe we should be grateful for the good things we have. And you?"

I tried very hard to think of something I was happy about, but I couldn't come up with a single thing. Raúl was waiting for me to answer. I looked up into his clear brown eyes, and I wondered if he would still like me if I told him the truth. "It's not so easy living on Paíta. Not for me."

Raúl nodded. "Yes, it is a hard life. I did not think your family would last this long. No one did."

"And everyone hates us. That's the worst part about living here. If I could change that I would."

Raúl looked down at me with concern. "No one hates you. The problem is, your papa is not fair to the people."

"How so? He pays them for their work."

"But he gives them no respect. He treats them like animals put here to labor for him. And he does no work himself. Why should he when he can make everyone else work for him?"

Again, I felt a little sting of shock at the way Raúl talked about Papa, but secretly I knew he was right. It hurt to know that everyone saw Papa that way, not just our family. Luckily Raúl said, "Let's not talk about it anymore. He's your father, and I am sure you must show him the same respect I show to mine. That is how it is for you. For better or for worse."

He was right again. It put me at ease that Raúl was willing to back down. "My family wouldn't have survived here without the help of the . . ." I almost said "*indios.*" "So what should I call the islanders?"

"The people. They are the people of Paíta. Just like you are now, Little Girl." Raúl gently touched the tip of his finger to my nose.

"Raúl, please don't call me 'Little Girl.' It's an insult and I don't like it!"

Raúl laughed again. "I promise, I won't call you that anymore. Are we agreed now?"

We talked until I was sure Mama would be getting mad that I wasn't back with the water to do the wash. "I have to go," I said. "It was nice talking to you."

"Yes, Benita. See you tomorrow." It was the first time he had used my name.

But the next day I felt nervous about seeing Raúl, now that he knew I would be coming. So I decided to spy on him instead. In the midafternoon I went the long way up the back side of the cotton field, which bordered a low hill. I climbed high enough to reach a clearing and sat cross-legged on the ground there. Although I was too far away to hear what went on in the field, I could see everything. All the people were there, bent over the rows. I spotted Raúl, his strong brown back bare to the sun.

Before long, I saw my father enter the field on horseback. He had just purchased this old horse with money he'd made from the cotton operation. A cranky old nag, it fought my father in the mount, skittering sideways and snorting and rearing back a bit. Papa barely had the horse under control as he rode in along a ditch, near where Raúl worked. It made me nervous to see how close the horse's stamping hooves were to Raúl.

Papa dismounted, and Raúl stood to speak with him, shielding his eyes from the sun. Their conversation began to look like an argument. My father raised his arm and gestured toward a portion of the field. Raúl pointed in the opposite direction. I crept down the hill so that I could hear them.

Papa reached down and grabbed a wad of raw cotton and held it under Raúl's nose. He shouted, "Did you think you could hide this from me?" Raúl slapped my father's hand out of his way, and the people in the field started to gather around.

My father threw his hat onto the ground. "It will all be ruined. We should have sprayed." He mounted up and kicked his horse hard, galloping out, leaving a cloud of dust surrounding the cotton pickers.

"Don't worry about him. It will be all right," Raúl said to everyone. He waved to me and I came down from the hill.

Once we took our seats together on the slope, Raúl let out a heavy sigh. I hated to see him like that.

"What's wrong? Why was Papa so mad?"

Raúl just sat staring at the ground.

"Won't you tell me?"

He snorted. "You wouldn't understand, Benita."

"I can't possibly understand if you don't talk to me."

Raúl took in a deep breath and said, "Your father thinks this is *his* cotton field. But he's wrong. It belongs to all of us on Paíta."

Now I was speechless. I believed it was Papa's field; that's how he always talked about it.

"He can't tell us what to do. There're going to be big problems if he can't get that through his thick head."

I knew exactly what Raúl meant. "You're right. Papa is very stubborn. He has a hard time seeing things the way everyone else sees them."

Raúl turned to look at me then, and his smile was warm. "I'm glad you understand, at least." Raúl unwrapped his lunch and ate it quickly. "We have too much to do today, Benita. I'm sorry, but I must get back to work now." He stood then, and so did all the other islanders.

"I have to go, too." When I stood up, I realized I was shaking. I didn't know what bothered me more—that Raúl was up-set, or that I had just turned against my father.

That night at dinner, Papa said to Mama, "We have pests in the field that could destroy the whole crop. And that Raúl. He is a pest too. I'm telling you, he is going to cause me some serious trouble."

Mama glanced my way, and she put her finger to her lips. So I didn't say a word. But that night in my bed, I couldn't stop thinking about what Raúl had said.

Papa didn't seem to have a clue about how things worked on this island.

CHAPTER

12

One evening that summer, a surprise visitor interrupted life on Paíta. All the families were preparing their evening meals and putting children to sleep when a wild jungle cat walked right into one of the village huts without making a sound. It took a quick look around at the startled, frozen faces of its hosts and calmly walked back out.

We heard about it from Joam. It was so strange for a wild cat to come into the village that everyone feared the cat was not a cat at all, but an angry spirit that took the form of a cat to walk the island. They called the creature Ay Pook. And now they believed something even worse was going to happen. The only thing they could do was kill the cat to ward off the danger.

I was shocked by just how superstitious the people of Paíta were, and that their beliefs would lead them to destroy the cat. I complained to Papa. "It didn't hurt anyone, right?"

"It's dangerous to let a wild animal roam free in our midst," Papa said. "It probably came to the village because it was hungry and looking for an easy meal. There's no predicting when it might attack a person, if it gets hungry enough."

Since the cat had appeared at the end of the day, the village elders decided that from dusk to dawn no islanders were allowed to leave their homes. Papa set a curfew in our house too. No going outside after sunset until the cat was caught, not even to wash at the cistern out back behind the kitchen.

A hunting party was formed, six men with the best skills at bow and arrow. Raúl was among them, and I wondered if he believed that the cat was an evil spirit. I hoped the hunters would just frighten it away.

The next several days were quiet, with no sign of the cat or the hunting party. The men finally returned a week later, exhausted and dismayed. They gathered all the people together to tell them what had happened. Papa and I took my brothers along to hear about it, and while Joam translated, I realized I was picking up some of the people's words on my own.

The party had set out from their camp that first morning, hoping to find the cat sleeping in its lair somewhere. They tracked the cat throughout the entire day, following paw prints and huge heaping piles of scat, but they couldn't find its den.

To aid their efforts, they used a cat caller, made from the hollowed-out hard shell of a calabash fruit. A taut piece of leather was fastened over the wide open end with some twine. It looked like a small drum, and inside was the dried peel of a plantain, waxen and stiff. When a hunter rubbed his thumb across the skin, the caller produced a sound that was like the low-bellied growl of the cat. As they told the story, they made the sound, and my stomach turned over. The deep growl chilled me to the bone.

The men walked through the jungle for days, listening for a cat to answer the call. But they never even got a glimpse of it.

And each morning when they set out, they found fresh cat tracks inside their own footprints. The cat spent every night tracking them!

A few of the hunters grew tired of the chase, and others were spooked. They decided they were wasting their time, because it wasn't just any old cat they hunted. It was Ay Pook and it would never let itself be caught. It was best to return home to Subidalta. But should the evil creature ever venture into the village again, they would be ready for it.

Each family hut was prepared with a jar full of rocks that could be used to make a terrible sound, guaranteed to scare the cat off, and a reed whistle to alert the rest of the village. Everyone was still nervous for the first few days, so the evening curfew would stay the rule until we were sure the cat was gone. It didn't matter to me. I preferred to stay in and read my books.

A few nights later I was wide awake, just reading and enjoying a cool night breeze that swirled in through my open window. I felt it enter my room on swift wings. But then it changed direction without warning and went straight after the candle burning on my bedpost and blew it out.

I tried to make myself go to sleep in the dark, but I lay awake listening for the cat. Would it meow like the street cats in Guayaquil? After a long time with no sleep and no cat, I decided to read some more. Slowly and quietly I got out of bed and crept into the kitchen with my candle. I couldn't find the matches anywhere. Perhaps they were on the porch; Papa liked to smoke out there. I looked out the window and saw the pack resting on the front railing.

When I opened the door and confronted the gaping darkness, I remembered the curfew and why we were told to stay inside. But those matches teased me to come and get them. I wasn't actually leaving the house. In one swift move I could have what I wanted and quickly return to the safe indoors. So I went out.

But the night was so lovely that I didn't want to go back in. I stood in the dark at the porch railing, swaying with the breeze, and breathed in the salt air. It was heavenly.

Then I heard a deep grumbling sound coming from the bushes between our house and the beach. I was shaking a little bit, but it wasn't fear that made me light up a match and put it to my candlewick. As I held my arm out over the railing, the flickering light caught something that seemed to watch me from the bushes. A pair of glowing and golden eyes gleamed, like two headlamps trained on me. I was held by that stare, unable to move.

A large animal stepped out from the cover of the bushes and came toward the house, straight for me, its movements fluid and light, as if its paws barely touched the ground. It was a cat, all right, but nothing like a gutter tabby. Spotted fur rippled over its sleek, thick muscles. It halted directly below our porch and stood looking up at me. That jungle cat was the most amazing thing I had ever seen—like a queen in the night. I did not fear it. No, I dreaded the moment would be over too soon.

I heard Papa cough as he got out of bed. I tensed and so did the cat, and then it slowly moved off. I turned around to go back before Papa caught me in the doorway, but it was too late. "Didn't I tell you to stay . . ."—his voice trailed off as he looked out over my shoulder—". . . inside the house . . ."

Grabbing up the whistle, he made it shriek, and the cat leapt away through the high grass, tearing toward the jungle. "Get in your bed!" Papa yelled, and like the cat, I ran for it.

It was pitch-black in my room but not as quiet as before. The night air was ripped to shreds by the sound of whistles. All the people of Paíta were awake now, blowing their heads off. They probably thought they were blowing that cat straight back to hell.

I was reminded of the day I ran from the village women, and how the sound of their voices had chased me down the beach. I understood now that fear made them treat me the way they did. Not hatred or meanness. Just pure fear of all the bad things in the world. To them I was one of those things.

I lay there that night, wishing there was some way I could change their minds and make them see me as something other than my father's daughter.

I thought too about the superstition that the cat was evil, a bearer of bad tidings. But I felt lucky to have seen it. I decided that a cat visit would bring good luck. Now that we'd met, I was sure that only good things would happen to me, even though I couldn't say when.

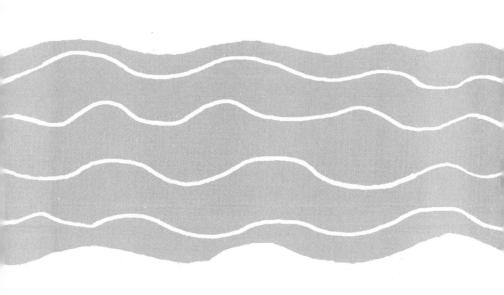

PART 4

HARVEST

CHAPTER
13

Every week Mama would send me to the village store to pick up supplies. I liked going there. The fishermen of Paíta spent the slow, hot midday hours talking over the hum of the generator, drinking their beer. Raúl usually took his place among them.

Not long after the fight in the cotton field, I found Raúl standing alone at the counter. As soon as I saw him, everything around me seemed to quiet and slow down. The fishermen kept their conversation in the corner low as I walked up to the counter. On the wall behind Raúl's head, the picture of Jesus hung crooked in its broken frame. Raúl seemed lost, standing silently by my side as rivulets of sweat crept down his neck. I felt nervous for him and turned away to look at a stray wasp that buzzed up high, banging itself against the tin roof.

Little Carlos took my grocery list and put my purchases in a brown paper sack. I paid and turned to say goodbye to Raúl. There was a smear of engine grease on his face. I had the urge to wipe him clean with my bare hand. As he bent toward me, his eyes had a message to deliver—*you will be mine*. I stood looking back, still as a stone, knowing it was true.

"The fish harvest happens this afternoon, yes?" he said.

I didn't know what he was talking about. "I guess so. Um, are you looking forward to it?"

"I want you to go. With me."

"Yes. Yes! YES!" I said, barely giving him the chance to tell me to meet him at the saltwater lake at three o'clock. I shouted goodbye and left in such a rush that the fishermen tilted away from me in their chairs, and I made the dull bell peal as I flew out the door of the store. Tearing down the beach toward home, I felt as though a rising tide was pulling me out to sea, not threatening but deliciously insistent. I would be taken away, and by what I had been waiting for all along.

I had no idea what the fish harvest was, so I asked Papa about it. Just as Pepito had told us the day we arrived on Paíta, the ocean tide sent salt water shooting up the beach in a fast-moving shallow channel that made a lake behind the village stocked with schools of fish. Papa said the islanders planned to poison the waters so that all the fish, ahi and snappers, would float up to the surface to be harvested and smoked. They'd keep for weeks like that.

"How did you hear about the harvest?" Papa asked.

"Um . . . the fishermen were talking about it at the store."

I started to fret that Papa might be planning to go himself, and he'd see me with Raúl. Luckily he said, "We'll buy some fish from them tomorrow. Best to stay away until then. I'm told they like to go crazy after the harvest."

But that one worry unleashed others that were new for me. All this time I'd been waiting for Raúl to like me and now that it seemed he did, a little nagging voice in my head was telling me I was doing something wrong. I was sneaking out. Raúl was so much older than me. I hadn't even gotten permission to be with a boy, much less a man of his age.

And that wasn't even the biggest problem.

Raúl was one of them—a Paíta native. That's not how I saw him; he was special, of course. But what would my parents think?

I might be able to make Mama understand. After all, she'd married a man older than her, a man who didn't come from the place where she grew up. But Papa wouldn't be so easy to convince.

Everything about what I was doing was bad, except for the way it made me feel. I was so happy, I wanted to climb on top of the roof and sing. If my parents knew what was going on, they'd probably want to chain me to a post. It would have to stay my secret. For now.

I spent the rest of the day wondering what to wear. I didn't have much to choose from. Mama kept her one decent-looking outfit wrapped in tissue paper. I'd never get out of the house in it. Other than that, I had a clean white cotton T-shirt that used to belong to Papa. The fabric had shrunk, and it didn't fit him anymore. I put it on. It was long on me and the men's deep V-necked front dipped down low on my chest. I tied up the extra fabric in a tight knot just below my ribs.

Standing on my bed, I could see my body in the small mirror hanging over my shelves. I thought the knotted shirt showed off my flat brown stomach, but my breasts looked lopsided. I hated how the left one stuck out sideways and the other drooped down. It was time for me to get a bra but I hadn't needed one back home and Mama said I would fit into hers soon enough so there was no reason to buy one for me. I had a woman's body now, but I still didn't feel all grown up.

Could Raúl truly like me? Looking at myself in the mirror, I felt a glimmer of doubt. But why else would he ask me to the harvest or stare at me in the store that way? As I was turning back and forth in front of the mirror, a knock came on my door. Mama walked into my room and caught me standing on the bed.

"What are you doing, Benita? Why is that shirt tied around your waist?"

"Oh, no reason," I said, and jumped down to the floor. "I . . . I just wanted to look different, I guess."

Mama just stood there nodding, waiting for me to go on. "You *do* look different."

"Yeah, well . . . I don't want to look the same every single day."

"Is there something special about today?"

Mama was giving me this look like she knew exactly what was going on, so I told her the truth. "Well . . . ," she said, "Raúl is much older than you. But that's not unusual."

"So I can go?"

"I want you to know, Benita, that I always hoped we'd find a better suitor for you. But our circumstances have left us no options."

"Mama, I'm just going to the harvest with Raúl; that's all."

"Sometimes I forget how young you still are. Listen to me. I know what I'm talking about. Things between a man and a woman can happen very fast. Before you know it, you're tied to a man who's come calling for you."

"But Raúl is wonderful. He's so strong in so many ways, and I *really* like him."

"I can see all the things he is, Benita. And I think he could be the salvation of this family. But . . . "

"But what?"

"Don't you think we should have him over to the house first? That's the proper way to do this."

"Ugh! NO. What do you expect him to do, sit down with Papa to talk about his prospects? That's ridiculous. I just want to go to the harvest with him. Please?"

She sighed. "Even if I told you not to go, I don't suppose there's any way to stop you from seeing him some other time, if your heart is set on it." Mama smoothed my hair, her eyes dark. "My parents couldn't stop me."

"Please, Mama, can I go to the harvest? Please?"

"I can't let you go alone. Just imagine if your father found out. I insist you take your brothers as chaperones."

I could tell there was no changing her mind. "Thank you, thank you!" I hugged her.

"Now take that skimpy shirt off and put on a skirt. Brush your hair. And make sure you're home in time for dinner." Mama left my room and I heard the boys getting noisy in the front room. They'd obviously just heard we were all going to the harvest.

I changed and looked into the mirror once more. "Oh, why even bother!" I said to myself. It wasn't going to be a real date with my brothers tagging along. I ran the brush through my hair fast and was out the door.

By the time we got to the lake, the people were already throwing the poison. My brothers and I stood together watching all the activity, like the unknown guests at a boisterous wedding, who wait uncomfortably until someone asks them to dance. The villagers chanted some kind of working song, their arms moving in unison as they tossed the stuff out over the water.

José shouted, "Raúl's here!" and I turned to see him coming toward us.

Raúl didn't seem surprised to see the boys. "Ready to lend a hand?" he said, smiling at them. He seemed his old self again, with none of the nervousness I had seen in the store earlier that day. I felt so relieved. The first thing he did was send my brothers to the north side of the lake, where Pepito would supply them with the poisonous barbasco weed. The boys scattered like dust in a brisk wind, and we were left alone.

"Are you ready?" Raúl said to me.

Ready for what? I wondered until Raúl handed me a burlap sack. Inside I saw the poison—green flakes that looked like some type of seasoning. He came up close behind me and pointed to the far side of the lake.

"Go between that tree and that patch of reeds. Do you see where I mean? It's a big area to work. You might be worn out by the time you're done. I can find you another spot if it's too much."

I shook my head. "I'm glad to do it."

"Go on, then."

The people I passed waved to me as I walked by. I wasn't sure whether they did it because they knew Raúl had sent me or because they were just happy to see someone from my family lending a hand for a change, but it felt good to be welcomed. I walked faster, eager to start. As soon as I got to my place, I began to throw the poison, tossing the weed out as far as I could. By the time I reached the area where the reeds grew, I was very warm and sweat clung to my skin. There was still some poison left in the bag so I knelt to sprinkle the water at the base of the reeds.

As soon as I stood I saw Raúl. He had been watching me. A breeze rustled the reeds and I lifted my hair to cool my back. He walked forward, solemn and strong. We looked at each other without moving. Very slowly he reached out and traced his finger down the front of my body from the base of my throat to my navel. My heart was pounding so hard it felt as if it might burst right through my chest. He traced with his finger once more, his touch crossing my body from shoulder to shoulder, leaving a fiery trail on my skin.

"We should go back," he said, a bit hoarsely. I didn't want to go, but I put my hand in his and let him lead me away.

It was getting dark and from the outskirts, the village looked as if it were on fire. But it was the light and heat of a bonfire burning on the beach, the flames leaping higher than the tops of the huts. Everyone was caught up in celebration and I spotted my brothers running around, their faces and bodies covered in mud. Raúl was greeted by cheers. He held his hand up in the air and my hand was still in his, so the gesture seemed to announce to the crowd that we were together. Raúl went to dance with the men. He did a crazy stomp and spun and spun in circles. Though they looked as if they were going wild, I could see they were really just having a lot of fun, laughing the whole time.

The smoke from the fire was burning my eyes and so I stepped away. On the outskirts of the party, a group of women sat in a circle scaling and gutting a huge pile of fish. I watched them from a distance and gathered up my courage to join them. Not one of them seemed to mind as I stood observing them work, and when I sat down in an empty spot in the circle, one woman handed me a knife and showed me how to strip the silvery scales off the fish.

Soon I could do it as fast as they did. I listened to their voices, but didn't understand much of what they said. I guessed they were talking about me from the way they kept smiling and nodding my way. I didn't mind that at all. I just smiled back and listened as the women spoke to one another and sang songs. The time passed quickly. Night fell all around and when the stars came out, Raúl returned, placing three large red snappers into my arms.

"For you and your family."

A feeling of disappointment washed over me. It was time to go home. "I should go back, for dinner. Papa will be wondering . . ."

He whispered in my ear, "Do you still hear snakes in the thatch at night?"

"My father uses the poison the people gave him. They don't come anymore."

"You should listen more closely."

"I will," I said. *What does he mean?*

When I was a short distance down the beach, he shouted to me, "Don't forget to tell your father who gave you the fish!"

I walked along quietly while my brothers scampered ahead, jostling each other down the beach. How unfamiliar the trip back home seemed, although I had taken the same steps a thousand times. I felt that everything in my life before that day was meaningless, a bad dream. I would only have to sleep for just a little while longer before the dream would end and my real life would begin. The three fish I held by the tails were proof, and tonight I would eat them and my body would remember my future. I walked into the kitchen of my parents' hut and placed the fish on the table.

Mama's eyes went wide.

I smiled. "Raúl gave them to us."

"What a thoughtful young man."

I ate my dinner slowly and quietly, partly because I was savoring the fish and thinking about the person who had given it to us, and partly because I was listening in on my parents' conversation. When Mama told Papa that Raúl had provided the meal, my father's only reaction was to clear his throat be-fore he said grace.

Then he announced, "I have good news. The pest problem is solved, and the cotton will go to market at the end of the week." He'd be taking all the undyed bales to Guayaquil, fill-ing Pepito's boat. He'd done this twice before, and he would be gone for a night, possibly two.

"Can we go this time?" Alfonse asked.

"You are too young, Alfonse," Mama said.

"I'm not," said José.

"I'm not either," Manuel added.

Papa turned to me. "What about you, Benita? Do you want to go too?"

The last time Papa went, I'd begged him to take me but it had been too expensive to put us all in a hotel. Now the cot-ton sales had given us enough money for that kind of extrav-agance. And now I didn't want to go. I tried to look as if I were contemplating an answer to his question. "I think I'll stay," I said as nonchalantly as possible.

My father looked surprised. Mama did not.

Papa said, "I thought you were—now these are your words, Benita—'dying to get off the island.' "

I sighed heavily. "I don't want to go with the boys. I'm with them all the time and this trip will be the same: 'Benita, watch out for your brothers.' "

"You should love your brothers," my father said.

"I do. But what's wrong with wanting to be without the boys for a little while?"

"Nothing. What do you think, Pilar?"

"She's old enough to decide for herself."

"Fine. I'll take the big boys," he said, smiling at them.

"YEAH!" José and Manuel shouted.

I finished eating in a state of total joy. After dinner I cleared the table and Mama helped me wash the dishes. She said nothing more about the trip and nothing more about Raúl, but I somehow felt her silence to mean we shared a secret. When she handed me a dish to dry, she placed it in my hand; she didn't shove it in my direction. She spoke softly when she asked me to empty the bread bowl so that she could wipe it. "The fish was delicious. You must thank Raúl for us, won't you, Benita?" I promised her I would. "Good girl," Mama said.

When I finished my chores, I found my father smoking on the porch. I sat down beside him on the wooden planking. He stroked my hair and together we looked out at the ocean, which gleamed like a silver cloth in the moonlight.

"What will you do to keep busy while we're gone?" Papa asked.

"Same things as always. Do my chores, go walking about. I don't know."

"Sounds dull. You live like an *indio* now."

"I do not! Besides, they don't like to be called by that name, Papa."

"How would you know what they like and don't like?"

"I just do," I answered vaguely.

"There're a few things you could do for me in the grove while we're gone."

I rolled my eyes. "Oh, Papa. Do I have to?"

"Of course not. Think you'll change your mind and come with us to Guayaquil?"

"I don't think I will."

"You sound very sure." Papa took a deep puff on his cigarette and blew the smoke slowly into the air. I was tempted to tell him about Raúl, to share that little secret piece of myself in the hopes that it might bring us close, as we used to be. But it was too soon. I would tell Papa, but I wanted to wait.

"I can live without you for a day or two," I said.

"You'll be watching the beach for Pepito's boat to come in."

"Why? Are you going to bring me a present?"

"I suppose I could. What would you like?"

The first thing that came into my mind was the particular type of undergarment I'd wished for earlier in the day, studying my body in the mirror before going to the fish harvest. Something I couldn't say to my father. So I had to come up with something else. I remembered that photograph in my encyclopedia of the Parisian fashion model, the one wearing an elegant black dress.

"Papa, do you think I'm beautiful?" I asked.

He took my chin in his hand and tilted my face to the right and left, pretending to examine me for defects.

"You look like an angel."

I jerked my chin away. "No! I mean if you were a boy and I was a girl, and if we were close to the same age, would you think I was beautiful or just sort of pretty. Or not at all?"

"That is an impossible situation for me to imagine."

"You have to tell me."

"I made you. To me, you are perfect. This goes beyond the question of beauty."

"Well, I want to be beautiful, and I want to sew a special dress for myself. Would you please bring me four yards of the softest black linen you can find?"

"You'll have no place to wear such a fancy dress here."

"I won't be here forever."

Papa had a stern look on his face. "Is that all you'll be wanting, young lady?"

"There *is* something else," I said, and then I just blurted it out. "I need a brassiere." I wished I could disappear in a puff of smoke.

Papa took a look at my chest, and then he quickly turned away, as if the sight had stung his eyes. "You'll have to discuss that with your mother. But I think you shouldn't rush away from being a girl, Benita. You'll be a grown-up woman the whole rest of your life." Papa took a deep drag on his cigarette, then yawned in an exaggerated way and patted me on the head. "Time for your bed, I think. Sweet dreams, my girl."

I had been dismissed, so I leaned over to let my father kiss me on the forehead and I left him to get ready for bed. That was the hardest thing I'd ever had to ask Papa in my whole life and he practically ignored me.

I took the metal pitcher and dipped it into the fresh water of the cistern just outside the kitchen, then brushed my teeth roughly and washed my face in the basin in my room. I combed out my tangled hair, pulling until the comb ran through easily. I let the clean white cotton nightgown float down over my naked body. I drew back the sheet and crawled into bed, punching at the cotton mattress in those places where it had bunched up.

As nighttime took over, my anger at Papa floated away and I remembered my day. Raúl watching me from behind the reeds, his dark seriousness. I remembered how together we had joined the music, fire, dancing, the heat. He made me feel a part of everything. He made me feel grown up and in love.

I thanked God, or whatever spirits were out there listening, that I now had something to be grateful for on Paíta.

CHAPTER

14

Two nights after the fish harvest, I woke to the sound of a snake capturing a rat in the thatch of our roof. Soon I heard another shrill call, not as loud as the first, which didn't seem to come from our house at all. Then I remembered what Raúl had said: *Do you still hear the snakes in the thatch?*

He had come for me. I lay there stiff in my bed, my pulse racing in my veins, listening for more of the same cries. All I heard were my mother's sighs and my father's snores. I counted to one hundred and sat up. Slowly, I put my feet down, ever so quietly, and went to my door, where I checked the main room to see whether the boys slept. They were all stretched out in a corner, legs and arms flung about like driftwood. On tiptoe I reached the front door, pausing to be certain no one inside was awake. Then I went out.

Raúl was waiting at the edge of my father's property. The long cotton nightgown I wore flew out behind me as I ran to him. Raúl ran toward me, too, grabbing me up and twirling me around in a storybook way. I went dizzy under the stars.

"Let's go to the beach," he whispered in my ear.

We dashed down the path, hand in hand. Settling into the sand, I lay my head on his big round shoulder and we watched the water silently. Our breathing was louder than the sound of the waves. After a while Raúl took hold of my chin and turned my face up toward his. I knew he was going to kiss me, and so I got ready to kiss him back, but I leaned forward too far and our lips bumped. Startled, Raúl pulled away for a second, but then he kissed me for real. He was very gentle about it. His wet lips touched mine so lightly that I barely had a sense of them before the kiss was over. He stared into my eyes with great intensity but I had no idea what he was thinking. It was all so overwhelming and I started to laugh.

"You are a silly girl," Raúl said.

"No, I'm not. I love you." The words gushed from my lips and I meant them completely.

But Raúl gave me a look that said he didn't believe me. "You only *think* that you love me."

"Raúl! That's not true. I've always loved you, from the first moment I saw you, when I *was* just a little girl." I described that day for him. How he'd helped us get to shore and I'd gotten mad when it was decided that he would carry Mama, because I wanted to go with him. "I hated everything about this island, except for you. But I decided that if you lived on Paíta maybe it wasn't such a bad place after all."

"I'm going to need more proof than that," he said playfully.

"Like what?" I asked.

"If you love me . . ." He pretended to be thinking. "Go jump in the lake!"

"That's too easy. I'd do that even if I didn't love you."

"You're right. Why don't you travel to the far side of the island and back again?"

145

"Right now? But I want to be with you."

"Go wake up your parents, then. Tell them you love me and are going to live with me from now on."

I laughed.

"I'm very serious."

"About what?"

He sat me up, patted the nightgown down around my knees, then reached for my hand. He took a deep breath before he continued. "It is time for me to have a wife. And I choose you."

I gasped. Maybe he thought I disapproved, because he started to talk quickly, as if rushing through a speech he'd rehearsed.

"You will be good for me because you are young. When I show you things, I feel like I see them for the first time even though I have seen those things a million times before," he said. "And when I tell you things, you listen to me with fresh ears, and I hear that what I tell you is the truth and I feel happy."

"Raúl, that's a beautiful thing to say."

"Listen to me now. I have more to tell you. You talk about the day I carried your family here, but you don't understand how that day was important because I proved you could depend on me. That is what love is. And I will take care of you, better than your father can. But I promise to do more than that. I will take care of your family, too. Fish for them, earn for them. I can make the coconuts grow. You tell me your life here is hard. I can change that. It will be even better than your happiest dream."

I was held in a web of silence, listening to him speak. With every last cell in my body, I had hoped to one day hear him profess his love for me. But that wasn't exactly what he was doing. Instead, he seemed to be talking about making a good deal, or a sound contract, and I was very confused.

As for the last thing he said, about my life on Paíta, the problem was that I didn't want to have a life on Paíta. I wanted to leave this place.

"Where would we live?"

"We will go away together."

Whew! Much better.

"We will leave the village and go far away, deep into the jungle on the other side of the island. I will plant a small garden for us and hunt for our meat. We will make ourselves a shelter. My mother's family has done this for generations. *Enraizado.* It means "rooted." It is done so that two people who want to get married may see each other in a pure way, with no outsiders watching. It will be difficult living outside the village, but it will unite us."

For some reason, the image of the wild cat came into my head, the night I saw it bolt away into the trackless jungle. I could follow and be free like her, escape from my dull life on the plantation. But everything was moving too quickly. It was just as Mama had warned me it would be. After all, we'd only been alone together once. And now marriage?

Raúl was waiting for my answer.

"I wished for this, Raúl, that you'd want to be with me . . . but I never expected . . . I'm just not sure."

Raúl let go of my hand. "Will you think about what I've said?"

"Of course. I'll think of nothing but this. You know I'll have to talk to my father."

"Why don't I speak to him? He'll never allow it if I don't face him myself."

"No! You have to let me tell him. I can make him understand."

"You don't know your father as well as you think you do, Benita. He doesn't like to listen, especially to something he doesn't want to hear."

I sighed heavily. "I don't know what to say to you about Papa."

"Your father is not always fair. He will not be fair to me."

When I looked into Raúl's hurt and serious face, I fell in love with him all over again. I threw my arms around his neck, put my lips onto his and kissed him hard. He pressed into me and our lips opened to each other. I felt his tongue come thrusting into my mouth. I leaned back and Raúl followed, putting his hand out to touch my breast. I arched up to meet it. He held me tightly like that, and we lay there aching, coiled around each other.

Then, without any warning, I felt myself being wrenched out from under him, pulled to my feet. Papa had me by the hair, and he was screaming, "You little fool! What do you think you are doing?"

"Papa, you're hurting me!"

"Not as much as you've hurt me." He let go and gave me a hard shove back toward the path. "Go to the house. Now!" My scalp stung.

Raúl was on his feet. "Keep your hands off her, Mariah." He took a step, and Papa backed up.

"You don't understand. We love each other, Papa."

"Tonight I'm sure it's love. And tomorrow he'll forget all about it."

"You underestimate me, señor," Raúl said.

My father got very calm. "Benita, go to the house right now and get in your bed."

148

The three of us were locked together, Papa and Raúl staring at each other with pure hatred, and me too shocked to move. Papa had never once raised his voice to me, certainly never his hands. And now he stood glaring with murderous intent at Raúl, who stood before him unafraid.

"Who do you think you are?" Papa said to Raúl.

"The man who wants to marry your daughter."

Papa started to pace in the sand, keeping his eyes on Raúl the whole time. Finally he stopped. "I can see right through you. I know what you really want. You're a filthy peasant. Filthy. Did you think I would give her to you?"

"No," Raúl said. "I hoped to prove myself. I . . ."

"Was tonight meant to be one of those opportunities? You drag her to the beach, pull her down into the sand . . ."

"We shared a kiss. That's all."

"And from that sort of behavior am I to be impressed? Stay away from my daughter. You are unworthy of her." Then Papa called Raúl by that insulting name I'd warned him not to use. "You stupid *indio*. Benita is meant for someone much better than you."

Raúl looked ready to roar. "Better than who? You brought her here. You make your living here. How are you better than me?"

"She *will* do better. I can promise you that."

"I can take better care of her than you can, and you know it. Your farm is dying. Everything you touch suffers. Your family, too. But the truth is that you cannot keep your daughter forever. There's nothing you can do to stop me."

"I will not stand here arguing with a peasant." Papa grabbed me and turned me back toward the path.

Raúl was shouting after us and halfway up the path we could still hear him. "You'll be sorry, Mariah!"

149

The full moon had risen high above the ocean. It hovered above Papa's shoulder, a cold rock in the sky. Papa said to me, "Go to your room now. In the morning I shall give you your punishment." I ran, slammed my flimsy door shut and felt the walls of my tiny bedroom closing in on me.

* * *

The next morning when the island's cocks began to crow, I got up and found my parents dressed and waiting for me at the kitchen table. Papa just glared at me, but I looked him in the eyes and refused to turn away, even though I was trembling as I sat down across the table from him.

"Your behavior of last night was inexcusable and you must be punished," Papa said.

As soon as I opened my mouth to defend myself, he bellowed, "Don't you dare say one word!"

Mama said, "Josef! Don't be so cruel."

"Since you have made it abundantly clear that you are all grown up," Papa continued in a steely tone, "it's time for you to start acting like an adult. To begin with, your responsibilities in the running of the plantation will increase. I'll expect you to work alongside your brothers. You'll be expected to care for our livestock as well, to feed them and clean their pens. And you are forbidden to see or speak with Raúl ever again. If I catch you anywhere near him . . ."

"I'm sure she understands, Josef."

I just sat there staring at my parents. Mama looked as miserable as I felt.

"Do you have anything to say?" Papa asked.

"Yes, I do. I want you to know that my punishment started when we moved here."

"Let's go, Benita," Papa said. "It's time for you to get to

work." He led me out the back of the house, and I followed him into the pigsty. Inside the dark and dusty outbuilding, he told me, "I want you to fertilize the field while we're gone. You know what to do. You've seen your brothers do it. Mix up two parts compost to one part pig waste. Half a bucket per tree. Do you have any questions?"

Fertilizing was the messiest job on the farm. It meant collecting the waste from the pig's pen every day and mixing it with the food garbage coming out of the kitchen, then hauling it out bucket by bucket to spread around the trees. José and Manuel did this job every three months. To do it alone would take me at least a week.

"Benita, I think it would be better if you came to Guayaquil with me when I deliver the cotton," Papa said. "I trust you to do as I say, but I don't trust Raúl to leave you alone."

"I'm not going anywhere with you ever again," I told him. I was instantly sorry I'd said it.

He raised his hand high into the air. I winced and waited for it to come back down on me, but when I didn't feel the blow, I opened my eyes. What I saw was almost worse than being hit. Papa was crying. Tears had filled his red eyes. He turned away. "You'd better get started fertilizing," he said as he left the pen.

I was knee-deep in pig dung by the middle of the day. I'd neglected to tie up my hair before I began work, and it dangled down in the muck every time I bent over. My arms and shoulders ached from the shoveling. And I stunk. I could smell myself even when I pinched my nose closed.

My father came to check on my progress. He probably wanted to make certain I was doing the job. I'd seen him supervise enough workers on Paíta to know he thought this way. And that's how he was treating me, as a worker who had to do what she'd been told. So while he watched me, I worked like a machine, scooping up the muck, pouring it into buckets. I would not let him see that I was tired already. Satisfied, he left me alone.

I worked until it was almost dark. I gathered up all the dirty buckets and brought them back into the sty. The stinking stuff was practically baked onto my skin. As I cleaned myself at the cistern outside the kitchen, I overheard Mama and Papa. I stood frozen to the spot, watching them through the window.

"What are you saving her from with this punishment, Josef? Why not just chain her like a dog?"

"She has been spoiled."

"Spoiled? Look at the squalor that we live in. No one here is spoiled."

"I've never given her any real responsibility, and so she has no sense of her own worth. She was ready to throw herself away on that worthless peasant."

"What did you expect?" Mama said. "She's a young woman now, and it's natural for her to want to find a husband and to start a family of her own. On Paíta, Raúl is her only choice. He is the best man she'll find on this island. He can provide for her. And for us, I might add. Don't you know anything?"

"Are you suggesting that Benita should be with Raúl?"

"Yes, as a matter of fact, I am. Think of it as a gain for the family."

"Are you insane?"

"And what if I am? WHAT IF I AM?" Mama was screaming at the top of her lungs. "Who would blame me?"

"I refuse to discuss this any further with you."

"No, you are going to listen to me. For once in your life." Mama moved close to Papa, inches away from him. The look she gave him frightened me, as if she were going to spit venom. "I want you to suffer, Josef, the way your family has suffered ever since you brought us here. I want you to lose the one thing you love. Your precious daughter will leave you, and there's nothing you can do about it!"

"Listen to me, you crazy woman. Benita will fertilize the field. And she'll stay away from Raúl."

Mama roared with false laughter. "You wait and see what happens."

"I don't care how hard it is for her!" Papa bellowed. "I'll make the both of you even more sorry when I get back if you do not do as I wish."

"I'm not going to do anything of the sort." Mama left the room, and that was the end of that.

I didn't go into the house for nearly an hour. I just sat in a stupor, too stunned to move. Mama was using me as a sword to inflict her deepest blow on Papa. I'd had no idea she could be so hateful.

✷ ✷ ✷

Papa and my brothers left for Guayaquil the next morning, and I spent the entire day in the field. Fertilizing was more difficult now that my body was worn and sore. My thoughts had gotten no rest either.

Images of that moonlit fight played in my head. The terrible look Raúl had turned upon my father told me his anger was like a living thing, hard to kill. And I knew that Papa would always look down on Raúl. They hated each other. They probably always would, and now I was the dividing line between them. Each man wanted me on his side.

And I had a choice to make.

Raúl was an islander. I couldn't deny that we didn't have much in common, but still I felt so much for him. He was everything Papa was not. He was young and strong. He was kind and had the respect of all the people. He was the man I'd wanted for so long, and now he'd changed. He wanted me, too.

My father had also changed, but for the worse. He acted like the sovereign ruler of the island, whose word must be obeyed as law. It was as if his heart had shrunken and died. I didn't want to think that way, because it was so hard to hate someone you love. It hurt more than anything. But now I did hate him. And with all my heart.

There was something else to consider. If I went away with Raúl, I would no longer be the girl who stood silently watching other people live. It would be the start of a life that was all my own. But would I be happy with Raúl? Did I even want to be married? What was the right thing to do?

I didn't have any answers. And I didn't feel as if I had nearly enough strength to find them, standing there in a field of dung. Sore and aching in my body and soul. Without anyplace to call home.

CHAPTER

15

Papa returned from Guayaquil late the next afternoon and came out to the field to find me.

"Ah, there you are, Benita! I was surprised you didn't come down to see us land."

"I have too much work to do."

"Good girl. I knew I could count on you. But come into the house now. I have some surprises for you."

I didn't bother to clean up before going in. Papa had brought back trunks full of supplies that would sustain us for another few months—soap, tins of coffee and tea, bottles of whisky for him and new sandals for me and my brothers. There was a hefty bolt of black linen, expensive fabric that glistened as if it had been spun with metal thread. He held it out to me, not even noticing that I was covered in mud and dung. But I didn't want to take his present, to let him think one gift could fix everything. "I'm all dirty. I can't touch that now."

"Of course you are. How silly of me." Papa put the weighty bolt down on the table.

But there was an even bigger surprise. A large white man stood in the doorway waiting to be introduced. He wore a gray tunic that dusted the floor, and his hair was long and shaped like a bowl sitting on top of his head. Papa said, "Say hello to your new teacher, Brother Pantomon."

I looked at my brothers. They weren't exactly jumping for joy about this bit of news, but was it because they'd have to pick up their schoolbooks again, or was there something else bothering them? They seemed as wary and uncomfortable as Papa was buoyant and full of energy.

"Hello, Brother Pantomon," my mother greeted the stranger for us. "Josef, how did this happen?"

"Well, it was a stroke of great luck. I sold all the cotton in the first hour at market, and for more than we've ever gotten before. I thought, why not stroll around the city, take the boys to buy some new clothes? We were walking through the plaza outside the Church of La Merced when I saw a large group of beggar children surrounding Brother Pantomon. They were making quite a ruckus, and I overheard how he was teaching them to count by handing out bits of candy. It struck me then, that he could probably provide similar lessons for Benita and the boys."

"We already know how to count," I said to Papa.

"Well, of course you do," Papa said.

Pantomon spoke up. "I was schooled in Spanish, French and English by the Franciscan Church in Barcelona, Miss Mariah. I'm qualified to teach languages, penmanship, ancient and modern literature and the history of Europe. Do these subjects interest you?"

"He's a monk," Manuel said.

"Yes, we can see that," I said.

"Speaking of counting," Mama said, "I am wondering, Josef, how you plan to pay this man for his services?"

"That's the best part of the story. His trip has been sponsored by his church."

"You see, I was sent on assignment to Ecuador," Pantomon said, "but as soon as I got here, I found that the soup kitchen where I was to work had been converted into a lumber warehouse. That's why I was sitting in the plaza. I had not yet been reassigned. But when I met your husband and he told me about Paíta, I made contact with my order. They were delighted to send me here, once I told them this was an undeveloped island with a primitive native population and no church to attend."

"Extraordinary luck, isn't it?" Papa was running around nervously. "Look here, Pilar. I bought this coffee grinder. . . ." Something made me think he was frightened. He was blabbering as he had the day we arrived on Paíta, the day he was afraid we'd all leave him alone in the blue shack.

"Josef, how can we afford all these things?" Mama said.

"Don't worry, Pilar. I have the cash. I told you. We did very well at the market. Better than ever. Thanks to my quick thinking." Then he turned to me and my brothers. "That's the end of show-and-tell, children. Let your mother and me speak alone together now. Pantomon, if you wouldn't mind, please wait for me on the porch?"

My brothers and I left the room then, said good·day to Pantomon and started walking out to the field. Once we got away from the house, José let out a big sigh. He looked miserable, his lips pressed tightly together and his face grim. I'd never seen him so distressed.

"What's the matter?" I asked him. "Didn't you have any fun in Guayaquil?"

"There's going to be some big trouble," said Manuel.

"What are you talking about?" I said.

"Should we tell her?" Manuel asked José.

"I don't know," José said. "Maybe it's all over now."

"I don't think it's over," Manuel said. "Not a chance."

"Tell me *what?*"

"Papa and Pepito had a huge fight," Manuel said. "I mean, they were screaming and threatening each other. The old man didn't want to let Papa into his boat."

A fast-moving chill ran right through me. I could guess what they'd fought about. It had to be me and Raúl. "Oh no! Tell me what they said!"

"Wouldn't you like to know?" Manuel teased.

"Tell me, Manuel."

"You can't make me."

"That's what you think. If you don't start talking right now, I'm going to tell Papa you haven't watered the trees for days."

Manuel hesitated for a moment, then said, "That's a lie. How would you know, anyway?"

"Dummy, I've been working in the grove since you left. I've seen for myself how the soil is turning to sand. Did you just forget to water, or did you think no one would notice?"

José spoke up then. "All we heard was that Papa did something Pepito didn't like. The fisherman was saying things like, 'You don't deserve to live on Paíta with the rest of us.'"

"And Papa was calling Pepito ugly names," Manuel added. "You know, trying to bully him and make him feel bad. It was really terrible."

"We have no idea what started it," José said. "At the end of the day, Papa told us to wait in the boat because he had some business to do, and when he came back with Pepito, they were already mad."

158

"I might know what they fought about," I said.

"The heck you do!" Manuel said.

"How would you know?" José added.

I looked at them and thought about whether to tell them the truth. They seemed so young to me, and I knew that once I told them what was really going on, things would be changed between us forever. But they would find out sooner or later. "Raúl asked me to marry him."

They were stunned into silence.

"I haven't said yes. Yet."

"Are you going to leave us, Benita?" José asked.

"I don't know."

"Well, you don't seem very happy," Manuel said.

Right then we heard Mama calling, "Time to wash up for dinner. Benita, José, Manuel? Let's go!"

"Don't say anything, to anyone, about what I just told you. Will you promise, boys?"

"Who would we tell?" Manuel said.

"Don't worry, we can keep a secret," José said. "But what about the teacher? Don't you want to start school again?"

"I don't give a damn about that now."

"Well, me neither," said Manuel.

"No, Manuel. You mean, 'I don't either,'" I corrected him.

"That's what I said."

Pantomon joined us for dinner, and he and Papa chatted away about the friar's impressions of Guayaquil. He compared our old hometown to other cities in South America, talking about the beauty of the architecture. I got so lost in their conversation and remembering the place where we used to live, I almost forgot everything that was going on. But then, while the adults were having their after-dinner coffee, I got a sudden, startling reminder.

There was a knock on our front door. Papa answered it. My breath got stuck in my throat when I saw that it was Raúl and Pepito. I wanted to run from the room. I wasn't ready to have a family discussion about my marriage to Raúl. I hadn't made up my mind.

Raúl did not look at me. He spoke directly to Papa. "You have been called to come to our village council. We are meeting tonight."

Papa said, "We have a guest here. I'm not going anywhere."

"It's about the cotton," Pepito told him. "You must come with us. Now."

A brief flicker of realization crossed Papa's face. "I see. Well, let's have it out then."

I looked at Mama and saw that she was worried. My brothers seemed afraid to look up from their plates. I looked at Raúl, whose warm eyes told me he was still waiting for me.

"I'll be back soon. Carry on without me," Papa said, and they left the house quickly.

Mama stood up. "Everyone to bed now. Pantomon, do you have a place to sleep?"

"Oh, don't worry about me. I'll be fine on the beach. Good night, everyone." He took a candle with him, along with his rucksack.

I went to my room and thought about getting ready for bed, but I didn't want to put on my little girl's nightgown and pretend to sleep. For several minutes I just sat there full of worry, and it was too much to bear. I had to know what was going on. I crept out my bedroom window and ran into the darkness, down the beach. I could see my father walking between Raúl and Pepito. They stopped at a fire that had been built in the sand. Many people were crowded around. Moving carefully, I went in closer and saw that there were only men at this meeting. They formed a circle around Papa, who sat down with his back to me. Slowly I made my way around the circle, moving closer so that I could hear what was being said.

Papa sat listening to a man with long gray hair. Joam was at Papa's right. I looked around the circle then and met Raúl's eyes. He was shaking his head at me, urgently trying to tell me something without making a sound. I thought maybe he wanted me to crouch down out of the way, so I dropped to my knees, but that only made him more agitated. He mouthed, "GO HOME!"

I heard a voice yell something that sounded like "HALT!" and then the entire tribe of men turned to look at me huddled there. The man who had been speaking to my father turned to Joam angrily.

Joam interpreted. "This is not a meeting for children. This girl must go."

My father was silent, as if he was too stunned to speak. He just looked at me helplessly, or as if he didn't know me. I didn't know whether I should go over and shake him awake or just leave.

The old man stood up, shook his long stick at me and shouted. All the men in the circle started saying the same thing to me. Chanting "Hoti! Hoti! Hoti!" or something like that. Raúl was saying it too. I took a last look at my father, who sat still as a statue, and then I ran away as fast as I could.

It was late when Papa finally came home. We all got out of our beds to find out what had happened. He was very calm and told us that the islanders were simply upset because they didn't think he was getting enough money for the cotton. "They're greedy people, *los indios*."

"What did they say?" Mama asked.

"They have no idea how the marketplace sets the price. They think it's up to me."

"Josef, did they find out about your arrangement?"

"I told them, they'd be lost without my help."

"Josef, answer me!" Mama yelled.

Papa walked away and twisted the cap off a bottle of whisky. He poured himself a drink and drank it down before he spoke to my mother. "I have been banned from the cotton operation. My cotton-farming days are over."

My mother collapsed in a heap on the floor. "Oh, this is terrible. What will we do? How will we live?" She wrapped her arms around herself and rocked back and forth. Papa poured another drink, and then he left the room without another word, as if he'd simply forgotten we'd all gathered around. As if our being there didn't make one bit of difference to him.

CHAPTER 16

The next morning the sun rose just as it did on any other day, but everything looked different to me. My tiny room was quiet, still and dusty, almost as if I were already gone from it. My diary was on the windowsill next to my bed, exactly where I'd put it the night before and every night before that, but now it was more than just a book I wrote in. It was a tale of travel and change. I opened it and began to read backward in time, all the way to the day we shut the doors on our old life in Guayaquil. It seemed like a million years ago, but that didn't bother me. A new life was waiting.

Mama came into my room. She had been crying and her face was all red and puffy. "We have to talk," she said. A sob escaped her as she closed the door behind her. "Everything, everything is ruined." She stopped to wipe her face. "There's only one way we can survive now that your father has fought with the islanders. Unless we find some way to get back in their good graces, we will starve here. That's the truth."

I knew there was a reason she was telling me all this. "What is it you want me to do, Mama?"

"You must marry Raúl. To save our family. It is our only hope."

My mouth hung open. Even at her weakest, my mother had an incredible survival instinct. Here she was, utterly distraught, but she was still able to see a solution to her problems.

"Listen to me, Benita. If you are married to him, they can't possibly let that happen. They will see you as one of them, and us as well. It will unite our two worlds. Please, please, my daughter."

I remembered something Olga had said to me the time she visited Paíta. She had been talking about her mother. *Getting married is the only way I'm ever going to get away from her.* My way to avoid Mama had been to throw myself into my chores. If I did what she asked, I heard less from her. But now marriage might be a better way to get clear of her.

"I have work to do now. Remember?"

"Yes, you stay strong. Think about what I've said. We're depending on you now."

I didn't eat breakfast with my family. Grabbing a piece of fruit, I headed for the grove.

In the midmorning, Papa came out with the monk Pantomon to show off his plantation. They stood at the perimeter fence while I shoveled the dung. I could overhear their conversation, but I didn't think Papa knew it. He was drunk as a skunk and blathering on and on about the farm as if he were born to it. That my father wasn't sober didn't alarm Pantomon, who seemed to be listening with a focused sort of kindness.

"This land has been in our family for generations . . . ," Papa was saying.

164

That is a lie.

". . . but I was the first to realize its true potential."

To ruin our lives.

"Although the trees will not bear coconuts for many years—I know that from my research—when they do, we'll make a fortune here. There's nothing stopping us. . . ."

There would be no coconuts for years? Why had I never heard him say that?

Surely the friar could see that the farm was nothing but a ruin. All we had to show for all our work was two hundred spindly sprouts poking haphazardly out of the ground. I wouldn't even call them trees, since they stood no higher than my chest. They looked as if they would barely survive in a strong wind. Let Papa live here and slave. He could fool himself, but not me. Not anymore.

"Listen, Pantomon." Papa continued with his sloppy speech. "I need your help with Benita. Girl's gone native on me. She's turning into one of those disgusting *indios*. Puts me to shame just to look at her, but we can turn her around. We've got to. You'll help me do it, all right?"

"I'll do what I can, of course," Pantomon said.

I dropped my shovel when I heard my father talking about me like that. The last of my doubts about leaving dried up and blew away.

Papa called out to me, "Tomorrow's the first day of school, Benita. Don't say your Papa doesn't know how to make you happy!"

I didn't even bother to answer.

When I took a break for lunch, I found Papa on the porch, smoking a cigarette and reading from an old magazine on agricultural production. "Come talk to me, Benita," Papa said, patting the seat beside him. "Like a nice girl." He reeked of alcohol, so I stood by his side instead and looked over his shoulder at the pictures in the magazine. A man wearing farmer's overalls was pouring thousands of cranberries into a huge metal contraption.

"What is that thing?"

"It's a fruit press. It squeezes the juice from the berries."

"Will it work for coconuts?"

"That's what I'm reading to find out."

"Are you planning to buy one?"

"No, we can't afford anything like this."

"Papa, are you sorry that there aren't any coconuts yet?"

Papa turned to look up at me and said, "You know, success doesn't happen overnight. It takes hard work and patience."

I didn't respond.

"You have to understand that, Benita."

"How much patience and time?"

"As much as it takes."

"You should have told us that from the beginning."

Papa stared at me as if he couldn't believe what I'd just said.

"I'm going to have my lunch now." As I walked away, I realized that Papa hadn't really answered my question about whether he was sorry.

José came to visit me in the grove that afternoon. He watched me work for just a little while, and then he brought out an extra shovel and started to help me lay the compost at the base of the trees. "You don't have to do that, José," I said. "I can manage."

"I want to help. There's nothing else to do around here."

I stopped working and pitched my shovel into the dirt. "Do you want to do something for me? Go tell Raúl I wish to talk to him."

"Are you sure?"

"Yes. I need him."

166

When I finished for the day, I brought my tools back to the sty and found Raúl waiting there for me. He had hidden himself in one of the stalls. He picked me up, although I tried to stop him. "How can you stand to touch me?" I said. "I'm disgusting."

"Not to me. Do you have my answer?"

"When do you want to leave, Raúl?"

"You tell me."

"I will be ready to go tonight, after everyone has gone to sleep. What will I need in the jungle?"

"Don't worry, I'll bring everything we need. Three days of clothes for you should be enough."

I sweated out the rest of the day in the field of dung, quitting early, before the sun met the ocean, and cleaned myself thoroughly with cold water from the cistern. I could not rid my hair of the bad smell, and back in my bedroom that night, I boldly cut it to my chin with a sharp kitchen knife. Raúl was shocked when he first saw me in the moonlight, but then he laughed and I laughed with him.

I said, "I am a new woman."

His horse Tara was tied at the back gate. Raúl put me onto the mare's back and mounted up behind me in the saddle. Quietly and swiftly we took off for the island's interior, fast as birds fly across the sky, as if we knew what awaited us was paradise.

PART 5

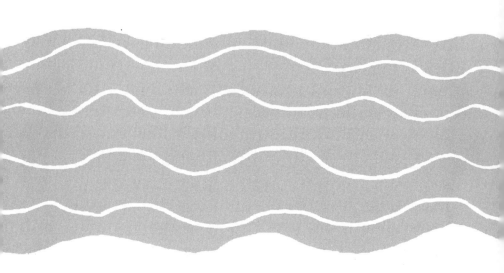

A HOME
AWAY

CHAPTER

17

Raúl and I rode under a deep blue dome of evening sky crowned by a delicate crescent moon. The sounds of the jungle that night were like music. Monkey noise chittered from tree to tree. The swaying branches caressed the air. A gentle wind whispered to me, and I thought I heard it say, *Here they come. Together. In love.*

In the dark I smelled dewed earth, evening orchid and Raúl's warm skin. I felt so small, tucked against him in the saddle, my head leaning back upon his chest. Tara was rocking us together, carrying us to a place I hoped was far away.

"Raúl, will we ride for a long time tonight?"

"No, not too much farther. But first, I want you to see the view from the top of Asiento del Rey." He pointed ahead at Paíta's enormous flat-topped mountain looming up before us. We rode for another hour or so, and then we arrived at the edge of a dry ravine lined with thick genipa bushes that threw a tart sweetness into the air.

Raúl halted the horse where the ravine broke open into a deep, empty gorge. "There used to be a river running here when I was a boy."

"What happened to it?"

"It dried up not so long ago. Four . . . maybe five years ago. There have been many dry seasons now. Too many."

I was thinking about how my father always complained that the grove was too dry. But the whole island suffered, not just his farm.

Raúl nudged Tara's flanks gently and we traveled on, but at a slower pace. The trees near this ravine were much taller than any others on the island, and had thicker trunks. They looked ancient. But what struck me most was that these trees seemed to breathe, and I sensed life flowing through them as surely as if they had veins. As if the bark was their skin, their branches were the tender arms, and the leaves sent sensory impulses across the entire tree.

Was I seeing things as they were, or just imagining?

The ravine eventually closed up on itself at a point several kilometers south, and soon we were on a diagonal path climbing up the steep mountainside. Tara was laboring under our weight, all her effort concentrated in her heaving shoulders and grinding front legs. Raúl shouted words of encouragement to Tara, and she pulled even harder. I tried to make my body light. The last few feet were the hardest on the horse. There was a bit of trail for Tara to use as a foothold, but at the very top she started to slip backward. Her legs kicked away at the dried dirt and her breath came out in violent snorts. I closed my eyes and heard the loud crack of Raúl's switch on the horse's hard buttock. In a burst, Tara heaved herself forward and pulled up over the ledge to the top.

When I opened my eyes I saw that the mountain fell away on

all sides and exposed us to a view of the entire island. It was fantastic to see. Paíta was just a round stone in the midst of a swirling ocean. The top of this mountain was a vast open plain, and at the low point in the center was a pond that caught the moonlight. Little blue flowers bloomed here and there.

Raúl helped me to dismount. We stumbled forward holding hands, pulling at each other and moving toward the edge of the cliff. He hugged me to him, fit me neatly under his arm. We watched the moon for a long while as it settled over the ocean. Then we followed it down, dropping to the ground, and closed our eyes when we could see it no more.

* * *

The cool, damp morning found us curled up on the hard earth, pressed against each other. I peered at Raúl in the pale light, but I was so tucked in to him that all I could see were the parts of him closest to me: the breadth of his fleshy chest, a jaw and chin roughened with beard growth, one bushy eyebrow, the tip of his nose. Far away to the east, from somewhere deep in the jungle, I heard the growl of a wild cat.

"I know which animal makes that sound," I said.

"Don't worry, Benita. I'll protect you."

"I'm not worried." I only hoped it was the same cat that I'd met on my porch.

We ate a breakfast of berries and some cornmeal patties Raúl had packed for us, and we set off again. The way down the back side of the mountain was equally difficult but Tara took the slope steadily and quickly. At the base, Raúl directed her to travel away from the mountain, and we entered a steep and narrow valley. Flowers bloomed among tall black evergreens. Moss grew thick on juniper trees. A small black pond containing orange fish no bigger than my pinkie finger was surrounded by cattails with silvery white tips. I reached out sideways to stroke them as Tara walked us past. The air smelled of lemon.

But the strangest sight of all was the huge bloodred palms that dominated the landscape. They were everywhere, crowned by spiky-looking flowers, and had enormous red leaves that looked like hands with long, narrow fingers. They towered over Tara's head.

"What are they?"

Raúl said, "It's a type of cane. But don't try to eat it. Too bitter."

"I've never seen anything like them before. They look fake."

"And don't touch them. They have thorns. When they cut, it stings enough to make you crazy."

Raúl stopped the horse. I looked out over the strange new landscape, realizing my passage was complete in more ways than one. We were on the other side of the island, on the other side of my childhood. I felt that if I were to turn around and look behind me, I would see everything that I once was.

"Do you like this place?" Raúl asked. "Because this will be our home while we're away."

"I feel like I just figured out a big secret," I said to Raúl. "That it's possible to be born into a new life."

Raúl looked puzzled.

"I think it's fantastic," I said. "I can hardly believe it."

"Good." Raúl eased himself off Tara and helped me dismount. He tied the horse to the copal tree. "I'm going to make camp for tonight. You can explore, but stay where I can see you. Until you learn your way around, it's best. Understand?" he said.

"Yes, Raúl."

He unstrapped the leather saddlebags, and Tara stomped the ground when the weight was released from her back. Unrolling two cotton mats and placing them side by side on a flat, high piece of ground, he said, "Rest here if you're tired."

I lay down, crossing my arms behind my head to watch him work. Raúl unpacked the tools first. They were wrapped in a canvas cloth he'd sewed by hand that folded up neatly and protected the metal blades from scraping against each other. Taking out his machete, Raúl marched over to a patch of the strange red palms and started cutting furiously, whacking at the stalks with sure strokes.

The only personal possession I'd brought along was my diary. I wanted to write down everything that happened while we were away. Lying there on the mat, I described our midnight ride, and how strong Tara was, and the beauty of the valley we were in.

After a while, I started to feel restless. I stood and began to meander through the camp. Gazing into the dark fishpond with its invisible bottom, I thought about my father. I didn't need to wonder what his reaction to my leaving would be. I could almost hear him bellow in anger. This gave me a pleasant thrill. Would he come looking for me?

"Raúl, how far are we from Subidalta? In kilometers."

He figured in his head. "Almost sixty."

"How do you know someone won't find us?"

"It's a safe spot. I've hidden in this valley before."

I felt my confidence drain away. If we were hiding now, had we done something to be ashamed of? Or had we made a mistake?

"Why were you hiding?"

"Sometimes it's good to go away."

A moment of silence passed between us. "But why don't you think they'll find us?"

He stopped working to answer. "This is a very hard place to find. The only way to get here is to go over the mountain, and you must take the trail or it is impossible. But the trail does not make it easy. Do you remember how hard it was for Tara to climb?"

"They could go around the mountain instead."

"No. All around us the jungle is very thick. Many men would have to come for us with machetes, and it would take a long time. And why should they do this when they don't know we're here? Not many people leave the village, and not even the hunters want to travel up Asiento del Rey. Your father could not find us."

"He could come by boat."

"He could try, but he couldn't land on our beach. There's a reef offshore. It is long, and at low tide it rises out of the water. No boat can get through. Do you see? This place belongs to us."

Raúl returned to work then, ramming the stalklike trunks of some of those red palms straight down into holes he'd dug for them. He framed a roof with four shorter pieces squared off to each other and woven across with red fronds. The thorns had scratched his arms and legs.

"You're streaked with blood!"

"I'm fine," Raúl said. "Don't worry so much, Benita."

I watched Raúl hoist the roof up onto the corner posts. He tied it down with more of the palm. The shelter cast a warm red shadow on the ground. Raúl placed our sleeping mats in the center, in the flushed glow. "Come inside," he said to me, as formal as a white-gloved butler at the front door.

Settling down on one of the mats, Raúl tenderly pulled on my hand to take me with him. I moved stiffly.

"So! We made it, didn't we?" I sounded panicky, so I took a deep breath to make myself calm down. "Raúl, I want to ask you something. You said you hid in this place once. When was that? And why were you hiding?"

174

"When I was ten I came here," he said. "It was after my mother died, and I was very sad. My father thought the cure was for me to work harder. So he took me fishing with him, on very long trips for weeks at a time. I hated it; the endless movements of the sea made me sick. One time we battled a storm and we almost sank. To me it was a taste of hell. But my father wouldn't take me back to shore. He loved the ocean and everything about it, even the rough weather. But even the memory of the smell of a day's catch made me want to cry. So I ran away. I found this valley."

"Then what happened?"

"I got lonely and weak. Remember, I was still a little boy. I went back."

"And you became a fisherman?"

"What choice did I have? But there are other things I'd rather do."

"Like what?"

Raúl stood and picked up the ax. "We can talk about that another time. Let's make a fire for tonight." I got to my feet. "Build a circle of stones," he said, pointing at one just outside the hut. "Find more that size."

"That rock looks like a coconut," I said, and then I wished I hadn't. Why was I still thinking about Papa's world?

Raúl marched away into the woods. I did as he asked, like a proper soldier in his tiny army. He brought back a spindly tree he'd chopped down and hacked away at it, making smaller pieces of wood from the trunk, which he then placed in the middle of the stone pit I'd built. Raúl lit the wood using a match from his supply, and soon a fire started up. The flickering light now coming from the shelter was like a signal in the closing darkness. My hand was back in his and he squeezed it hard.

Dropping onto one of the mats, he motioned to the empty

place next to him. "Sit beside me," he commanded gently. Again, his strong fingers and roughened palms pulled me down.

I found myself wishing I could hesitate, prolong our lazy day into the night. But Raúl had that look in his eyes again, the one I'd seen that day in the village store. I didn't know much about the act of sex, other than the fact that the man puts his thing inside the woman, but my sinking heart told me I was about to find out a whole lot more.

Raúl said, "Sometimes when I look at you, I see the child you were when you first came to Paíta."

I turned away and stared deep into the fire pit. I didn't want to be childish right then, but I couldn't help it.

Raúl spoke softly into my ear. "Do you want to take your clothes off?"

"Not yet."

Raúl kissed my cheek and then rolled back onto his mat. He put his hands on the waistband of his shorts and dragged them off in one swift move. I now had a view of him stark naked. I took a quick look down at his crotch. The hair there was very black, and his male thing was thick around and pointed up at me. He was leaning backward, propped up on his hands, in a position that encouraged me to continue my exam. I turned away.

"Maybe I should tell you a bedtime story, Little Girl." He sat up then and gave me a hug with his big naked sweaty body. His hard member pressed gently into my ribs. The feeling was kind of sweet and silly at the same time.

"Have you heard the story of the dragon goddess?" he asked.

I shook my head. "I don't think so."

He snuggled me in close to him. His skin smelled smoky from the fire. "At the beginning of time, there was a male god, a warrior. He was hunting in the woods and crossed the path of a goddess ten feet tall. She appeared to him in the form of a fire-breathing dragon. She did not want him to be in her woods, and so she challenged him to a fight. The warrior had no choice. He would have to fight with her or die on the spot. It was a long, hard battle, but the warrior won, inflicting a fatal blow with his sword. He split the goddess dragon's carcass in two and flung the pieces away from him. Those two parts of her body became the Earth and the Sky."

"And that was the end?"

Raúl was looking down at me. "No. It is the beginning." He reached out to touch my face. "You are that goddess. The heavens cross your forehead," he said, and smoothed his hand across my brow.

I froze with his caress. I couldn't even blink.

"The stars are your eyes." He kissed my lids shut.

"The far horizon rests upon your breast." Raúl placed his palm flat on the bony part of my chest and patted me twice. A deep hollow sound came out my open mouth.

"The round Earth revolves at your hips and belly." Then, gathering me in both arms, Raúl pushed me over onto my back and fell on top of me.

He was heavy and the ground was hard. He held me so tightly I could hardly breathe. Raúl fumbled with my clothes but was having trouble taking them off. I did not move to help him. We were eye to eye, locked in our embrace. If it's going to happen, then let it, I thought. My shorts came off.

Raúl placed his hand firmly between my legs. His palm was hot and he rubbed me there, and I got a sensation of shivery weakness. I didn't want it to stop. His tongue wet my ear as he said, "Now?"

I nodded and braced myself. A stinging sensation spread and flooded into the middle darkness of my body. The pain made me wish I was strong enough to kill him. I forced myself to think of something beautiful to make it go away—a perfect red rose in full bloom. Picturing the petals opening up, I felt the pain less and less.

Inside I was hotter than fire could be, more red. As I clung to Raúl, I felt the muscles tight in the small of his back, his hot breath at my throat, and his head heavy against me. He was moaning, "Oh . . . I . . . Oh . . . I," and then he hunched and held me tight for several seconds. Then it was all done. My face pressed sideways against his chest, I watched the dust settle all around us inside the shelter.

Raúl lifted himself away slowly. "Now you are my girl," he said. I crawled out from under him.

Standing by the edge of the shelter, I discovered a little blood running down my leg, but I wasn't due.

"Why don't you come lie down?" he asked, sounding sleepy.

"I need to wash myself."

Raúl told me about the beach, not far from our shelter. I found it at the end of a soft sandy trail. As I dipped into the ocean, I felt the swift dark tide pulling at me. I cleaned myself, and the warm water turned silky and then washed away.

Back at the red hut I stood over his sleeping body. He was snoring lightly. I found myself wishing for something but I did not know what. There was nothing left to do in the night, so I lay down next to Raúl.

Am I grown up now? I still didn't know the answer to that question, but I couldn't keep my eyes open a minute longer.

CHAPTER

18

During our first few weeks in the camp that fall, we worked from morning to night. But I didn't mind. Raúl was very good at living off the land, and as he'd promised back in Subidalta, he seemed to have brought everything we needed to survive.

One morning we took an ax and went into the jungle. We had to build a better shelter. Our red palm sleeping hut had been good for a while, but it was set right on top of the ground and we shared it with the bugs. Raúl wanted to find a few good eucalyptus trees to use as the main supports for this new hut, because the wood was soft and easy to chop. I liked the way the speckled bark felt smooth, almost like a pelt, and that I'd be able to touch it from the inside of our hut. We picked the four straightest ones we could find, and Raúl chopped them down. He hacked away the branches so that the wood was clean.

"We'll take them back to camp one at a time," Raúl said as he lifted one end of a log and hoisted it onto his shoulder. "I'll need you to pick that end up."

I wrapped my arms around the log, and with a grunt I managed to get it off the ground. But I didn't have enough strength to lift it as high as my shoulder.

"If it's too hard, I can harness Tara to pull this wood for us."

"No, no! I can do it."

"Are you sure?"

"Yes, but I have to put it down first." I knew my arms weren't strong enough to lift it like that. "Keep your end up," I told Raúl, and I walked down the length of the log to where it was about three feet off the ground. I squatted down beneath it, got it placed on my shoulder and stood up. The log stayed balanced there.

"Well done, girl! Well done."

Unfortunately the trunk didn't get any lighter on the way back to camp, and I had to stop and shift it from shoulder to shoulder a few times, but we brought all four trees to the camp together.

Raúl got right to work building the frame for our hut with bamboo. My job was to gather leaves from the yarina palm. Once I had a huge pile collected, he showed me how to weave them together to make the hut's walls by crisscrossing the fingers of two leaves and then pulling each one tight, to close up any gaps and make them hold on to each other. I spent five days weaving yarina palm. I would see the pattern of the dark green leaves in my sleep, like endless wallpaper plastered behind my eyelids. My hands were raw and red from weaving.

I'd never seen a man work harder than Raúl. At night, I could barely keep my eyes open, and it was hard for me even to hold the pen to write in my diary in the disappearing light. But he stayed out, binding the bamboo stalks for the hut's frame with lianas vine. Not only that, he made everything look so easy. When I asked whether I could work on a section of the roof's frame, he warned me that the vine was very stiff, hard to bend. He was right. I tried to wrap it around the two pieces of cane the way he did, but I couldn't even get it to go over the stalk properly. That made him laugh and he took it out of my hands.

"You're doing a great job with the palm leaves, Benita. Keep doing that."

I didn't want to complain, but I couldn't help it. "My hands are burning, Raúl. I don't think I can do any more weaving today."

Raúl took my hands in his and turned them over to look at my palms. They were slashed to bits, and red and hot as if I'd grabbed a frying pan right out of the fire.

"You'd think my calluses would protect me," I said. "But the yarina cut me right through."

Raúl kissed both of my hands. "Benita, why didn't you tell me?"

He quit work for a while and we went for a swim. Getting into the salty surf nearly killed me. The water felt like a thousand needles in my hands. But Raúl held me up like a bride crossing the threshold, so I didn't have to tread water, and we just rocked together in the surf. After a few minutes I felt better, and by the time I got out, my hands didn't hurt nearly as much.

I wanted to swim in the ocean with him the rest of the day. That moment was like a really good dream, and so much better than when we had sex. I hadn't really got to liking sex yet, though I hoped I would soon. I just didn't think it was nearly as nice as everything that came before, when we just kiss or hug each other. And I never knew exactly what I was supposed to do.

I should have asked Olga about this when I'd had the chance. I wondered if she was engaged by now. I wondered if

she had sex and if she liked it. Or did she just do what was expected of her, as I did out here in the jungle? Either way, I bet
she knew how to do it exactly right. This had to be my secret
from Raúl, because I didn't want him to figure out that sex was
another thing I couldn't do properly.

Luckily he hadn't seemed to notice.

But that was my only real worry so far. I couldn't help com-
paring this time away with my family's early days on Paíta,
when getting settled had seemed so difficult. The difference
was like night and day. I wasn't sure whether it was because
Raúl made this rough life seem easy, or whether my expecta-
tions had simply been lowered long ago by Papa, who knew so
little about how to live in a place like this. Thinking about all
the mistakes he'd made, I felt a little sorry for him. But I
quickly remembered all the things he'd done that I was angry
about still, so I put those thoughts of my old life with him out
of my head.

Our house was finished only one week after we'd arrived,
and I was very proud of the work we'd done. It was just four
walls and a roof, but when Raúl hung two hammocks that he'd
brought from the village, I realized that this place was all mine
and his and we could do whatever we wanted. We got into
the hammocks and swung side by side for the rest of the
afternoon.

"It's a perfect home away from home," I said. Raúl was
beaming.

He'd brought food supplies for two weeks. We had beans
cooked with rice and cornmeal patties. He'd brought a sack of
pork jerky, which was tough to chew, but tasted very good.
There were several tins full of coffee, and Raúl drank only one
cup a day, in the morning, to make the supply last. Just as back

in the village, there were fruit trees that provided us with bananas and mangos and lemons. And the pond, of course, was our supply of fresh water.

But Raúl's plans for our extended stay in camp included a vegetable garden. There would be corn, yucca and three types of beans. For greens we would have some lettuce, spinach and celery.

"That's not all we'll plant, Benita. Guess what else I have."

"I can't possibly imagine anything better than this."

He slowly pulled a seed packet from his back pocket but hid the picture on the front to make me guess.

"Peppers?"

"No. Guess again."

"What else could possibly grow on this hot and dry island? It has to be potatoes."

"Nope. Do you give up?"

"Yes! What have you got there?"

He turned the packet around and I saw a picture of a red heart-shaped vegetable that I hadn't tasted in a very long time because they wouldn't keep in the cooler at the island store.

"Tomatoes! Oh, I can't believe it. How long do they take?"

"Twelve weeks usually. But I think they'll grow much faster. Look at how healthy everything else is around here."

"Do you think we'll be away that long?"

"No, no. I said, I think we can harvest sooner."

"I hope so."

Raúl looked surprised. "Do you want to go home already?"

I shook my head at him. "No, I was only saying that I can hardly wait for the tomatoes, not that I'm ready to leave."

"Good. I hope you like it enough to stay for a while."

I wanted to ask him just how long we would be staying away,

but now didn't seem like a good time. He'd think I *did* want to leave. I put the question out of my mind. After all, we had just gotten there.

We worked at starting the garden from dawn to dusk and did nothing else for nearly a week. First we cleared a piece of ground equal to the size of our camp, just on the other side of the pond. Then Raúl harnessed a short-stemmed hoe to Tara to make ten furrows. We planted the whole field in one day, poking all the little seeds into the ground with our fingers and then adding a shovelful of dirt back on top. We'd water the plot by hand. It was small enough that we could manage it.

I was so tired from all the work that I barely wrote three lines in my diary each night before I had to blow out the candle and get some rest. But as hard as it was, I liked doing a man's work. Housework was dull by comparison. You clean something and it only gets dirty again. You cook a meal, and it is eaten quickly and forgotten. Even though working like this made me more tired, I knew I was getting stronger. I could feel muscles in my arms and shoulders where there hadn't been any before. And I must have been growing in other ways too. I didn't have a mirror, but my clothes didn't hang so loose. And when I asked Raúl about it, he looked me up and down approvingly and said, "Now I really can't call you Little Girl anymore."

Just like me, the vegetables we'd planted were growing fast. A week after we'd put in our seeds, they started to sprout and we had to build racks to shade the new plants from the harsh midday sun. We made these from bamboo and more of that yarina palm and placed them over the furrows.

One day as we were watering the field, a wild turkey came into our camp. I saw it first and called out to Raúl, who jumped into action, grabbing his bow. He chased the bird through the woods and I followed as close as I could. That bird was so fast! Lucky for us, the turkey made the mistake of heading into a small meadow and trying to hide in the underbrush. Its bright colors were easy to see through the grass and Raúl got it with the first arrow. I couldn't believe it. I ran over and jumped onto Raúl's back.

"You did it! You did it!" I shouted.

"That was easy," he said, but I could see he was swelled with pride. He held up the bird for me to admire. "Hungry?"

"You bet I am."

"Yeah. Me too. Let's cook it."

It was just in time. Our food supply was running low. Raúl showed me how to pluck the bird clean of feathers, and while I finished this job, he started up a fire in the cooking pit he'd built outside our hut. He set some large boulders beside it and took a metal rod from his canvas tool kit. He used this as a roasting spit, skewering the turkey and setting it high above the flame.

"The rod was a good thing to bring."

"We always cook game outdoors like this. I'll have to hunt for us from now on. But I didn't want to go so soon. I wanted to make sure you felt safe here."

"I feel safe whenever I'm with you."

He smiled. "I'm glad to hear that, but when I go to hunt, you'll have to stay here by yourself."

"Can't I go with you?"

"Women don't hunt, Benita. They can't keep up with men."

"I can run fast. I was right behind you when you shot this turkey. I saw you do it."

"No. It's not safe to take a woman on a hunt when she can't

protect herself. A turkey is harmless, but I'm going after big-ger game that could charge and run you down. Or might attack."

"Why don't you teach me how to use your bow? Then I can protect myself."

"It's not so easy. I practiced for more than a year."

"Well, I can try, can't I? You can't be against that. I under-stand you want to keep me safe, but I'll be even safer here alone in the camp if I know how to shoot."

He was laughing now. "Okay, okay. You win. I'll teach you, all right?"

I didn't think he was mad, but he was staring at me, and I couldn't tell what he was thinking until he teased me a little. "I bet you have very good aim."

I just shrugged. "Always aim for the bull's-eye, right?"

"Who knew you could be so tough?" he said, but he was smiling.

The turkey was the most delicious meat I'd ever had. As we pulled the flesh from the bones, I started to get thirsty. Raúl fetched some water for us from the pond and sat back down. "I wish we had some *chicha*," he said. "Then everything would be perfect."

"What's that?"

"You never had *chicha*? Everyone on Paíta drinks it."

"I've never heard of it."

"Ah, I know why. We would drink it at night, when the work was done and you were safe in your bed."

"Where does *chicha* come from? Is it a fruit?"

"No, it comes from the manioc plant. I'll teach you to make it. It's my favorite drink." He finished his drumstick and threw it into the fire. He stood up then and shouted at the top of his lungs, "I love my *chicha*!"

186

His voice echoed against the dense canopy of trees. He was so loud that it was hard to believe no one could hear him. But we were all alone out there.

In the morning Raúl drew a red circle onto a tree with a smear of clay for my target practice and placed my hands properly on the bow. I could tell he was nervous to have me handle it. He threaded the arrow for me and stood behind my back to help me pull on the sharp, tight wire slowly and evenly.

"Draw back and try to touch your fist to your chest," he said.

I used all the strength I had, but my hand trembled as I tried to hold the bow steady, even with his hand there to guide me. I was afraid the wire would slice off the tip of my finger when I let it go. On my own, I couldn't even pull it back more than an inch. Raúl took the bow from me and came around from behind my back.

"Here, watch me. This is what you must do." He moved to stand directly in front of the target, and I stepped aside. "Aim the fist that holds the bow directly at what you want to shoot and turn your body away." He looked like the perfect archer— straight out of a Greek myth. "Keep your hand steady when you pull back." The wire bent like taffy for him, and he pulled so hard he made the bow bend back as well. "Let go fast. Don't let your fingers get in the way." When he released the arrow it flew straight and faster than the wind. It sunk into the tree and hit the target just left of center.

"See? Even I need to practice."

"Show-off!"

Raúl put the bow back into my hand. "Try again."

I worked at it for nearly half an hour and then I had to stop because my hand was sore from pulling on the wire. "That's enough for today," Raúl said. "You did very good for your first time."

I hadn't managed to hit the target once, though I'd shot a couple of bushes nearby. "But now you won't take me on a hunt with you."

"I'll have to make you a bow that's easier to bend."

"Or I can kill whatever tries to attack me with the machete."

Raúl just laughed. "We'll see. Let me think about it."

Or maybe I'll just sneak after you, I thought. *But I hope I won't have to. I hope, I hope you take me along.*

That night I sat by candlelight and recorded my defeat in my diary. I was so glad I had that book with me. I hadn't brought anything else to read, so I had no other written words to keep me company.

Raúl was watching me. "Every night I see your hand fly over the page. What do you write about?"

"Well, first I write down the date. Today is September tenth. . . ." I turned the book around so that he could see for himself, but he didn't glance at the page. "Then under that I write about what happened during the day. About all the work we do and how I feel about the things that happen to us."

"Why do you need to write this?"

"I suppose it sounds kind of boring. But I want to be able to remember everything."

"What is so important about remembering? Why not just live and be happy?"

"Because writing makes me happy."

"You write in that book like a squirrel storing nuts away for the future." I knew he was only teasing, but I wasn't sure why. "I should throw your diary in the fire and turn your memory black."

Maybe he was questioning me this way because he thought the diary was where I kept secrets from him, so I put the book in his hands. "Read it. There's nothing in there you don't know."

Raúl shoved it back at me. "I can't."

"Go ahead."

Then I saw the embarrassed look on his face, and I gasped. "You *can't* read, can you?"

"No, I cannot."

I don't know why this hadn't occurred to me before. He'd grown up on Paíta. How in the world would he have learned? I thought about all the other things he'd never know because every book was closed to him. But I was excited, too. Finally here was something I knew how to do that he didn't.

"Raúl! I can teach you."

He turned away from me and blew out his candle. "No. I'm too tired."

"I don't mean right now," I said to his back. "But it's easy to learn and I do it really well."

"I don't need to read. I never have. Go to sleep, Benita."

I stayed awake after that, and I felt just terrible. I should have apologized, but it hadn't occurred to me to do so until after his light had gone out. It was amazing how someone could tell you how he felt without using any words at all.

But then I started to wonder if the real reason he didn't want to learn how to read was that he didn't want *me* to teach him. That made me mad, especially since I spent every minute of every day learning from him. What a big baby he was!

In the morning he woke before I did. I rose to find him packing the things he'd need for his hunt. Tara was already saddled for the trip.

"How long will you be away?" I asked.

"I'll be back before dark."

"What will I do here without you?"

"You're a smart girl. You'll figure something out. But in case you get scared, I sharpened the machete for you. It's there in the sack." Raúl kissed me quickly and he mounted up even faster, spurring the horse out of the camp.

I just stood there and watched him go. Then I picked up the machete and ran my finger along the blade. It was very sharp and it drew a sliver of blood. But the funny thing is that I hardly felt it at all. It was just a tiny cut on my hand, proof that I'd already gotten much tougher since we'd left the village.

CHAPTER

19

Raúl was gone only for a few hours, and he bagged a small deer not far from our camp. The little doe still had her pretty white spots. He took her body into a grassy clearing and it was hard to look at the bloody mess he made of her then, but I didn't turn away. He removed her insides with his knife and dug a hole to cover them up; then he skinned her and hung the pelt to dry in a tree. The flesh under her fur was purple-blue and looked slick to the touch. He cut it all away from the bone.

My stomach was churning and I didn't know how I'd get over the sight of the poor creature, flayed out in the field. "I don't know if I can eat that," I said.

"You'll change your mind when you smell it cooking on the fire."

When Raúl was done, he washed off in the ocean and came back to me wearing a clean pair of shorts. "I'm sorry I couldn't take you on the hunt, Benita. But now we have food for a few days, and so we have time to explore. If that would make you happy."

"Oh! I would really love that."

"Good. We'll go tomorrow."

Even though I knew Raúl was trying to please me once again, he didn't seem like his old self. He spoke stiffly, as if we'd just been introduced. I couldn't help wondering whether he forgave me for pointing out that he couldn't read. Or was he simply trying to forget about his anger? I decided we were just tired. We needed to take a break.

We spent the entire next day foraging. At the cove we speared some huge crabs and cooked them on the beach. In the jungle Raúl showed me how to locate a variety of wild mushrooms. Some were good to eat raw, others needed to be boiled. I tasted the wild blueberry for the first time and it became my new favorite. I was so glad to learn about all these new things.

But Raúl also taught me how to make *chicha*, which is the most disgusting drink imaginable. He pulled several manioc plants from the ground, cut off the roots and sliced them into a few pieces that he put in his mouth. He told me to do the same. Then we started chewing. And chewing. It tasted like some kind of raw potato, which wasn't too bad, but the flesh was tough, almost meaty.

"How long do we have to do this?" I asked.

"Chew it good. Till it turns to pulp and the juices in your mouth flow right through it."

We munched on that first mouthful for at least ten minutes and then Raúl spat his out into a pot and so did I. Now I understood why the islanders sat around spitting into cans all the time. When we'd chewed through the pile of manioc pieces, Raúl directed me to boil a pot of water and when that was done he added it to the pulp, until the can was filled to the brim with hot, bubbling spit.

"Now what?"

"We let it sit like that for a couple of days until it's ready."

"What happens to it?"

"It gets thicker and a lot less sweet and turns into the most delicious drink in the world."

"Well, there's no way I'm going to drink that stuff even if it was my saliva that made it."

"I want you to make it for me every week," he said.

"Yuck."

Now that our camp was completely set up, things got a lot easier. Raúl hunted for our meals and chopped wood. I did all the cooking and I kept the fire going. Together we weeded the garden and picked whatever was ready for harvest.

One chore I looked forward to was taking caring of Raúl's horse. I didn't have to make up any grub for Tara, as we did for the livestock back in the village. There were plenty of leafy things all around us that were good for her to eat. But Raúl didn't want to let the horse roam loose, so I took her by the reins and walked her around the perimeter of the camp twice a day.

Tara and I became good friends. She was always glad to see me when I untied her from the copal tree, and I liked to think it was because she enjoyed having her coat brushed even more than she wanted to wander about and eat. I'd whisper in her ear, "You pretty horse," as I ran the stiff brush hard along her thick neck. And she'd answer me with a snort or a whinny while I'd watch a shiver of pleasure travel just under her skin, down the entire length of her body from head to rump. Usually goose bumps rose on my own skin just to see it. What I loved most about Tara was the way she moved: Her huge muscles would shimmy with each delicate step she took. Just for fun, I'd pretend to be a horse, and I'd stroll alongside her, moving in the same languorous way that she did when she was grazing, as if I carried two stones of mighty flesh above my dainty ankles.

Sometimes I felt I got along better with Tara than I did with Raúl. After that one bad night with my diary, it was as if the ground beneath our feet had suddenly got as narrow as a track and we had to be careful where we stepped or we might fall off the edge. It wasn't hard to say something that would make him mad. The worst fight we had happened in the garden, which was thriving under his care.

I was picking beans that were as thick as my fingers. "I never would have thought it possible to have such a healthy garden on this island," I said. "How did you learn how to farm like this?"

"I learned a lot from the people. They know much more than you think they do. They know what grows well on Paíta and how to help it along."

"Still, it can't be easy." I was thinking about Papa's plantation and how hard farming that piece of land was. "Maybe you're just very lucky," I said.

"No, it's not luck. If you look at the plants, really look, they will tell you what they need. I got very good at seeing them."

"You spent most of your time fishing, though, right?"

"I would fish with my father almost every morning, but when I wasn't in the boat, I was working in the field. Now I'm the best farmer on the island. Everyone knows that. The people depend on me to grow their crop."

"Uh-huh."

"I *am* the best farmer on the island. Everyone knows." He said this as if it were an indisputable fact, even though I wasn't debating with him, like he was pushing at an invisible wall and couldn't give up.

"Yes, you are the best farmer. Just look at this garden."

"Your father wouldn't listen to my advice. He was afraid. Afraid I was right, and when his plantation got healthy he would owe me something for that."

"It'll take a miracle before Papa's plantation produces any coconuts. I just know it."

"Oh, no. Those coconuts will grow. Because when we go back, your father will have no choice. He will have to let me work there because I will be your husband. Then he will learn who is a better farmer." Raúl said these words as if they were a rule to be carved in stone, and a little flare of hatred for him fired in my heart.

"When we go back, are you going to stay mad at Papa your whole life?"

Raúl yelled, "Why do you always stick up for him when you know he's wrong?"

How dare he accuse me of sticking by Papa? I'd left because I thought Papa was so wrong about everything. I was getting madder by the second, and so was Raúl. I should have kept my mouth shut.

"I'm not defending Papa. I hate the plantation. It can wash away into the ocean for all I care."

Raúl threw his hoe into the ground. It stuck straight up like a flag. He walked out of the garden and away from me. I could practically see the smoke coming out of his ears. All of a sudden I wanted him to come back. But it was too late. He was gone, and so fast that I couldn't have caught up to him even if I wanted to.

I was so angry, my hands shook on the vines as I finished

picking the beans for our dinner. There was so much anger around me and inside me too. I felt as if I were choking on it, as if it fogged the very air I breathed. I realized that the question I'd asked Raúl was one I should be asking myself instead. How long was I going to stay mad at Raúl, and at my father, for that matter? I knew for sure that I didn't want bad feelings like Raúl had, to last for my whole life. I could see they were a great source of unhappiness for him.

We did not ever talk about that day. Again, Raúl seemed to have swallowed his anger, but this time I knew it was only a matter of time before it would flare up again.

Our days and weeks went by in a slow and steady way. He had us start to gather our winter wood supply even though it was only late October and the rain wouldn't come for another two months—if at all. We'd collect an armload of wood each day just in case. The wood from the achiote was good for cooking, and balsa wood was what we used for tinder. We kept a growing supply of it underneath the floor of the hut.

I kept on writing in my diary every night. Things like, "For lunch today I prepared fried plantains and a mango salad, and for dinner we had fish." Even though the days were uneventful, I didn't want to lose touch with myself, and that silly little book was the only outlet I had for my feelings.

I wrote about my family, which made me realize how much I missed them. Now that I was away from home, memories that were nice would pop into my head, and not just from our life before, but from our time on Paíta. When José and Manuel taught me how to surf the waves and we held hands under the churning water. When Mama gave me her pearl earrings because I told her I liked them. And good thoughts of

Papa crept up on me. He had given me the gold-plated pen I was using; it made me feel that the things I wrote about were important.

In my diary I also kept track of when Raúl and I had sex. There had been nothing between us for more than a week, and the truth was that I longed for it. But only because then I felt as if he was happy with me. He looked deep into my eyes, and when I looked back, everything seemed so much simpler. The only good thing about having less sex was that I was less worried about getting pregnant. I always marked the day that I got my period in my diary and counted the days until my next one, but when October became November and I was on day thirty-five, I panicked. Then all I could think about was how my life was going to turn out just like Mama's, and there would be a baby I didn't want that was mine and his. I did finally get my period on day forty, and I was so grateful I fell down on my knees to thank whoever was listening to my prayers.

After that brief relief a whole new worry gripped me. Just because I wasn't pregnant right then didn't mean it wouldn't happen the next time Raúl and I lay down together. I didn't know which was worse: worrying about getting pregnant, or worrying that the reason I didn't want to have Raúl's baby was that my heart was telling me I didn't want to be his wife. From then on, I decided it would be for the best to stay away from him at night, and then maybe I would stay safe.

Late one night, Raúl drank up his *chicha* as we sat on opposite sides of the fire, watching it burn down. We stayed there for a long time, and he'd had so much to drink that his breath stunk of it and even his sweat smelled like the sugary juice. I could smell him from where I sat, and I was reminded of the time Papa shook me awake on our last night in Guayaquil.

197

And I realized all of a sudden that *chicha* is a drunk man's drink. What a fool I was. I thought Raúl just liked the taste. That he seemed especially loud afterward, and that he usually pulled me to him after drinking a full can of the stuff, and that it took him longer to wake in the morning—none of this had alerted me to the truth about *chicha*.

Raúl reached for me but I didn't want to lie down with him, so I said, "I think you've had enough of that," and pulled the can out of his hand. He was so woozy that it wasn't hard to take it from him.

"Why don't you try it?" he said. "You want to do everything boys do. Are you scared?"

"Scared of what?"

"Of what might happen to you."

Just to show him, I decided to have a taste. I tilted the can up to my lips, but I made the mistake of smelling it first. I nearly gagged. I had to hold my nose to get the liquid down. That first sip was awful—the worst thing I'd ever tasted. A warm, gooey pap that burned my throat. But afterward my skin tingled, and Raúl seemed friendlier as I passed the can back to him.

"One sip isn't enough. Have some more," he said.

I took another sip. And a few minutes later I gulped down some more. I remember Raúl coming toward me, laughing and saying that little girls need to drink their *chicha* and cracking himself up over that joke. I remember I thought he was being stupid. We had another can. And then another.

I was sweating now; the fire seemed to roar up in front of us. I stood, and the wave of heat coming from the flames soaked into my skin. "I'm burning up!"

"Take off your clothes!" Raúl shouted. I pulled my shirt over my head, and Raúl cheered. I was standing there bare-chested, the sweat rolling down between my breasts, pouring off me. "Look at you now!" Raúl was on his feet all of a sudden, rushing toward me and the fire, but I easily dodged his outstretched arms. He came after me slowly, almost staggering.

"Benita, wait! I want to . . ." But he didn't finish his sentence and he just kept coming after me. I thought it was very funny the way he was chasing me but couldn't catch up. I peeled off my shorts and I was completely naked now. "Argh," Raúl grunted, and tried then to run, but I was still faster than he was, moving with the kind of easy grace I'd learned from Tara. It felt so good to be naked, like a burst of freedom. I dangled my wet shorts in front of him, teasing him to come and get them. Then I threw them at him. They only grazed his head but Raúl dropped to his knees and then fell over backward in the dirt.

Looking back, I stopped running. "Raúl? Are you okay?" I walked over to him slowly, certain that he was faking and would reach up and grab me. But he said nothing for a full minute, and when I went and stood by him, I knew he was dead asleep, his arm flung out dangerously close to the leaping flames. I was suddenly hit by a wave of dizziness, and instinctively I knew I had to keep moving or I would fall over too.

I dragged his body away from the fire and crawled into the hut. I don't remember too much else.

That night I had a dream about my father. It was all a big swirl of images. I saw glorious coconut trees heavy with large green coconuts. They were everywhere and all around me, as if Papa's field had gotten ten times bigger than it was. Papa was on his unbroken horse, kicking its flanks, the horse rearing up and trying to throw him. I shouted up at him, trying to tell him that Raúl could pick the coconuts, but Papa didn't hear me. He just rode his mad horse around the grove, jockeying back and forth between the trees, trying to stay on its back. And then all the coconuts turned brown and fell from the trees, hundreds of them. I picked one up. It was a pathetic little coconut, smaller than the palm of my hand.

The next morning my head felt as if it were being clamped between two boards. And I was freezing cold, though the temperature of the air had to be at least ninety degrees. I couldn't even wake Raúl. What nasty stuff that *chicha* was. Although now I understood why he drank it, I thought I'd probably throw up in the can the next time I had to make it for him.

As I put his coffee on the fire, images from my dream came back to me. Coconut trees with rotting fruit. I realized that my dream wasn't just about Papa. It was about how time is passing for all of us on Paíta. I didn't think Raúl and I were facing ruin, the way Papa was in the dream, but just like a field ready for harvest, we were done here.

We had lived as a man and a woman, built our home together, planted our food and harvested it. Although I wasn't sure what should happen next for us, I knew that our plan wasn't to live alone in the jungle for the rest of our lives. What was the next step? What would our future be?

I brought Raúl his coffee and watched him drink it. He didn't speak.

I could have screamed into the silence that fell around us, but my head hurt way too much.

CHAPTER

20

Raúl always took care to make sure we wouldn't be found in our hideaway. And though nearly three months had passed with no sign of a scout, he didn't want to leave trails in the hills surrounding our camp, because that would make the search easier if someone was coming. For that reason he preferred to exercise Tara in the ocean. Tara's hoofprints melted away in the single sandy path to the beach, so our secluded camp remained safe.

But Tara despised the ocean; anyone could see that. She would not walk through the water, but like a fancy dressage horse, she lifted herself one foot at a time above the waves, prancing and snorting in dismay when the surf washed at her belly. Though Raúl was her master and she let him pull her into deeper water, he could never get her in so deep that she would swim. She could not be yanked or cursed into submission, nor charmed with a kindly word. And the equally stubborn Raúl would not give up. Every day they went to the cove, and every day the result was the same.

Then one morning Raúl asked me to help him. He never let me ride her on my own, so I couldn't imagine what he had in mind. "If you lie across her back, Benita, with your arms around her neck, she will not feel the ocean because your body will break the wave as it rises on her. But you must hang on tight when the ocean swims over you. Do not float free. That will be your job."

Raúl led us on foot to the water, the three of us together for the first time in a long while. My naked legs straddled Tara's hot unsaddled back. She made my hips swivel, up and down and left to right, as if I were joined to her. Her hide got slick with sweat from the hot sun that beat down on us both. It felt good.

At the water's edge she gave out a whinny to let it be known that she did not want to go in. She allowed Raúl to lead her but she kept her head held high.

"Take hold of her mane now, Benita. Close to her neck," Raúl said.

I grabbed two black clumps of horsehair in my hands and wrapped them around my wrists. Leaning forward, I crossed my ankles over Tara's wet and steaming rump. Raúl pulled on Tara's bit to lead her out. The blue ocean, bright as a gem on that morning, tickled my dangling knees. Tara shivered. "Good horse," I said in her alert right ear.

When I looked up for Raúl, I found him dancing ahead of us, the water at the height of his chest. He clucked at Tara, tongue to his teeth, and suddenly the horse burst into her paces. Circling Raúl at a swift clip, she rushed forward into the swelling sea. She moved like a wooden carousel horse, lurching and rising with the contours of the sandy floor beneath us. The ocean turned to white froth at her sides. We were moving so fast and I was dizzied by splashes of color, sunlight on the sea. The ocean flowed in beneath me and across the horse's withers. Tara seemed to sink as I was lifted up.

"Hang on!" I heard Raúl command, but my body was slipping sideways. A rough wave came and threw me off in a single sweep.

"Quick, quick! Get back on! Pull yourself now!" Raúl was shouting and Tara was bucking, scared of the deep water. Clasping her trailing mane like a lifeline, I dragged myself to her flank but I couldn't remount the enormous horse in the pulsing ocean.

It was all so beautiful. Tara's chestnut brown hide. The spinning clear surf. The heavenly sun. I laughed out loud, and as I did, Tara reared back, loosening a rain of spray over our heads. When she came down, her front legs buckled a bit and she dropped low in the water. In that moment I flung my leg, hooking it over Tara's back. We circled in this awkward hold. Me, like a trick rider of the old rodeo, spinning sideways off the mount and spitting salt water; the horse with a wild eye shooting ahead.

"C'mon, c'mon, you can do it!" Raúl bellowed at us. Using every last ounce of my strength, I managed to yank myself onto Tara's back and off we went again. Raúl took us deeper and deeper, and soon the pounding of her hooves was replaced by a smooth motion, the horse no longer bounding but swimming, her slim leg bones turning the water, the massive body free for once of all its weight. I linked my hands around the horse's neck and let my legs float out behind. I didn't try to hold her quite so tightly with my body. Raúl kept Tara in the turn, but the ocean was calm now. There were only the cawing of frigate birds, Tara's rhythmic inhalations. I heard my light breath whistle in the air.

"You've got it," Raúl called out. He let loose with more rope and Tara took a wider arc. Before long, I realized Raúl had let us go. I directed Tara away from shore, set her roaming out into deeper water, locked on a course for the deep ocean that was empty and waiting, promising freedom at a point just beyond. I wished that I could head straight out into that forever blue and swim the horse to the mainland of Ecuador, but even if I could, I didn't know which way was home. We were in deep water by then, and Tara's snorting breath was becoming more rapid.

"Come back. You'll hit the reef!"

There before me was a long, low wall, partially submerged. The crashing ocean frothed up where it met the reef, forming a bright white boundary line that enclosed our cove in its embrace, and I understood why Raúl had told me that a beach landing was impossible. So was a beach escape. The reef's jagged points sliced the waves into shards and shot them up in the air.

"Tara, we have to go back." I pressed my left thigh into her flank and the horse turned, her nose pointed to shore.

When we got close, Raúl shouted, "Throw the rope!" We didn't stop for him. I gave Tara's flanks a nudge with my heels and she bounded out of the ocean, leaping into a run like thunder moving sideways. The air hit us hard and drove the salt water from my body. At full speed Tara moved smoothly, almost as if she were immersed again, her back a flat steady plain above the pounding of her legs.

But we had to halt where the sandy beach ended, only a half mile away. Tara, frustrated, walked herself in a circle in the sand, and I realized instantly that the circle was the shape of her bondage, the shape of the limits he'd set for her. In a flash

I saw myself in the camp that Raúl had built for us, as I went around from garden to hut, hut to pond and back again. The way I circled the camp, going through the motions of the day, was just like Raúl's exercising of the horse. He created the illusion of movement for us both. The same way his having taken me from my father's house seemed like change, when in reality he had only roped me in.

I turned the horse and casually cantered back to where Raúl was waiting. He yelled, "Where were you going, Benita?" and as we got close he grabbed hold of Tara's bit, pulling her reins out of my hands. He petted the horse then, his hand upon her sleek neck.

"I love to ride her. So much! When can I go out again?"

Raúl didn't even give my request a moment's thought. "She knows how to swim now. No need to take her in anymore." He turned then and walked us slowly back toward camp. And though we were going back to what felt like nothing more than a holding pen in the open jungle, my mind began to wander, and I realized Raúl might have been right that night he proposed to me on my father's beach. When I'd said I loved him, I had no idea what I was talking about. And I certainly didn't feel that way about him now.

The rest of the day we worked in the garden. Raúl staked the tomatoes and watered them, and I picked the spinach, which came up strong as weeds. I had three baskets full and there was plenty more to pull.

In that quiet, peaceful moment right after our supper, I decided to try to talk to him about some of the things I was feeling. I couldn't hold them in anymore. The main thing I wanted to say to him was that I was beginning to forget the reason we ran away together.

I looked deep into his stony face, which was once so handsome to me that my heart would pound just to look at him. Now all I saw was his hardness; he looked unbreakable.

"Raúl?" The sound of the fire was almost louder than my voice. "Do you love me?"

Staring into the flames, he didn't answer right away. "Why do you ask such foolish questions?" he said finally.

"Because I can't remember the last time you told me how you feel about me and what we're doing together. You never say anything like that anymore."

"I am here with you. That should say enough."

"But it doesn't."

"Because you are impossible to please."

"Don't misunderstand me. When I look at what we've done here, Raúl, I can see it's a success. The camp works perfectly. The shelter is comfortable, the garden gives us fresh food. But between us there's so little that feels good. Do you know what I mean?"

Raúl sighed deeply and I understood that I had only spread my disappointment to him. "I can't give you more, teach you more, be with you more than I already am, Benita. Every day we do for each other, and I believe our life together is as it should be."

Raúl reached over to hold me in his arms. I closed my eyes and melted into the warmth of his body. As he stroked my head, his hand felt sad to me, heavy and slow and consoling. It was the tender moment I had asked him for, but I didn't feel close to him. I felt as if he was patting me down, silencing me and my doubts, which only kept them burning.

He fell asleep soon after, and he slept soundly while I wrote in my diary about all of our differences. It wasn't just that I liked to stay up at night and he liked to fall asleep early. I liked to talk and he liked to sit quietly staring into the fire. He came from a world where a woman served her man. I had been raised to think for myself. He wanted to be with a woman who would do as he said, I wanted to be with a man who understood what I wanted. I was a child of the city and he was born on the island.

The problem between Raúl and me was now perfectly clear. I didn't know why I hadn't been able to see this before. There was a gap between us and it was as wide as the ravine we had crossed to get to this hiding place. And there wasn't any way to bridge it because there was nothing I could do to change one simple truth about us.

While we slept in the same room, we lived miles apart in our hearts.

CHAPTER
21

I had been lying in my hammock just listening to the sounds of the jungle when the riotous chatter of monkeys trumpeted in my ears. It sounded like a call to adventure and I rushed out of the hut.

I found them perched high above my head in the copal tree, which was nearly bare from heavy winds that had been blowing strong for several days, promising the start of the rainy season. I crouched down to spy on them from behind a bush so that they wouldn't startle.

They had tiny little heads and black faces that fitted them like masks. They flitted around like birds, chasing each other all around the tree in a frenzy. Whenever they rested, they took turns grooming each other, head to tail. Or they'd sit huddled together at the shoulder, staring across the empty pit of the jungle. A queer look came over their small black faces then. I interpreted these looks to mean that they were very glad to have each other because the world is too big and strange for little monkeys.

When Raúl found me, I said, "Look at those monkeys. I think they're in love. It's like they were made for each other."

He crouched beside me and carefully pulled a bow from his hip sack.

"Don't!" I whispered.

Raúl stared at me, the weapon still held high on its target while he searched my face with a harsh look. "Why?" he asked. "Two monkeys, good for eating." He pulled back on the bow's wire and I pushed his arm away roughly.

"No! You won't be able to shoot them both. Think how bad it'll be for the one that survives," I said.

"No, I'll get the two. Watch me."

I sighed. "I believe you. I do. But don't do it."

"Is there some other thing you want for dinner?"

"Anything else. I won't eat a dead monkey."

Raúl softened then, his voice deepening as he said, "You know we have no meat. This is necessary."

"Please don't," I said. "There's something special about these two."

"Yes. They came to play in our camp. Only a fool would let them go."

"Just watch them for a minute. You think they don't have feelings? And for each other?"

"You silly girl. They've grown used to each other. That's all. Lucky for them."

Raúl's open bitterness felt like a slap in the face and I stood up from the bush where we hid. The monkeys came to a dead halt in the tree. They peered down at us, their eyes flickering with fear and decision. They were going to run. Instantly Raúl righted the aim of his bow and released the arrow. I screamed as the first one hit the ground. The other was gone in the next second.

Raúl burst into pursuit. I followed as closely as I could. The monkey never stopped moving, making it easy to spot even in the uppermost branches of the trees, and its howls seemed to rip the air as it went crashing through the foliage. Raúl kept pace below, craning his neck to keep an eye on his target.

If I hadn't been so furious with him, I would have been impressed by the way he moved through the dense jungle. Barefooted, he beat the earth as he ran, dodging fallen logs easily and pursuing his prey tirelessly until finally the monkey was exhausted. Raúl set himself up below with a clear shot to the animal's neck. The panting creature was caught helpless in his sight. Raúl held still for a moment, savoring his victory. Then he sent the arrow and the monkey dropped, a lifeless sack at his feet.

Once it was over, I turned back toward home. I knew that I would not eat the monkey, and that Raúl would not understand. He would be insulted and in a dark mood, but that was his problem.

Close to our hut's entrance I heard an animal sound. A pathetic squeak came from the place where I had watched the monkeys play, and I found the little monkey Raúl had hit, bleeding from the foot and in too much pain to get away. I crouched down, talking softly, trying not to scare it. After a while it no longer looked up at me desperately frightened, but just lay there like a little wounded warrior, ready to die.

I had to do something but I was afraid the monkey might try to bite or scratch me if I picked it up. I went into the hut and looked around for something I could use to capture it safely. The only thing I could think of was our blanket. If I wrapped the monkey up, maybe I would be safe.

Outside I softly let the blanket cascade down. When the monkey did not struggle beneath it, I gathered the tiny form off the ground and took the bundle inside the hut, placing it in one of the hammocks, then unrolling one edge so that the monkey could see out. "Rest there, little one. Don't move."

We were frozen then, just watching each other. The monkey broke our mutual gaze and began to look around the room until it spotted a pile of freshly picked fruit I'd placed on the table.

"Hungry, Monkey? You can have some." I walked slowly toward the table and peeled a banana. The smell of the fruit escaped and I saw the monkey's eyes open wide. I brought the banana slowly over to the hammock and broke off a piece. I dropped it onto the blanket. With a feeble hand the monkey reached out, picked up the slice of banana and greedily began to eat. I fed the monkey the whole thing piece by piece until it was taking each piece right from my hand. When it had finished, it still had that hungry look in its eyes.

It was time for me to begin making dinner, anyway. "Just stay there," I said. "There is more good food coming your way." I worked at the small fire inside the hut, starting up a stew of yucca and plantains.

Not long after that Raúl came home. The very instant he stepped inside our dwelling, the monkey jumped up and started screaming, letting loose with a barrage of crazy shrieks that rained down on him, and he lifted his arms to shield his head from attack. When he realized he was safe, he dropped his guard and looked around the room. The monkey was now perched at the edge of the table, teetering on its one good foot. I threw another peeled banana its way, and it stopped shrieking.

"What is this?" Raúl said, pointing to our guest, who stared at him with evil intent.

"Our new monkey," I told him. "The one you tried to shoot. You missed. Well, that's not exactly true. You did hit it, but the arrow cut clean through its foot. It was still on the ground when I got back, so I brought it in here. It likes to be fed. I think we're friends now." The monkey chewed meanly and stared at Raúl.

"It's possible the poison has already got into the blood. It may not live," Raúl said.

"That's an even better reason to take care of it."

Raúl shook a finger menacingly in the air. "I don't want that animal in my house."

The monkey chittered a low warning at him.

"Your house?" I said.

Raúl paced back and forth a few times and then halted. "I won't live with that monkey," he said.

"I told you not to shoot it. I'm not going to leave it out there to die. When it's better maybe it'll go. You should have listened to me, Raúl."

"I want it to go now!" Raúl banged his fist on the table. The monkey leapt into my arms and climbed up to nestle against my neck.

"Go outside, if you're going to act like that. This is my house too, and this monkey is my pet and we don't want to be yelled at."

Raúl, glowering, punched the front door on his way out. I heard a lot of banging noises outside, and I snuck up to one of the windows to have a peek. I realized I didn't completely trust Raúl.

He had furiously thrown himself into the business of making a fire in the pit we kept outside the hut, hauling a long log out of the forest and hacking it apart in large chunks. When he finished with that, he rampaged through the brush, gathering dried branches in his arms. He looked like a walking thornbush. He threw these on the ground, took an armload of our cooking wood and laid that on top. Then he held a match to the kindling at the bottom of that massive pile of wood and set it ablaze.

Soon a bonfire was going. Raúl stood back and admired his handiwork. "Thinks she's better than everyone else," I heard him say in the face of the immense flame. "Just like her father."

"Who is more like Papa, me or you, Raúl?" I said. But he didn't hear me.

After a while he sat on a stump and busied himself with the work at hand, to dress the monkey meat for his dinner. His movements were quick and angry as he sliced with his bowie knife, making a slit along the inside length of the fur-covered arms and legs. Scraping back the pelt's edge, he yanked it downward, dragging the hide off all the way to the neck. I'd seen him skin and gut many deer in exactly the same way, but he was pulling the monkey apart as if it had wronged him. Though the animal was dead, I feared for it, and me.

He kicked out one of the burning logs, set up his spit and put his dinner on to roast. Within half an hour the monkey meat began to smell good. I could hear the juices sizzling on the charred wood. When it was ready, he sliced into the cooked flesh and ate it all off the tip of his knife. His meal finished, he lay down and quickly fell asleep in the intense heat.

I kept the lamp burning for a long time, way into the night, but by morning it was out. The hut was cold. I rose to start up a small fire and heated a pot of coffee. The monkey lay wrapped in the blanket where I'd left it, in Raúl's empty hammock. I found Raúl outside, curled in a tight ball beside the smoldering fire.

I handed him a cup that was full to the brim and said, "Here's your coffee."

He did not bother to thank me, but while he drank it, he told me of the hunting trip he had planned and said that he would be away for nearly a week.

"Will you take me?" I asked.

Raúl explained that he would be traveling far and there would be no room for me on the return, as he planned on bagging a large carcass that he'd have to carry across Tara's back.

"Why do you need to go on such a long hunt this time?" I asked.

"This place is hunted out. I have to go or we may run out of food. I will stay away for five days. And when I get back, I hope you will learn that you need to have me near you. That it's important for us to stay together. And you'll see, Benita. Need is greater than love. This is what is important between a man and woman."

"So this trip you're taking is meant to be a lesson for me?"

He didn't answer.

"I wonder what I am to do while you're away," I said.

"The same things you always do. You have your chores. You can go for a swim." The echoes of a former conversation I'd had with Papa came to me. *I'll do the same things as always. Do my chores, go walking about. I don't know.* What a funny circle life could be. But I didn't laugh. Papa had wanted me to go with him.

Raúl stood then and began preparing for his trip. He packed his canvas sack of tools, whistling, but unaware that he was doing so. With a shock I realized that he was happy to be leaving. Oh, how I hated him right then. I peeled my clothes off and jumped into the pond, knowing that this would upset him. He'd said to me more than once that a fresh water supply was crucial to our survival, and that swimming in the pond would destroy our source.

"Benita! Haven't you learned anything? Get out of there!" he yelled at me.

I swam to the opposite side. I made the far edge in a single stroke and came out of the water slowly, as if I hadn't heard him. Beads of water rolled down my body, and when I shook my head they flew all around. I looked at Raúl and I could tell that he was mesmerized by the sight of me standing naked and proud before him. I also knew that my body had changed since we'd been together. I was taller and stronger. The parts of my body that had been soft and round were lean and hard. I felt as rangy as a colt. I stretched my arms over my head and reached toward the sky. Then I went into the hut and left Raúl alone.

He finished packing up the horse without making any more whistling noises. Then he entered the hut and said, "Come give me a kiss goodbye." His look was mournful. "I will miss you, but this is for our good. We'll be happy when we're together again."

I sat at the table with the monkey, eating a breakfast of fresh beans with mashed bananas and feeding the creature from my hand. The acrid, fleshy smell of the green vegetables filled the air.

"Are you leaving no tools behind for me?" I said without looking his way. Raúl came over and placed the bowie knife with its small but useful blade, on the table in front of me. "Goodbye, then," I said. He bent down for a kiss, received my cheek and left.

"What happens to us now?" I said to the monkey, equal parts terror and excitement running through my veins.

"Chi, chi, chi," said the monkey.

I held to the routine of the camp while Raúl was gone, harvesting vegetables and cooking my meals, swimming and playing with the monkey. I wrote in my journal at night. Our separation was not as difficult as I thought it would be, and I enjoyed being on my own.

But a few days later I was returning to the hut after my morning swim, the monkey riding upon my shoulder, and I saw something very strange. A trail of dark drippings was splattered across the sand; it looked like blood, as if someone had slaughtered an animal and carried it through our camp, but Raúl was too neat and careful to do something like that. I followed the trail and found that it led into the hut.

"Raúl?" I called out. "Are you back?"

I was answered by some grunts coming from inside, and I entered cautiously. I found Raúl sitting on a wooden bench and cutting an old sheet into strips. "You're back early," I said. He jerked his head toward me, and I could see the tears streaming down his twisted face.

"Help me," he cried.

I ran to his side and saw that his thigh had been opened up in a deep gash. A dreadful pool of blood had gathered beneath where he sat. He collapsed onto me and I laid him onto one of the sleeping mats as gently as I could, for he was quite weak.

"What happened to you?"

"We have to stop the bleeding," he whispered roughly.

I grabbed the sheet from his hands and continued tearing it up into long narrow pieces. Following his instructions, I wrapped his leg tightly above the open wound. Then I covered that jagged gash of flesh with more white fabric and saw the blood seep through almost instantly.

"My God, Raúl. How did this happen?"

"I was attacked. By a cat. No, that's not right! An old witch in the woods got me in her trap. Oh, it hurts!"

He was making no sense. Now I was even more worried than when I'd first looked at his leg. "Talk to me, Raúl. You must tell me what happened."

"I will try. The day I left, I went south. The woods were quiet and all the animals were hiding. The animals know when a hunter is after them. But it wasn't me that frightened them."

"Tell me what you saw."

"Something moved in the trees. I turned Tara but I saw nothing. Then there was a snap of twigs. I took my boar spear from the saddle. When I looked up again, I saw what it was I hunted."

"Was it a cat?"

"No! It was an old, old woman! She stood in front of me, beneath a bent tree. But then she was gone, and all that was left was a thick smoke in the air where she'd stood. And that's when I knew she was *Ay Pook.*"

"That can't be, Raúl."

"Listen to me! Ay Pook! She's an evil witch."

"You don't believe that, do you?"

"The people say she can turn into a cat. She brings death to anyone who looks at her. And I looked her right in the eyes."

"Raúl. There must be some other explanation for what you saw. Maybe other people live on Paíta. You've just never seen them before."

"Then why was Tara so scared? She was bucking, trying to get away. I let her run. We climbed a hill but when we got to the top, a terrible roar filled the air. Tara reared up, and below her flank I saw spots of brown on gold. Then there were teeth at my thigh. They pulled me off Tara's back and a searing pain burned my leg, hotter than a brand!"

"This is terrible. What did you do?"

"I hit the ground, Benita. And Tara ran. My spear was at my feet. I picked it up. That's when I heard a growl, lower this time, ready for blood. I waited and waited, until I heard the animal in the brush moving away from me. I sat with my spear in hand until I was sure I couldn't hear it anymore."

"How did you get back here?"

"When I stood, the pain felt like lightning. One hour's ride took me two days on foot. But I worried about you. When I found the hut empty, I thought *Ay Pook* had gotten you, too. That you were gone forever."

"You poor man."

I felt so sorry for him, but I didn't know what to think about the story he'd told me. The part about the cat had to be true. His leg was badly torn. The fact that he believed in evil spirits just like all the other islanders—that was almost as shocking as anything else that had happened. But he did.

"Don't worry. You survived the fall, and I will take care of you." Raúl wept again and I held him to me. His head fell heavy as stone against my breast.

PART 6

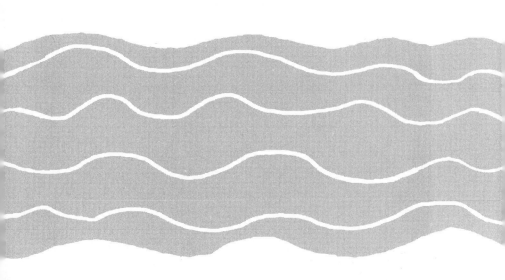

YANASA

CHAPTER

22

According to the date in my diary, we'd been gone for almost four months. It felt more like a year. I never saw Tara and she didn't take any of the food I left out for her, so it seemed unlikely that she was roaming anywhere near our camp. Our own food supply was shrinking. The rainy season was threatening us with high winds, and in the evenings, dark skies gathered and a light drizzle fell.

But when I'd suggest to Raúl that it was time to return to Subidalta, he'd always say, "I must heal first. I can't walk that far on my own." He was just like Papa, stubborn as a bull when he'd made up his mind about something. But I didn't think his wound was healing very well. He managed to hobble around, but he wouldn't let me see it, and he had to change the dressing every day.

Raúl was also certain that Ay Pook stalked the area and that our lives were in danger. He didn't want me to go any farther than our garden, and even then he'd get uneasy if I stayed out too long. I found it maddening to stay in the camp all day. I'd clean the hut and pick vegetables for our meals and help Raúl chop wood. Most afternoons I'd lie in the hammock until it was time to make dinner.

That was because after his fall in the forest, he spent his afternoons sleeping on a cotton mat on the hard ground. He often had trouble falling asleep and I had to stay quiet or he'd complain that I was keeping him awake with my noise. So I'd just lie there and watch him struggle to get his leg comfortable, flapping around from side to side and cursing under his breath. When his closed eyelids fluttered and his lips trembled, I knew he was dreaming, and that was good because I could move around then and nothing I did roused him.

Day after day, watching him sleep like this, I'd think about the many things I wanted to do. Go for a swim, take a walk, just leave the camp for a while. And it occurred to me: Why couldn't I have a brief escape and be back before he woke? I decided I would help him go down into a deep sleep so that I could be free.

I knew that Raúl slept best in our old red shelter that glowed in the shade. I set him up in there one afternoon with a water canteen, some fruit and fried plantains.

"Why do I need these things?"

"In case you get hungry or thirsty. This way I won't have to disturb you and you'll get even more rest. Get healthier."

But as soon as he lay down on the mat he fussed about the pain in his leg. To take his mind off his trouble, I told him a story about our first night together, the night we left Subidalta. I felt as if I were telling a fairy tale to a child. "The moon was bright and the stars were shining as we rode away. . . ."

When I finished, he was still awake, so I sang to him then, letting my voice grow more hushed from one song to the next.

Finally he fell into sleep, and I stood up carefully so as not to wake him. I recalled the night I'd sneaked away from my father's house and left my sleeping family behind. This time I did not pause in the doorway on my way out.

I stepped out from under the shelter's roof and the world expanded before me as if I'd escaped from a tunnel. Dappled sunlight illuminated particles of a fine powdery seed that drifted through the air. A light wind moved around the hem of my shorts and tickled the hair on my knees. I took a step in the silken sand and heard the sound of waves gently lapping the shore, barely audible.

The little monkey was sitting on the roof of the main hut, looking right at me. We stared at each other for just a moment or two, and then it jumped down from its perch and hopped a few steps away, toward the beckoning woods.

I nervously called out, "What if the cat comes after me?"

The monkey chittered. "Nonsense," it seemed to say.

"Easy for you. You can escape into a tree."

The monkey shook its head at me.

"Okay, okay. But let's not go too far."

For protection, I slung Raúl's machete through my belt. The weight of it hanging off my waist made me feel tough. I touched my finger to the sharp edge and felt it ready to slice. Any animal that tried to attack me was in serious danger. *Just let one try,* I thought.

I walked slowly away from camp while the monkey skittered up ahead. I took my time; there was so much to see. The rain of the night before had wetted the leaves of the trees, and I drank the rainwater, letting it flow down the center vein and onto my waiting tongue. Paíta was becoming a wet place for the first time since I'd lived there, and I could sense that the island was responding, as if it were breathing a sigh of relief for the first time in a long time. The jungle floor was soft beneath my bare feet. The air seemed to tremble with wonderful and strange possibilities. I ran my hands up through my heavy hair and a pleasant breeze cooled my scalp.

Moving deeper into the jungle, I searched between the thick trunks of trees for any sign of a predator, but there was nothing. Raúl's hunting drills came back to me. "Take care," he would say. "Keep your eyes open. Do not forget how the trail looks or you won't find your way back." But I felt that the jungle was gently urging me to play and discover, not to hunt or mark my territory.

The monkey led me onward. Worries about a predatory cat came and went through my mind, but I watched the monkey for a sign. I knew it would alert me if one was near. But the monkey showed no fear and no hesitation as it leapt from tree to tree.

We were on a steady course and had long ago left behind the worn path out of camp, as well as the familiar turnoff that fell away to the beach. I scaled a small hill and continued to climb, higher and higher around the curves of a steep knoll, hacking my way through thick brambles with the machete. The sharp bushes pricked at me but I kept going. I ran down the other side of the hill and found myself wading through a marsh, with its sharp grasses growing past my waist.

My feet were sore, and the blade of the machete was awash with the juice of the many plants I'd dispersed. How far had I traveled? I'd covered a good distance; I knew that much. And how long had I been away? Hours had passed but the sun was still high in the sky, as strong as when I'd set off.

Walking on, I found myself on a trail that weaved back and across the jungle, from east to west and back again, very much like the strange trails I'd once discovered behind Papa's house. When the trail ended, I found I was in a pine forest where the trees looked as black as ink against the sky, and I stood directly in front of a large round black rock with a flat top. Another altar. But this one looked as if it hadn't been used in a long while. It wasn't even burnt. Still, I took this as a good sign. Something familiar was something safe.

The flat rock was almost fully surrounded by a dense circle of evergreens that formed a curving wall. It felt like a special spot. The jungle seemed to get quieter in that moment, and all the sounds were far away, as if I were in church.

I wasn't sure where to go next. Directly behind me, the way that I had come, was sunlit jungle, untouched except for the clear-cut trail I had made with the machete. Turning around again, I noticed that there was a gap in the curving evergreen wall. The monkey had waited for me, but now it went in the direction of this gap in the trees. The little head disappeared from sight. I parted the wall of trees and passed through, following its lead.

On the other side I saw that the hill fell away and that there was a trail through thick woods that went steeply down. I stowed the machete in my belt to free up my hands for the descent. The path was strewn with loose rocks and clumps of dried clay. In those places where it was impossibly steep, I slid down the hill on my backside.

I came out of the woods at the edge of a grassy cliff, high above the ocean. I gazed at the sea for a while, watching it break upon the colossal rocks below. From that height they looked like mere stones scattered on the beach. Looking ahead, I saw that the steep and narrow path continued across the face of the cliff. The end of the trail was not in sight.

I thought of all the commonsense reasons to turn around. If I kept going I would be late getting back, and Raúl would know I had wandered away. I had no idea where I was, or what might be waiting for me below. A dangerous encounter with a wild cat was a real possibility. But my instincts told me I was alone, and I felt safe. The hills I'd climbed were steep, but they were only hills, not insurmountable peaks. The marsh was wet, but it did not drown me. I'd had a great day and I didn't want it to end.

I took to the trail ahead, more heedless than before. I whistled, swinging my arms and letting my legs hurl themselves down the steep trail. I continued to pay attention to the natural landmarks all around me, just to make sure that I did not get lost, even though this path was most likely the only way back up. When I reached the bottom, I discovered that the trail ran along the base of the cliff. As I followed along, it took me to a cove that was unlike anything I'd ever seen before.

What a windblown and rugged place it was! The beachhead was a deep pocket of jet-black sand that glittered sharply in the harsh sunlight. Enormous driftwood logs were strewn around everywhere, thrown haphazardly up on the shore by the rough ocean. Waves crashed and spewed gritty froth into the air. The pounding surf echoed against the cliff walls, sounding out a slow drumbeat.

At the deepest part of the cove was a pile of logs. I walked over to have a look at it and saw, to my surprise, that it was a neatly-stacked collection of tree-sized driftwood, bleached pale gray by the baking sun, gathered together to form a dwelling of some sort. A roof and three walls were made from logs stacked against each other and supported by enormous boulders. The structure had been carefully built: The natural bend in one log met the curve of another so that the entire mass—and there were too many of these logs to count—looked woven together. It was nothing like the huts back in Subidalta. Who lived here?

I bent over to peer into the dwelling through an opening. It felt queer to be looking into a stranger's home, but I doubted that anyone lived there still, given how barren it looked, so I ducked and crawled inside. It was dense and dark, like an animal's den. Thick seaweed carpeted the floor and the low ceiling pressed down on me. A couple of chunky pieces of driftwood were set around and might have once served as furniture, perhaps a table and chair. Several gourds had been cut in two, like discarded dishes or bowls. There were no other signs of life.

At the center of the dwelling, I could stand upright. I noticed a long pole hanging on the back wall. I took it down and found that it was nothing more than a long and delicate branch, more than twice my height but it fit my hand nicely. There was nothing else to see in the hut, and now it was time to leave.

But I didn't get two steps when a hot pain seared my foot and I jumped, hitting my head on the roof of the hut. "Yow!"

A cooking pit was set into the ground and within it some charred wood still burned. If the place was abandoned, it had not been that way for long. Maybe a day at most.

I jumped around the hut, my spirits suddenly lifted. It had been so long since I'd seen another person. But here was proof that I wasn't alone with Raúl in the jungle, and that the woman he saw probably did exist.

But then I froze. What if those people came back now? And what if they weren't natives of Subidalta, and what if they weren't friendly? Better to be found outside the hut. I stepped out with the pole still in my hand.

I waited for some time to see if anyone would return and kept myself occupied trying to figure out what this pole was used for. It narrowed at one end to a wisp, where the supple green wood bent like a whip tail. I played with it, thrashing the bushes, and discovered I could hit whatever I aimed at— a leaf, a stone—and my hand had found the perfect spot to hold on to it, just below a knot in the wood that bulged out to keep my fist from sliding forward.

I looked out to the ocean and saw a cormorant drying its wings on a pointed rock; it was a bird that swam underwater to catch fish. Like a signpost left for me to read, it made me suddenly understand that the pole I'd found was meant for fishing. Flexible at one end so as not to break when the fish struck, long enough to set the bait beyond the roughest surf. I looked closely at the tip and saw that a tiny hole had been pierced through it, perfect for threading with a bit of fishing line. Now I really wanted to keep it.

But as much as I wanted it, simply taking it seemed wrong, and I liked the driftwood too much to do that. I could trade for it, but the only thing of value I had was Raúl's machete. "What a fool," Raúl would say if he found out. "Trading a valuable tool for a piece of wood."

Perhaps I could leave a note for whoever lived here. I would write to tell them that I was only borrowing the pole, and I'd have it back to them very soon. Of course, I had no pen and no paper to write this note on either. And none of the people on the island could read my writing anyway.

Where I stood at the entrance to the hut, there was a huge split log. Its flat face was the perfect surface for writing, but all

I had was the machete. It would take hours to write a sentence with it. But I could carve my initials. Leave a signature of sorts. It wasn't stealing if I was letting whoever lived here know that I'd taken the pole. Maybe I'd even get the chance to tell them myself when I returned. I knelt down in front of the log and scratched into the surface of the wood, and when I was done I stood to admire my work.

"Let's go, Monkey!" I called out. The sun was beginning to descend behind the darkening clouds. I turned around and saw it scampering into the bushes, leading the way back for me.

The trip back to camp occurred as if within a dream, taking less time than I'd expected. I found myself at our hut well before dark. Raúl was awake and whittling on a large piece of cooking wood with his hunting knife. "I called for you, but you didn't hear me. I told you not to leave the camp, Benita. It's too dangerous with Ay Pook out there."

"Are you hungry?" I put a pot on the fire and began preparing the cornmeal patties, hoping to take his mind off all that superstitious nonsense. The smell of roasting corn soon filled the air.

"Where's the machete?" he asked. "This knife is no good for carving."

"I have it." I handed it over, glad I hadn't left it behind.

"So, where did you go?"

I told him about the pine forest I'd found and the cliff overlooking the jet-black beach. He'd never seen this place I spoke of, but I had so many details to report that he was drawn in. I didn't tell him about the driftwood hut. I wanted to keep that special place to myself.

After dinner, sitting cross-legged on the ground with Raúl's knife, I made shallow markings along the entire length of the pole. I worked for hours, talking out loud: "To make it mine I plant this line." I worked intensely at it, as if I could endow the pole with a special power. I wanted it to work even better than Raúl's store-bought fishing rod. Soon a diamondback pattern emerged from the carving, snakelike and menacing. At the thick end I carefully etched a pair of keen eyes. I collected a bucket of blackberries, crushed them and painted the insides of the slashes with their dark juice.

When it was finished, I showed my pole to Raúl. He bent it hard. It didn't break but instead straightened right out again. "It's just a branch," he said, handing it back.

"Oh, no. It's more than that," I said. "Just wait. You'll see."

Raúl shrugged, as if he didn't care to see anything I had to show him.

CHAPTER

23

It had been only a day and a night since my discovery of the driftwood hut, but time passed like sap through a spigot. Every minute felt like an hour. Every day things got worse.

Raúl's wound got infected. I smelled the foul reek whenever I got close to him. He could walk, but I could tell how much it hurt to stand on that bad leg. And he was angry all the time. He threw a rock at the monkey because its chittering woke him from his afternoon nap one day. The monkey did not return to camp. Although I was sad about this, I knew it was probably better off.

I wished I'd never promised to stay and take care of Raúl, but he needed me now more than ever. I did most of his chores, everything except hunting for our food, of course. I knew I had to find a way to get us out of there, somehow, but his injury moored us to the camp.

During those endless empty hours I thought mostly about the driftwood cove. Maybe there was another way back to Subidalta from there that was easier than going over the mountain. If only I could get away, maybe I could find it. But after my last trip Raúl kept his eye on me like a hawk. My only hope was for him to fall into that deep, dream-filled sleep. Then I knew I could go.

It had been a very long time since we'd been together as a man and woman, and that act of love was the last thing I wanted to do, but I knew for certain that his sleep would follow fast when it was done. I prepared food for Raúl, tidied the hut, tore up more fabric for fresh bandages. By early in the afternoon I was ready. His skin had a bad smell and soon I would have to help him wash himself, but I lay down carefully beside him, held his face in my hands and kissed his temples. His smile did not hide his pain. I kissed him again.

"Enough now, Benita."

"I can help you rest," I said, and kissed him some more.

Raúl pushed me back. "I said to leave me alone!" he yelled.

In the silence that followed, I stood and brushed the dirt from my clothes.

"I am sorry, Benita. Please forgive me, but I'm afraid . . . you could hurt me. Can you understand?"

"Of course I do. I won't disturb you then," I said, and left the hut. I packed a canvas sack with fruits and my diary and a pen, grabbed the special fishing pole. I also took the machete. I didn't fear a cat attack, but in case I encountered an unfriendly stranger at the driftwood hut, I'd be prepared. Once more I tucked the blade into the waistband of my shorts and headed out of the camp.

"Benita!" I heard Raúl calling.

"Get some rest!" I answered as I picked up my pace.

If not for the trail I had made on my first trip, I wouldn't have found my way. The twists and turns I had taken went up the steepest parts of hills, across a creek I didn't remember.

Not long after departing from camp, I came into territory I didn't recognize. I must have been in some kind of daze that first day, but there was the trail I'd cut, straight through a patch of thorny bushes.

I began to draw a map using several diary pages; then if the trail became overgrown later on, I'd still be able to find the cove. With the sun as my guide, I counted the steps I took and began to mark my route. Now I knew I traveled south and west. For my starting point on the page, I drew a blue X, but I realized I had no idea where our camp was located on the island. I decided to ask Raúl about this when I got back.

Continuing to climb, I ignored everything except the trail, stomping up hills sticky with mud and then slithering down, marching across a marsh, with its stabbing grass-blades that pricked at the soles of my feet. I planted one foot firmly after another until I was across.

Finally I was in the black piney woods again. Looking all around, I found the same landmarks that had caught my attention the first time. I walked out along the bluff and saw that the waves still crashed violently on rocks far below. On this day, however, a thin, steady stream of wood smoke rose into the sky from the cove.

Someone was in that hut.

I felt for the machete in my shorts. It was still lodged against my sweaty stomach. My heart was racing but I knew I had to think clearly about what to do.

If someone was down there, then there were two possible outcomes to my visit. A friendly person with a horse might help me get Raúl back to Subidalta. But what if they were unfriendly or, worse yet, hostile?

I couldn't even imagine that. I had yet to meet a bad person on the island. Even though those women in the village didn't greet me kindly on the day I surprised them, they never attacked.

I took to the steep trail ahead, moving slowly and carefully so as not to loosen any tumbling rocks. I didn't want to disturb anything that might announce my arrival on the way down. I held tightly on to the fishing pole, my sweating palm darkening the bark.

It was cooler at the bottom of the cliff. Halting where the trail curved around the ridge, I peered into the cove. I saw no one, so I moved forward again. Once completely inside the cove, I squatted behind a shrub with a view of both the hut's entrance and the trail I'd left behind. But I couldn't stay like that forever. I stood up on the sandy ground and took in a sharp, shallow breath. A wisp of smoke spiraled out through a crack in the hut's roof. If there was a fire, the owner was keeping it low. There were no splashing or chopping sounds, no noise of feet clambering on beach stones. No singing or talking, not a pot being stirred.

Slowly I stepped out into the open with my pole in hand. I took two steps toward the hut and looked around. Nothing happened. I picked up a stone, pretended to examine it. Threw it down. Sat on a boulder next to the hut, looked at the ocean. No one was there. I stood once more and looked down at the split log into which I'd carved my initials.

Someone had left a mark next to mine. It looked like a cross or a plus sign; I wasn't sure which, but someone had definitely been to the driftwood hut, and now they knew I'd been there too. I scanned the dark interior of the hut. It looked no different from the first time I saw it, except that now there was a small fire burning in the pit. No one was home. Placing the pole on the ground, I walked closer to the entranceway and stood there trembling slightly.

I studied the slash marks in the log where this cross was carved. It wasn't a crude drawing at all. The bars of the cross were thick and curled up at the ends and it looked elegant. How odd. What could it possibly mean? I reached out to touch the cross, and as soon as I did, I heard the sound of stone cracking against stone, directly behind me. I whipped around.

Before me stood a tiny woman, a wrinkled crone. She was only half my size and wore a garment of black that covered her breasts and belly and hung down to her knees. Each of her ankles was bound with cord, and her hands and feet were painted bright red. A plug of wood jutted out from the loose skin below her bottom lip, stuck straight in there somehow. Long gray hair hung in greasy braids to her waist. In her right hand she carried a short spear.

She charged at me then, both hands on the spear, and drove me backward into the driftwood hut before I could reach for my machete. And she was shouting, her voice twangy and hysterical. I tripped and fell onto the seaweed floor. She circled and jabbed the space between us with the spear. Her tiny teeth were filed to points and blackened.

She put the razor point of the spear to the heel of my left foot and whispered venomously, *"Cha nanaca."* I felt the sting and saw a tiny spot of my own red blood. I quickly pulled my feet underneath me for protection.

The crone was studying me now, even sniffing the air. She walked around behind me and rubbed a clump of my hair between her fingers, then gave it a tug.

"Ouch!" I rubbed my head.

She came around to face me, grabbed my right breast, gave it a shake and dropped it with a shrug.

"So now you know I'm a girl," I said. I was too shocked to move.

She lost interest in me and turned to inspect the contents of my canvas bag. She grunted at the fruit and put it into an empty gourd at her feet. She cracked open my diary cautiously, as if fearful of unleashing a caged animal, and flipped through the pages. Bringing the book closer to her face, she studied my roughly drawn map. It occurred to me that now she would know where our camp was. Without thinking, I stood up to stop her and she snapped the book shut, tucking it away under her arm. She searched the bag one more time, found the pen and tossed the empty sack.

The hut had grown dark by now. Gesturing sharply with the spear, she stabbed the air around me a few times. She said something and tied my ankles and wrists with strands of hemp that she pulled from a twig basket. Then she backed away and left me alone in the hut. I heard her rummaging around outside, and she came back with a load of driftwood and dropped it next to the cooking pit. She placed some kindling into the pit and it was quickly set ablaze.

A completely terrifying thought came into my mind. Was she planning to cook me? With my wrists tied behind my back, I couldn't grasp the machete. *Don't panic*, I said to myself. *Think!* Then I noticed she hadn't tied my ankles tightly. I wiggled my feet discreetly and the twine loosened a bit more.

She set a wooden spit in place high above the hot logs and took six dead, limp, fat frogs from her basket. After skewering them on a twig and placing them to cook, she sat herself by the fire, spinning the meat and observing me, her prisoner, as if curious to see what I might try to do.

I had never seen a woman quite so old or so strange. Her arms were sacks of wrinkled skin but clearly she possessed a mighty strength. She'd carried those logs as if they were no heavier than one of my encyclopedia books. I now understood why Raúl said he'd seen the witch Ay Pook; he'd seen this woman. Were there more like her on Paíta?

She cleared off a large log and then fetched two empty gourds that she polished clean with the hem of her garment. She set them opposite each other atop the log, as though she was fixing up a spot to eat dinner. She took the twig of frogs from the fire and pulled off four for herself, two for me. She then cut the twine roping my ankles and led me to the table, motioning for me to sit. I shook my head. Frog was not on my menu.

"*Chatsa,*" said the crone, and shoved me toward the floor.

I landed in a lump and then sat up, with a straight back and my legs tucked beneath me, hoping to indicate that I was no threat by being polite. She went around to her bowl, kneeled and promptly ripped into the frog meat. It was a disgusting sight, but awesome. Her lips pulled back and I could see her pointy teeth. Gnawing like a rodent, she devoured the meal with great ferocity, wheezing ecstatically. The frog meat did smell good, and ignoring the way the waxen eyes stared blankly from the animals' cooked skulls, I thought about having a taste. If my hands hadn't been tied, I might even have tried one myself.

The crone had finished two before she noticed I hadn't even started on mine. She reached into my bowl, lifted one, separated the leg from the body and held it toward me.

"No, I can't, thank you," I said.

She snorted and gestured again that I should eat. I looked at the shapely thigh meat and suddenly remembered I hadn't eaten anything but cornmeal before my trip to the cove. Hadn't Papa once told me that frog legs were a delicacy? My empty stomach leapt to answer. I opened my mouth and she helped me take a bite. The juice from the meat flowed directly to my blood, firing it, heating me up. I realized I'd been desperately hungry for days. But she wasn't interested in feeding me like a baby. She stood and cut the twine holding my wrists and we ate together. I tore into that frog meat just as she did and also grunted with equal pleasure.

Afterward we both pushed back from the table. I pointed to a tooth necklace she wore. "Is that monkey? I'll bet you eat monkey, too."

"*Patcua*," she said.

I tried to pronounce it, got it wrong.

"*Patcua*," she repeated.

I made an attempt to get my lips around the word, but it was hard. She said it so fast that the word sounded like musical notes, not a collection of vowels and consonants, or even syllables. She kept trying to make me say it, but I couldn't get it right, so I just hunched over at the table, scratched myself in the armpit and hooted like a monkey. She slapped her hand on the log table. Startled, I jumped back, but she was laughing. She copied me doing the monkey, and soon the two of us were shrieking just as my furry friend used to.

I leapt away then and imitated a monkey walking on two legs. At first she watched, slapping her hands together and cackling; then she joined in, running behind me until I collapsed onto the seaweed floor, breathless from laughing. And the strangest thing of all happened. She flapped her hand at me as if to say, "You're so silly." It was a gesture I easily recognized. How could this be? We came from completely different worlds.

She walked to the back of the hut and removed a dark roll of fabric from her basket. She placed it on the ground, and as she spread it out, I saw that it was the spotted furry skin of a large cat. No wonder the jungle felt safe; the cat that had attacked Raúl was dead. I wished I could ask if she'd killed the animal herself. She sat on the skin and signaled for me to come toward her. When I got near, she pointed at the ground and said, "*Chatsa*." I sat myself down, without her assistance this time.

It seemed she wanted to talk. Pointing to herself she said, "Yanasa."

"Benita," I replied, although I had no idea whether we were exchanging names.

The woman tapped on her chest and said, "*Cui*," then poked me in the chest and said, "*Cha*." Because of her gesture, I assumed that *cui* meant "me," and *cha* obviously meant "you."

I pointed at the cat skin. The woman said, "*Imatini*."

I held up my hand. The woman said, "*Ichiosu*."

I was trying to find out whether the old woman used her hand to kill the cat. But I didn't want to make a clubbing or stabbing gesture, or act violently in any way. It could be a deadly mistake. So I smiled and nodded, and she smiled and nodded back.

"Can I have my diary?"

She did not understand, so I made the same gestures she'd made when the book was in her hands—the careful opening, the bristling of pages, the slap shut. She said, "Ay, ay, ay," and pulled the book out of her basket. I opened to a random page and read what was there. I had written out one of Papa's favorite poems by Pablo Neruda.

In you is the illusion of each day.
You arrive like the dew to the cupped flowers.
You undermine the horizon with your absence.
Eternally in flight like the wave.

The crone exploded with laughter. Even though she couldn't understand the words, she seemed to enjoy them. I read the rest of the diary entry for that day. I'd written about why I liked the poem so much: because it described how the pain of leaving is felt by both the person who leaves and the person left behind. I wondered whether Papa read this poem now that I was gone.

When I finished, she said, *"No pinocuche."* She took the diary back from me, placed it in her basket. Then she lay down. She waved me away with her hand and watched to make sure I settled down inside the hut.

I lay still for a very long time, until the old woman's heavy breathing could be heard. And I waited until after it died away, way past that. It was now just before dawn. I skirted the edge of the hut to avoid stepping on the dry, crackling seaweed and maneuvered to where she slept. Ever so gently I reached into her basket and found my diary and the canvas bag.

Before leaving, I stole a last look at her. Her ebony eyes were wide open and rolled back in her head as if she were in some kind of trance or under a voodoo spell or something equally awful. Maybe she was dead. She was staring right at me but she didn't move or blink. I was frozen, too scared to move, but then I saw her chest rise to take in a long, even breath.

I ran from the hut and blazed out across the rocky beach. I didn't stop moving, not even when I bent to pick up the fishing pole, nor when I was well up the cliff path. When I reached the very top, I was out of breath, but I had to make sure that woman, that witch or whatever she was, didn't follow me. I tripped out close to the edge of the cliff to check if she was down on the beach looking up, watching me.

As I leaned out, a fierce and overpowering gust of wind knocked me off my feet and I tumbled down the face of the cliff like a loose barrel. I desperately grasped at bushes but they pulled free as I took hold of them. Where the slope was less steep, I managed to turn my body around and to dig in with my heels to stop my descent. I was more relieved than frightened right then.

My knees were cut. Both had deep scrapes that pooled with my bright red blood. I patted some dried dirt gently onto the wounds. This hurt, but it worked to clot the blood. I stood up slowly and began to make my way back.

There was still a long way to go before I reached camp, and I had plenty of time to think. With a bit of pride, I realized that was the first time I'd ever been in danger or had any kind of injury, but I'd survived. A feeling of calm that was entirely comforting washed over me. And before long I was even laughing at myself for thinking that the crone was in a trance or that she watched me run up the cliff. Or that she was a witch. Now that was funny.

But there was something different about her. That much was certain. How could someone live out there—all alone—like a lost spirit of the jungle?

CHAPTER

24

The rough wind that had knocked me down the cliff kept on howling all that day, and the sky let loose with a hard rain. It was a struggle to get back to camp, and I was soaked to the bone by the time I got there, but I couldn't have been happier.

My mood changed the instant I saw Raúl. I found him propped against the wall of our hut, frantically carving at one of the eucalyptus trees that supported our roof. He had pulled it down and the hut was leaking rainwater, which formed a small puddle on the floor. If that weren't crazy enough, his face was contorted with fury and terror warped together.

His voice sounded dry in his throat. "Benita! I thought you were hurt. I thought you were dead."

"I'm fine, Raúl. See?" I spun around to show him that I was still in one piece and there was nothing he needed to worry about. Still smiling, I said, "What have you done to the hut?"

"I had to go find you!" Raúl placed the heavy eucalyptus trunk under his right arm and leaned hard against it. "I was making a crutch." He had a long way to go with his carving;

the trunk of the tree was nearly as wide around as he was. "Damn you. Where did you go?"

"I wasn't far. Just down the beach."

"At the cove? In the rain?"

"No, I went to the pine forest. Remember the one I told you about?"

"You're lucky to have made it back alive. You are a little fool."

I could see there was no trying to put him at ease. "It's a very good thing I made it back, considering I have no idea where we are. Look, I made a map," I said, and I pulled out my diary to show him the pages. He took it from me, studied the lines I'd drawn, followed them from start to finish with his finger. He saw that I'd crossed a river, gone through a marsh and still journeyed on. The end point was the crone's cove, a place he had no idea existed.

I looked over his shoulder at my map. "But this X that marks our camp could be anywhere on the island. Where are we exactly, Raúl?"

He ignored me. "What was in the cove? Where did you sleep?"

I thought for a moment. "I found an abandoned hut. It got dark, and I stayed inside for the night."

"What made you travel so far?"

"I don't know."

"I can't believe how stupid you are," Raúl said. "Did you stop to think you might be attacked by the same cat that tried to kill me?" He threw my diary against the wall.

I wanted to knock the unwieldy crutch from under him, to send him tumbling to the floor. But I crossed the room and picked up my book, now soaked through. It would probably warp when it dried. "That cat is dead. It's no longer a threat."

242

"How do you know?"

"I just do. I feel safe." I couldn't say more. It would panic him to know I had met the woman he called Ay Pook.

"You know nothing! You could have been killed."

"You're right. There are a lot of things I don't know. For instance, I know very little about this island. Particularly in terms of geography." I screamed at him, "WHERE ARE WE?"

"I won't tell you," he said, and turned away from me like a petulant child, intent on holding on to his measly secret. He stood on his one good leg, looking miserable. "The only reason you want to know is so you can go home to Subidalta," he said.

"Yes. The thought had occurred to me."

"So. You're ready to go. Ready to leave me here."

I went to his side and spoke as kindly as I could to calm him. "I would never do that, Raúl."

"I don't believe you."

A large spider crawled across his shoulder. He did not feel it. I plucked it off him, where it had crawled into the hollow of his throat. Pinching it between my fingers, I held it up for him to see and then flicked it away. "You have my word," I said. "I will not abandon you here."

He looked at me with new softness in his eyes and said, "I only want to protect you."

"If that's what you want, then you have to tell me where we are. Our lives depend on it."

He closed his eyes and turned away from me again. "We'll be fine," he said.

This type of talk reminded me so much of Papa. The thin and ridiculous lies. "I know you hoped things would turn out differently, Raúl. But we have to leave here now."

"I cannot make the trip back to Subidalta until I am better."

"You're not getting better."

"You're twisting things. Taking advantage of my weakness."

We were talking in circles. "Forget about going back for now. All I want to know is, where are we on this island?"

"Agh! You are wearing me out. I'm tired. Why is it so important to you?"

The steady rain had broken through the palm roofing by the back wall; it flowed into our hut and across the floor. I looked at the man in front of me, my almost-husband. He was keeping a secret. I knew for certain right then. I sensed it on him, like a costume I'd never noticed he wore.

I took one of the cooking pans and put it beneath the water running into the hut. "Won't be long before this pan is full," I said. "You'll have to keep an eye on it."

"Don't you dare leave!"

"You hold on to the knowledge of our location like it's the key to a door and I can be locked behind it. If my own father couldn't keep me on the plantation, what makes you think you can do that to me out here? And why would you want to even try?"

"I want us to learn to be together," he said weakly.

"I'll tell you what I want. Make me a drawing, show me where we are on the island. I'll give you plenty of time. I'm going to stay in the hut at that cove for another night. When I return, together we can make a decision about the route we should travel to go back to Subidalta. Do you understand me now?"

Raúl threw his crutch away from him. It hit the ground with a dull thud, and he followed it, dropping onto the dirty cotton mat. "It will all be ruined!" he bellowed.

It's already destroyed! I thought. But I was done talking. Trying to reason with him was a colossal waste of time.

I didn't leave right away. First I would prepare food for him and I'd stack enough firewood inside the hut to keep him warm for the night. I planned to bring a salad of green beans as a gift offering to the crone, but when I went to pick the vegetables, I found that the pond had overflowed its banks and our perfect garden was badly flooded. I stood in the furrows and the water swirled around my ankles. Raúl came out to help me. When he saw the water flowing through the garden, he cried.

I spent the remainder of the day salvaging what I could. We'd eaten through much of the first planting and hadn't bothered to seed the garden again. There were some corn and herbs. I pulled out the last of the green beans by the roots and picked off what remained of them, only a few handfuls.

I slept in the hut with Raúl one more night. In the morning I went out into the rain that poured down upon my head from the moment I stepped out the door.

"How long?" he said.

"Just one night. I'll see you tomorrow."

"Benita, are you crazy? What about the wild cat?" He grabbed for my arm but I got away.

"I'm not afraid," I said, and then I left.

I made the journey back easily this time, now so familiar with the terrain that I had to consult my map only at one or two places before quickly stowing the book in the sack to keep the rain from washing the pen strokes away. There was no threat or violence to the storm; the warm rainwater was like a bath. It soaked my clothes through and they clung to me, heavy as a woolen cloak.

I didn't know whether the old woman wanted to see me, and I remembered our first encounter and how scared I'd been when she first found me. And then again, when I'd left. But in between we had seemed to share an inexplicable understanding. I knew what had happened to us was a miracle, yet it was a mystery, too.

While she seemed related to the people of Paíta—the red paint on her body and the way she covered herself with a swath of cloth was the same—yet she was different. She seemed more ancient but more innocent. More fearless but more fierce. Who was she really? That's what I wanted to know.

But as much as I looked forward to seeing her again, I couldn't help thinking about Raúl. Our time in the jungle must come to an end, and hopefully in my absence he would realize this. I was going to have to get him back to Subidalta somehow, even if he resisted. But how? That was the question. If only I could ask the old woman to help me. She was my only hope, but there were so many obstacles. Could I make him understand that his terrifying Ay Pook posed no danger to him? Could I explain what I wanted to her? Would she be willing to make the journey to Subidalta?

Before I knew it, I was back at her cove.

I found her sitting in her hut on the far side of a roaring fire. Steam poured out of a huge clay pot that crowned the flames and I smelled a familiar peppery scent. It reminded me of the green powdery stuff on the altar back in Subidalta. She was so concentrated on her brew that she didn't notice that I'd entered her home.

"Yanasa." I said the name she'd called herself.

She let out a frightening wail that turned my blood to ice. Had I made a mistake coming back here? She rushed toward me, crying out. But when she got close, I saw that tears ran from her eyes. She patted and hugged me tight, and I got a strong wiff of the peppery scent. We held on to each other until she stopped her weeping.

I presented the supplies I'd brought. The green beans were

246

so tasty to her that she danced a little jig on the spot. I handed over a pack of matches, but I could tell she didn't know what to do with them, so I took one and scraped it quickly down the brittle bark of a dry log. When the red head burst into flame, I placed the lit match back in her hands. She nodded and accepted the gift with dignity, bowing slightly to me and watching quietly as the flame licked its way along the surface toward her pinched fingers. She blew the match out before it could burn her.

With the greetings behind us, Yanasa moved deeper into the hut and gestured for me to follow. She stirred the steaming pot and dipped one of the half gourds into the brew, then held it up for me to taste. The hearty smell of stewing meat hit my nostrils and I moaned in appreciation. I put my lips to the oversized spoon, blowing to cool the contents first, and then sucked down the liquid. It was still too hot, burning all the way down to my stomach, but I could taste the rich meat, not deer but some other game.

"What is it?" I asked her, not expecting an answer. But she put the gourd back into the pot, reaching in with her whole arm this time, and scooped up a big helping of the stew. She grunted at me. "Come look," she seemed to say. I peered over the edge of the pot to see that her ladle held up the big hairy head of a wild boar. The sharp little tusks gleamed white and stuck out from the boiled flesh.

"Oh," I said, feeling slightly sickened, and took a step back.

Yanasa dropped the stewed head back into the pot and laughed. "*Yari,*" she said to me and then sat herself on a drift-wood stool to keep stirring her concoction.

"Pig?"

She nodded.

We stared at each other and shared a few smiles, but neither of us attempted to speak. I felt a bit agitated because there was so much I wanted to know about her, but I had so few words to use with her, and also so little time. Just then Yanasa began to sing. Her voice was joyful, upbeat.

"*Faicani ani muran . . . Yarcani huanin uran . . . Iricandi aqui namaen.*"

I began to pick out the words she repeated. *Faicani. Yarcani. Iricandi.* They sounded familiar, and I realized I'd heard this song, or something like it, on the night I'd sat with the circle of women at the fish harvest. Had she learned it from them, or them from her?

Soon the song took on the quality of a chant as she sang it again and again. It was soothing and I let myself float away on the beautiful rhythms that poured out as she put her soul into her singing.

Yanasa sang and stirred the pot, and we remained like that until our food was ready. We ate the delicious stew, and then we went to sleep. I did not wake during the night, though I wanted to get up and see whether she slept with her eyes open again. But my own sleep was deep and dreamless and the next thing I knew, it was morning.

CHAPTER
25

Yanasa showed me all around her world the next day. We played together like children in the rain and didn't let it bother us one bit. There was so much to see and do. Although she showed me things I'd never seen before, there was nothing witchy or weird about her. But she *was* extraordinary.

I spotted her cross marks everywhere, on trees and scratched into the dirt; they seemed to mark her territory. We spent most of the first day exploring and hunting for delicacies. She had a sweet tooth for berries and tree sap, and fried ants were a favorite snack. Using a hollowed-out reed, she'd blow air down into the escape hole in an anthill, and when the insects came running out, she'd gather them by the handful and cook them up in a dollop of animal fat. They were peppery-tasting and I liked them almost as much as she did. I also found out what made her teeth so black. She tapped into the copal trees to extract a dark resin that she used as a stain. She did this every day, the way most people brushed their teeth. I painted my toenails with it instead.

Yanasa played an odd collection of improvised instruments to call all kinds of insects and birds to her. With a grass whistle she called the crickets. I heard them come closer and closer with their noisy chirping; they were so loud I could barely hear her playing her tune.

I was learning so much from Yanasa, but it was much more fun than the way I'd once tried to learn things—sitting in bed at night, reading from my encyclopedias. Now I knew that book learning was not the same as living, not one bit, and I was happier than if I'd owned all the encyclopedias ever written.

Yanasa took me to a pristine lake south of her cove, set deep in the woods. She had a balsa canoe stowed away there. It was so light that she could pick it up by herself. While we sat in there fishing, I realized it was nearly the exact length of Raúl's body. He would be perfectly cradled in it.

I knew I could get the canoe back to the camp, but I didn't know how to get Raúl to Subidalta in it. I couldn't launch the boat from our beach because of the reef. If we still had Tara, I could harness her to the canoe and she'd pull him to the village. I thought for a second about whether I was strong enough to pull him out of the camp alone. I didn't think I was, but maybe with Yanasa's help it was possible.

After I'd caught my third fish on the snake pole, she asked to trade the one she was using, another long, supple branch, for the one I'd decorated. I handed it over straightaway, happy to give back the tool I'd borrowed from her before we'd ever met. Both our rods worked like magic wands the rest of the day, and we easily caught several of the rainbow fish.

Not far from the lake was an open-faced shelter filled with small statues stacked up against the wall. They seemed to be made from the same dark red clay that we had back in Subidalta. Most of them were identical—a simple female figure that reminded me of Yanasa with her rounded belly and drooping breasts, except it had no face. There was a statue that was different from all the rest, with two bodies standing back to back and arched away from each other. One figure was the same rounded woman, but she was attached to a jungle cat standing on its hind legs, as if ready to strike. She held up this special figurine and let me admire it for several minutes.

Next to the hut was an odd little building shaped like a large beehive and made from the same red clay from the lake, dried to stone. Inside it was just one big charred pit, and a flat rock was mounted on the wall to hang over the center of the pit like a ledge. I assumed it was the oven she used to bake and harden her statues.

As Yanasa prepared our fish dinner and the sun fell in the sky, I thought about Raúl, and how I'd promised to return. But I would have to leave right then to get back in time. I decided one more night wouldn't kill him. I'd make it up to him somehow.

I took out the machete to cut down some bananas, and I heard a familiar chittering. A little black monkey was perched on a tree limb hanging over my head. I whistled to it, and it came right over and jumped onto my shoulder. It looked just like the one who'd kept me company back at the camp. I took the monkey down onto my arm and parted the fur on its foot. Sure enough, I found a scar there, where it'd been grazed by Raúl's arrow. The little monkey did not stay, and this time I did not mind letting it go. Yanasa and I stood together in the doorway of the hut and watched the monkey leave the cove. I waved a farewell, and this amused my friend. "I'm glad you didn't try to eat her," I said, but Yanasa had no idea what I was talking about.

Lying on the beach and watching the moon climb across the

sky, I made an effort to learn her language, but our conversation was more like a game of charades. I pointed to certain things and she gave me each object's name in her language. I learned that the rain was *humaro*, clothing was *shiro* and knife was *sapucua*. Firewood, *aishocua*. The canoe was *yara*. I wrote down all this crone-speak in my diary.

Some words were harder to learn than others. Family was one. With nothing to point to, I drew pictures in the dirt, starting with a small human figure and then giving her a sister (*cuina* was the word) and a brother (*cuinano*), and then a mother (*mamaja*) and father (*papajo*). For family, I drew a circle around the figures and then gestured for her to name the group. "*Chuna*," she said. When I asked about her family, pointing to her and saying, "*Cha chuna?*" she just shook her head. In turn, she asked about my family, and I did not know how to answer. I pointed somewhere away from where we sat. "Subidalta," I said, gesturing to nowhere in particular. "On the other side of the island."

Far, far away, I thought. How could I possibly explain that my family was lost to me and how I wished I could tell them I was sorry I'd left, that it was all a big mistake. What hurt the most was knowing they must have given up on me, since I'd been gone so long.

Suddenly Yanasa gave me a gentle nudge with her elbow. I looked into her face, thinking she had something to say. But she was only smiling at me, and so I smiled back, and it seemed to please her that I stopped looking so sad.

There had been plenty of times that day when we hadn't needed to talk at all. Like two actors in a silent movie, we let gestures and facial expressions speak for us—a smile or raised eyebrow, or a grimace or a shake of the head. And in the morning, as I packed up to go back to Raúl, Yanasa seemed to know exactly what I was doing.

"*Tai cha?*" she asked me. I slowly put together the words I had learned. *Cha* meant "you," and *tai* was the word for "go." "You go?"

I nodded.

"*Cuaca tai?*" Yanasa asked. She gestured to the top of the cliff and the jungle above. My guess was that she wanted to know where I was planning to go. I took out my diary then and showed her my map. She studied it and handed the book back. Then she shook her head at me, as if she were forbidding me to leave.

"But I have no choice."

While we stood looking at each other, I tried hard to think of the words I needed. *Come with me into the jungle,* I wanted to say. I knew how to say "go," and "you" and "me," but no other words came to me. Mangling together a little Spanish and a little crone-speak, I said, "*Cha tai con cui.*" You go with me.

Yanasa pondered my request as if she understood, and I tried to wait patiently for her answer. She was my only chance of saving Raúl, and I didn't know what I'd do without her help. "Please?" I begged her, putting all my hopes into that one simple word.

She looked at me doubtfully, but she agreed to the journey with a nod. Picking up the carryall basket she always kept with her, she gestured that I should take the lead.

I brought her straightaway to the north side of the lake, to where I found the balsa canoe tucked away beneath a bed of ferns. I hoisted it up onto my shoulder. Yanasa gave me a strange look, but she reached for the back end, and we carried it together into the jungle.

The rains came and went. My friend seemed to be on alert, ever-watchful and taking steps that were slow and sure. After a while she relaxed a bit and began to enjoy the journey. She picked some plants that had a white vein in the leaf and stowed these in her basket. A brightly colored macaw flew over our heads, and she called out to it, mimicking its squawk. The macaw landed in a nearby tree and twittered to us for a bit before flying off.

Yanasa seemed to love Paíta in a way that was especially tender, as if she were a part of the island. I had not once seen her cut a trail to make her passage easier, and she stepped lightly wherever she went. She treated everything as if it were sacred. Even Raúl, who knew everything about living on Paíta, did not show the same sort of feeling toward this place as she did. And no one I knew seemed to have such a peaceful heart.

Could I be happy living in the jungle my whole life? I knew the answer was no, but instead of feeling trapped on the island, I felt happy, almost as if I'd grown lighter. I knew without a doubt that I must figure out where I belonged. Where that perfect place was, or how I would get there, I had no idea, but this wasn't as important as knowing I must find it. Knowing this meant I was one step closer to being there.

When we arrived at the edge of the camp, I put down the canoe. "Here we are," I said, and gestured toward the tiny settlement Raúl had built. I'd been away only two nights, but it looked much worse than when I'd left. Rain had destroyed the red sleeping hut; the roof on the main shelter had collapsed in several places and the bare stakes that once held it to the ground poked up haphazardly. The pond had spread beyond its boundaries, and the irrigation channel that was once so docile flowed like a river over our garden plot. All the things that we used to keep in the hut—the cotton mats and the pots—were strewn around the yard like litter. There was no sign of Raúl.

Yanasa gave me a pitying look, as if to say, "Is this where you live, you poor thing?"

I nodded, then held up my hand. "*Ati*." That was the word she used when she wanted me to halt. I needed to check on Raúl and tell him about Yanasa before I brought them together. Walking toward the hut, I listened for him, but heard only silence.

I entered slowly, peering in from behind the door that now hung unevenly, ready to fall off in my hands. I instantly realized Raúl wasn't there. Panic rose in my throat. When I heard Yanasa scream, and then Raúl, I knew exactly where he was.

I ran out and found him barely managing to stand. He looked much worse than before, and he was as huge a shock to me as he was to Yanasa. He hadn't bandaged his leg and it was dripping with horrible greenish pus. His eyes were full of a wet and wild fear as he pointed at Yanasa.

"That woman, that witch . . ." Raúl was sputtering.

Yanasa ran to the base of a palm tree and climbed up as fast as a cat, not stopping until she reached the top, until there was no more tree to climb.

I tried to calm him. "What are you talking about? She is completely harmless. Just look at how you've frightened her."

Yanasa looked down at Raúl. "*Samaro*," she hissed, nearly spitting this word at him.

Raúl raised his fist and shook it at her.

"What is the matter with you?" I said to him, nearly in tears by now.

"That is the witch who attacked me," Raúl cried out, and then he fell to the ground, fainting dead away.

I stood looking up at her in the tree. She crouched low against the palm's trunk like a frightened cat and was just staring at Raúl. I tried to climb up to where she was, but I couldn't get high enough, so I climbed back down.

"Yanasa," I sang out. "Yanasa, come down." Her hands and feet were like claws fused with the bark of the palm tree. "Come now," I said sweetly over and over again, trying to coax her down, until finally she loosened her grip and lowered herself headfirst. Back on solid ground, she shivered. This seemed to relax her from head to toe, and she became more like herself again. I held out my hand but she wouldn't take it.

"You're fine now. No one will hurt you," I said.

She moved away and took a step toward Raúl. Standing above him, a few safe feet away, she let out a sound I'd not heard her make before, more ferocious than anything I'd ever heard in my life. It practically shook the ground beneath my feet, and it sounded very much like the roar of an angry jungle cat. I froze.

Then Yanasa turned her gaze on me. Staring into her fierce face, I was almost as frightened as the day we'd met. But when I looked into her eyes, she softened and gestured for me to follow her.

"No. I can't go with you now."

Yanasa turned away sadly and then she was gone into the woods, departing as quickly as a gust of wild wind.

256

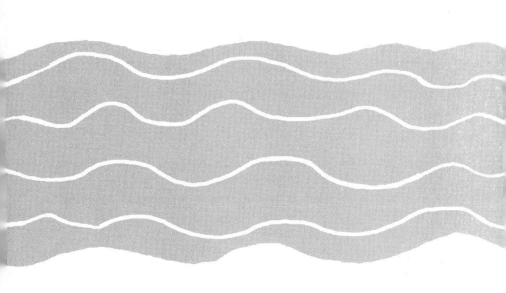

PART 7

FIRE IN
THE KILN

CHAPTER

26

The full fury of the wet season hit the island with heavy rain that fell all day long and most of the night, too. Standing outside in the storm felt like drowning, but sometimes at twilight, before the sky turned to darkest night, the weather would break for just a little while. That was the only time I could leave our hut.

I'd circle the camp and hear the earth recovering from the deluge, the water being sucked down into the ground and the insects chirping with relief. The balsa canoe was filled to the brim with rainwater. It poured over the edge and half sunk the boat in a pool of thick mud.

Whenever I went out of the hut, Raúl listened, tense and alert to my every move. In his mind Ay Pook was forever lurking outside, waiting for the chance to attack. I heard him calling to me one night, "Don't stay out there too long...." When I returned to the hut I found him with one eye pressed up to a growing crack in the thatch of the wall. As I closed the fragile door behind me, he jumped, caught in the act.

"Are you spying on me?"

Humidity clung inside the confines of the hut. The rank air was heavy, like a hothouse. "Not spying. Watching." He turned slowly onto his side with a wince. "You must not go out. There is a big cat out there and it will put a spell on you. Yes. To keep you prisoner."

It had been several days since Yanasa had left us alone. I'd look up at the sky and wish silently for her to visit, but she never came. I had no idea what to think about her true nature anymore, especially after hearing her roar like a wild cat. To think that she could transform herself was crazy, but why had she made that horrible sound? I debated with myself endlessly and secretly, but I tried my best to put his worries to rest.

"There's nothing to fear from a wild cat. I can protect us," I said. He closed his eyes then and pretended to sleep. I attempted to make us some dinner, but we had very little food left. The garden was completely washed away. This bad news made me furious. I wanted to pound on Raúl's chest with my fists until he was sputtering for air, until he came to his senses.

I stared at him lying on the ground, his weakened body practically lifeless. He looked more like a corpse than a living, breathing human being.

"We are going to die here," I said.

"No. That won't happen."

"Raúl, you have to listen to me."

"We'll be fine."

"There's no food."

"Tomorrow I'll be better."

"You're not getting better. And you won't get better if we stay here."

"I am better today than I was yesterday."

"Your leg is beginning to rot!" I shouted.

A look of stubborn resolve settled onto his contorted face. "You want to destroy me with your words. To steal my strength away."

"We need to get help."

"No one will come. Because of the cat woman."

"Stop it, Raúl!"

"The cat is not really a cat, but a witch. Ay Pook. At night she changes and prowls the jungle."

"That's impossible."

"I saw her with my own eyes. A few minutes before Tara and I were attacked. An old white-haired woman wrapped in black. I put Tara into a gallop, but she came after us. Your crone. Ay Pook."

"You were hunting. First you saw the woman, and later, on the hill, a frightened jungle cat attacked you. That's what happened. Okay?"

"Ay Pook! The cat woman! Oh, you must be careful." Raúl was moaning as he writhed on the ground. When I bent over to try to calm him, he struck out and hit me hard across the chest and shoulder with his forearm. I fell back onto the damp dirt floor. I was dazed for a moment and it was hard to pull air into my chest. When I could breathe again, I stood and felt my anger flare up like a flash of fire.

"I cannot be here with you anymore. I will *not* stay here and listen to you one more minute!" I ran around the hut in a frenzy, collecting my few belongings and shoving them into the canvas sack.

"You have the cat woman in you! Ay Pooooook!"

It was an accident, but I tore the flimsy door off the doorframe. "You're out of your mind!" I screamed at the top of my lungs. My voice echoed in the waiting forest.

260

I left him then, moving away fast with the fury of a new storm. I ran through the forest without thinking or feeling anything except for the earth rising up to meet my pounding feet. My anger was like fuel. I felt it combust and turn to pure energy in my veins.

I ran to the only person who could help me now. Witch or no witch, Yanasa was my friend. I trusted that much to be true. And before I knew it, I was back at the driftwood hut.

When I saw her I fell to the ground at her feet and cried as if a dam had burst inside my head. "I hate him, I hate him," I blubbered between sobs. She took my hands in hers and held them until I was finished. We gazed at each other for several minutes afterward. She questioned me with a look that was full of concern. "I have to go home," I said. "I must leave but I don't know the way back." She nodded at my words, and though I found some comfort in her presence, I wished so much that we could truly speak.

"*Cha Yanasa?*" she asked me finally.

I wasn't sure how to answer her question because I didn't quite understand it. I worked it through in my head. *Cha* meant "you," but I'd always thought "Yanasa" was her name. Was she asking me to be her? Was she saying, "Are you Yanasa?" That made no sense. It occurred to me that Yanasa might not be her name at all, but instead it might mean "friend." Maybe that is how she introduced herself to me when we first met, as a friend.

"Yes," I answered, nodding and holding on to her gaze. "I am Yanasa."

The crone stood and began to prepare some food that had an unfamiliar odor. When it had boiled and cooled, she removed it from the fire and sealed it in a tube of bamboo, corking both ends with a plug of wood.

"Tarique," the crone said. This word meant "tomorrow" and that night I dreamt of a better tomorrow.

* * *

Early the next morning, Yanasa led me up the cliff path. She had tied the cat skin around her neck like a cape, so that it trailed down her back to the ground, making her look like a wild cat walking on two legs. At the top of the path, she took off at a run and all I saw was cat fur darting through the trees. This had to be what Raúl saw the day he was attacked—Yanasa wearing the animal like a coat.

I caught up to her on that odd trail that weaved back and forth across the jungle, east to west. She had stopped rushing and was now taking very small steps, and I was suddenly reminded of the women's ritual that I'd witnessed back home, and the way they'd followed each other slowly and quietly. I got right in step behind her and walked as she did, and before long I seemed to have no thoughts anymore, as if they'd been washed out of my head. I felt emptier and lighter.

When we came to the end of the trail, we were standing before the altar rock. Yanasa climbed up to stand upon it, as if it were simply a platform and not an altar at all. She gave me a hand up and I stood next to her. The wall of green shrubbery that enclosed the rock created a barrier, separating us from the rest of the world. I felt protected, as if I were standing inside a temple.

Yanasa presented the straw of bamboo she had prepared and uncorked one end. We took turns drinking from it, a dark bitter liquid that smelled earthy, like a fungus. When we had finished the broth, Yanasa turned to face the deep green shelter of the trees. I did the same.

We were quiet for a long time. I listened to the birds happily chirping in the trees, until suddenly their shrill calls and whistles seemed directed at me. I stood completely still and listened even harder, until the chirping was as loud as trumpets, and I felt my heart race and flutter in my chest.

Yanasa was moving now. She shuddered slightly and stamped her foot. I called out for her but she didn't answer me. The jungle seemed to bend and swoop before my eyes, as if a dreamy wind had just blown through. My head felt very heavy and I let it droop.

Then I threw up; I hadn't even known I was sick, but as soon as I vomited, my head swam so badly it was impossible to focus. I fell off the altar, and Yanasa jumped down and wrapped her arms around me. My stomach was knotted in pain and I was so hot that my sweat made me shiver. Bird calls shot through me, high-pitched and harsh.

And then I saw and heard nothing.

When I became conscious again, the pain was gone but the jungle seemed to swell in front of my eyes and then subside, just like an ocean wave. On wobbly legs I stood before Yanasa. Looking into her face, I felt as if I were seeing it for the first time. She looked so old that she was ageless. She was older than the island itself. I laughed out loud at the very idea, and then I began to cry for joy, for having the eyes to see her as she truly was.

She took me by the hand and brought me straight to the lake. At the shore she dropped to her knees, and I did the same. My knees sank deep in the muck next to hers.

Yanasa scooped up two handfuls of the red clay from the bank and began to form them into two rounded female figures, just like the ones she had shown to me a week before. Then she handed me one to work on. I shaped mine to look like me, with a skinny waist and long firm legs like tree trunks. Yanasa watched, nodding and smiling.

When I was finished I held up my figure for Yanasa to

approve. She took it and pulled out a sharp flinty stone knife from her basket. She brought the knife up to the right side of my head, just above the ear, sawed off a chunk of my hair and began to embed the strands of my black hair into the back of the clay figure's head, pressing them down and covering them with wet clay to hold them in place. Then she handed the figure back to me, along with my hank of hair, so that I could finish while she worked on her own, decorating her statue with her gray hair.

Once our figures were complete, Yanasa reached for my hand and held it firmly in her own. She swiftly drew the flint knife straight across my palm. I tried to take my hand back but she was too strong. Blood poured out of my palm, and Yanasa had me rub my statue with it. Then she cut herself and worked her blood into the surface of her own clay figure. They both turned a brighter shade of red.

Yanasa took our two figures and placed them inside the kiln, atop the flat rock surface, so that they were standing back to back and leaning against each other. She filled the charred cavity with a pile of wood and set it all on fire using the matches I had given to her. She made a great ceremony of this act, until the whole pit was filled with burning, smoking wood. She danced around the fire in the kiln then, spinning and stomping, while I remained seated on the ground. As she spun and spun, she began to blur before my eyes, and her fur cape was all I could see, so she looked like a whirling wild cat. Just before she closed the kiln's earthen door, she lit a long twig of sage bush and filled the air with its sweet smoke.

Yanasa then led me to the open-faced shelter where all the fired figures were stored. She helped me to sit down on one side of the shelter with my back to the wall. I was very dizzy still. She moved slowly around inside the shelter, letting the sage smoke penetrate the air. I closed my eyes, inhaled deeply and felt the dusky fragrance engulf me.

She drew a line right down the middle of the shelter, etching it into the dirt with a long stick. Then she sat down, over the line and across from me. We stayed this way for a long time, staring into each other's faces. There was not much light and it was smoky, so I wasn't able to focus completely. Her shape looked as if it were changing, her body becoming less solid. The harder I stared, the less she looked to me like Yanasa and the more she looked like me, or a version of me. Peering across the hut, I saw a mirror image of myself sitting there facing me, staring right back.

I must be having some kind of vision.

A voice answered me. "We have come together," it said. These words, which were easy to understand, were spoken with a thick-tongued accent, and I realized it was Yanasa who spoke to me, but her voice was happening inside my head. The mouth of the figure across from me was not moving, yet I heard the voice as clear as day.

"I can hear you," I said.

"That is good," she answered. "Listen now."

Yanasa began to chant. "Great ones. Pity her. She searches honestly for the truth to come. I am glad. You will make her better." She repeated these words until I knew them too, and I was saying them out loud, along with her. Then Yanasa's voice ceased, and only I was speaking the chant, changing the word "her" to "me" so that I was asking for help for myself. Pity *me*. You can make *me* better.

All the while I was saying this prayer, I tried to focus on the very essence of the thing that troubled me. How could I save Raúl and get back to my family? Where did I want to live? What would become of me? I needed to find a question, just one question I could ask. I wanted a question to end all questions.

"Ask now. Ask what you want to know," Yanasa's voice said.

"I . . . I . . . I want to be free. Will I ever be free?" I cried out to her, to the gods, to whomever and whatever was listening.

There was no sound after that. Just the crackling of the fire inside the kiln, the sound of Yanasa breathing. And then came an answer. "You are free. Do you not know this?"

"Am I? I don't feel free."

"You have waited for someone to set you free. Who can do it for you? A person is only free who believes she is free."

I thought about these words. Was I free? Was I?

"But there is Raúl. He will die unless I can save him. This will be my fault, as much as his. And then there is my father. I can feel him holding on to me still."

"But *you* have already let them both go. They know the truth."

"They need my help."

"Then do it. Save them. And then save yourself. Be free. That is your path."

"My path? But I don't even know the way home. Raúl will not tell me."

"You must force him."

"How?"

Again there was a long silence, while Yanasa seemed to ponder my question. "I will lead you. Think of him now," the voice said. "As he is."

I concentrated on thoughts of Raúl as I had left him back at the camp. Images came to me in pieces. They played upon a screen inside my forehead, like a picture theater happening in my mind. It was as if I floated above him, near the roof of our old hut. I saw the wrecked room, our things thrown about. My snake fishing pole had fallen onto the ground next to Raúl, who lay with his legs twisted in the dirty blanket, his neck and chest filmed with sweat. He tossed and turned in a fitful sleep.

"He is afraid," Yanasa said to me.

Without warning, the vision I had of Raúl stopped wavering, as if it had now turned real. I felt the tension in his body, and I felt the muscles inside my skin go soft and sinuous. I swayed as I watched him. A low hissing sound filled the air. The sound rose in volume, and it circled him. He bolted upright and sat looking frantically all around. He inched backward on his rump, but his blanket was caught under an edge of the table. He yanked at it and made the table scrape against the ground. The angry hissing sound got louder. He tried to kick the blanket off him, but a loop of wool was stuck on the buckle of his belt. Raúl worked desperately, pulling at it. After a few seconds he finally managed to sweep the blanket aside, revealing a large snake with dark crisscross markings coiled at his feet. The creature's head was raised and its gaze was locked on him. With great pleasure I saw that Raúl was sweating fearfully.

"You must strike!" Yanasa commanded, and I concentrated very hard, wanting to unfurl all my anger on Raúl. The snake lashed out, but in one bold move, Raúl jumped up and away before it could strike. As the snake missed its mark, I felt myself falling forward where I sat.

Raúl landed at the hut's entrance and wrenched his body outside. I saw him pick up a stick and scratch some lines in the dirt beneath the overhang of the roof. He drew a compass first—two crossing lines with an arrow at one of the points, to show which direction was north. I'd seen one just like it on Papa's map of the island. Then Raúl scratched out a long line indicating a route that would travel over a large mountain and straight to the north from there. Where that line ended, he quickly drew a picture of a hut that looked just like the ones we'd left in Subidalta, and I knew he was trying to show me the way home.

I did fall over then, onto the ground, drained of all my energy. Yanasa came to my side of the shelter and put my head in her lap. I wrapped my arms around her waist. While she stroked my head, she sang the song I knew well by then.

"*Faicani ani muran . . . Yarcani huanin uran . . . Iricandi aqui namaen . . .*"

The words of her song were just as foreign to me as on the day I'd met her, as if our interior dialogue had never happened. But her voice was hypnotic, and I wanted to stay there, lying in her lap forever. To let the minutes, hours, weeks and years tick on and leave us behind. Yanasa smiled down at me kindly, and in that perfect moment I understood that the spirits the islanders worshipped were alive. I was convinced that they'd found a way to connect with these spirits. Just like Yanasa did. And like she'd taught me.

But she wasn't going to let me stay there in the protection of her embrace. She sat me up and brought over our statue from the kiln. I saw how our two figures had fused together to form a single object. Taking me by the hand once more, she led me into the calm water of the lake, up to our waists. As we stood, face to face now, Yanasa spoke. It sounded like a litany and a pledge and a farewell combined, and at the end of it she kissed me on the forehead and threw me over backward.

Water shot up my nose as I felt her hands release me, but it took more than a few seconds for me to find the surface, for she had shoved me under and away from her with great force. Sputtering and treading water at the surface, I spun around to make sure Yanasa wasn't standing by to give me another dunking. She was nowhere to be seen, and a new apprehension gripped me. Was she hurt?

"Yanasa!"

No reply.

Fearing she was trapped below, I took a deep breath and plunged into the lake with my eyes wide open. But the water was murky and I couldn't see beyond my hand in front of my face. I worked my way toward the shore, and as I was about to give up, I emerged to see a creature that shimmied up the far bank and shook the water from its body. Yanasa was alive.

I wiped the muddy water from my eyes but when I looked again, my heart skipped a beat. Sitting on the bank of the lake was a wild cat calmly licking its paws dry. The animal regarded me for a moment, exactly as it had that night on Papa's porch. There was no way to know for certain whether it was the same cat. But when I swam toward it, the cat stood up and roared with all its might. I froze in the water, afraid to take my eyes off it. The cat growled a low warning, then turned away. I watched as it gracefully padded into the jungle. I heard it growl again in the forest, as if making sure I got the message to leave it alone.

I sat in the lake as the rain poured down, and tried to make sense of it all. Could Raúl have been right? Was Yanasa a cat, or the cat Yanasa? After all that I'd experienced that day, I had the feeling anything was possible. I didn't know what to believe.

But after a while the rush of fear and adrenaline had run its course, and so had the bitter liquid I'd drunk that morning. I was sober now. Yanasa was gone, a wild cat had warned me to leave it alone. It was time for me to go. Simple as that.

I stood up from the water and took off through the rain-soaked jungle, heading back toward Raúl. *Save them; save yourself. Then be free.* The words played in my head like a marching tune, setting me into motion.

269

CHAPTER

27

I found Raúl sitting outside the hut, just as he had been in my vision. Tears streamed down his face and he didn't recognize me when I knelt down next to him. I slapped him—just a light tap to stop his sobbing—but it had no effect. I fetched some water and helped him to drink it.

Finally he spoke. "I want to tell you something. Now that we're together again."

"Yes, you poor man. What is it?"

"Do you remember how I said we should come to the jungle to live together because it would be good for us?"

"Of course I remember."

"Well, I meant that it would be good for me."

I looked into his eyes, which were clear and shining. "I have to tell you the truth before I die."

"Don't say that, Raúl! We will get back. I promise."

"Listen to me now. Please. What I've done is bad." He was shaking his head. "All because I wanted to ruin your father."

More of his crazy nonsense. "You should save your strength."

"You think I wanted to come here because of you. But there was something I wanted more."

"I don't understand."

"We all wanted him out of the cotton fields. We all wanted him off the island. But I was the one who wanted the plantation most of all. Do you remember the day I came to work for him? I heard him say that you would inherit it when he died. His words were like a seed, planted in my heart. It grew and grew." Raúl had trouble looking me in the eyes now. "And so . . . when the fruit was ripe, I plucked it from the tree. For that I am very ashamed."

I finally grasped the significance of what he was saying. "So . . . you never wanted to marry me?"

"No, I did. Because I knew that once you were my woman, all that you and your family had would also belong to me. And so I brought you here, thinking that as you grew to depend on me, things would work the way I wanted. But they didn't. As you know. Coming here only drove us apart."

"We should have left weeks ago, but you wouldn't listen to me."

"I thought if we stayed a bit longer, I might win you over. That's why I didn't want to go back."

We were silent for a moment, and I thought back to my life on the farm. Everything had happened so fast between me and Raúl from that day he worked on Papa's farm. He was so nice all of a sudden. He seemed to want me very much. I was such a fool. I wanted to smack his face hard this time.

Instead I told him, "You made a big mistake. You should have told me how important the plantation was to you. We all knew Papa wasn't going to succeed on his own. Mama practically insisted he let you help us. And I would have done anything for you back then. Something could have been arranged somehow. We should have stayed in Subidalta."

271

"Your father would never allow it. I knew I could not have what I wanted, not until his daughter was truly mine."

"But you didn't love me."

Raúl broke down in tears again. "Can you forgive me?"

All the bad times we had together came to me in a rush. The arguments and the silences, then being hungry and afraid. It was all too much. "We have more important things to worry about now. We need to find our way home."

"Yes, that's right. I made a map for you." He told me about the drawing he'd scratched out in the dirt. I went to have a look. It was just as it had been in my vision, and I stared at it for a long time. He might have drawn the map of his own free will, simply because he was ready to go home, but something told me that I'd made this happen—just like in the snake dream—and that I could do whatever I set my mind to. And the map was proof that Raúl was being truthful with me at last.

I studied his crude marks in the sand. The way home was up over Asiento del Rey and to the north. This troubled me. To travel up the mountain might be the shortest way back home, but I couldn't believe it was the easiest. I could put Raúl in the balsa canoe and pull him out of camp myself, but dragging him up the mountain didn't seem possible. If only I could go by water, I thought, but it was hopeless to try from our beach because of the reef. I thought about taking him to Yanasa's cove, but remembered the angry cat. I didn't want to meet her again, so the mountain seemed to be the only way. But would I have to climb it?

I returned to Raúl's side. "I need to talk to you about how we should go back."

He pointed back over his head. "Toward the north," he said, and folded his arms across his chest.

"We can't climb that mountain. Why don't we go around it?"

"The jungle will hold you back. Like a net."

"I'll tear it open with the machete."

"It will take too long. Trust me. There is a trail on the mountain. Look for a boulder covered with moss. You will find a cross marked there. At the start of the trail."

A cross! Yanasa's mark. It had to be a good sign. "We're wasting time talking. We'll figure out what to do when we get there," I said.

"Watch out for snakes, Benita."

"I will."

I packed our things as night fell, scouring the camp for whatever valuables were left. I gathered the tools, found their homemade canvas cloth. My special fishing pole with the snake markings was gone, but this didn't surprise me. After that, it was too dark to work anymore and I took my place with Raúl one last time and waited out the night.

In the morning I had to dig the canoe out of the mud. I blanketed the hollow of the boat with one of the cotton sleeping mats so Raúl would be more comfortable, and I fastened a length of hemp rope to one end of the hull, wrapping it round and tying it off in a type of sailor's knot that he'd taught me. I tested the hold and it seemed good. I worked quickly and when I was finished I came back to his side.

"I'm ready now."

"Why don't you just leave me here?"

I ignored him. "I need you to help me get you into the boat. Use your good leg to push off the ground." He did as I asked.

I tied a sheet around my waist and wrapped the rope on top of that to keep the rough hemp from cutting me. I heaved myself forward and managed to pull the canoe a mere foot or so.

The task was going to be even harder than I'd thought; I had to lighten the load in the boat. I threw out most of the tools, keeping only the machete. Raúl's bedding got left behind, but I kept my diary and a small supply of food.

We set off. When I could no longer see the camp, Raúl spoke with more than a touch of bitterness. "Is the cat woman still out there?"

I wish I knew, I wanted to say, because I had no idea what had happened at the lake. Not really. Perhaps Yanasa and the cat were kin, joined by an inexplicable force when she'd fused their statues together in the kiln. Maybe that's what made them seem like the same creature. And if that was correct, she and I were now bonded in the same way. One thing was definitely true. I knew that wherever, or whatever, Yanasa was— she belonged to me and I belonged to her. That was the magic of what had happened to us.

"I do think she's still out there. Though you have nothing to worry about," I answered him after a while, but Raúl was drifting out of consciousness, falling down into a sleep from which he might not awake.

"You must talk to me, Raúl. Don't let yourself fall asleep."

He moaned, his voice groggy. "What can I say, from inside this casket?"

"Anything that comes into your head. It doesn't matter."

I turned around to look at him and saw that his eyes were closed. "Raúl!"

"I'm so sorry, Benita."

"Just keep talking."

"No, no. I'm sorry about everything."

"I know that. You don't have to apologize anymore."

"But you don't understand what made me do it. I had no choice."

274

"A person always has a choice. I made a choice when I ran away with you."

"No! You're wrong. There was no choice. Not for me. When your father came to this island, he ruined everything. I couldn't let him get away with it. I had to stop him."

The canoe halted abruptly behind me. I turned and saw that it was stuck on a rock that jutted from the ground. Maneuvering the boat around it would not be hard, but I decided to take a short rest. "How did Papa ruin everything?"

"He took over the cotton fields. Deciding how much cotton we'd plant and when we'd go to market. We were all working for him then. And the worst was when we realized he had cheated us. Are you going to pretend you don't know what he did?"

I remembered how the islanders had got mad at Papa right before I'd left, and how the village council stopped him from selling the cotton. When he'd told my family that it was because the islanders didn't understand the market and were greedy, I had believed him. "No one on the island had ever thought of selling the cotton before my father came here. He put money in your pockets!"

Raúl was very calm. "Yes, Benita, he did. But he stole money that belonged to us too."

"I don't believe you."

"He told us that a bale of cotton sold for two hundred sucre. Five bales went to market, worth only one thousand, but another fisherman came up to my father at the market to congratulate him. The man said, 'Lucky you, you got a rich passenger.' Told my father he saw Josef put away two thousand sucre into his pocket. My father made your papa empty out his pockets on the spot, and there was the cash. Two thousand. And then he tried to lie about it! Said it was his money, that he always carried extra."

"You can't prove where the two thousand came from. What if my father was telling the truth?"

"But the other fisherman saw him take it in the market! What would you think, Benita? What do you think about what I've just told you? Do you trust your father that much?"

"I don't know," I admitted.

"Ask your father yourself, if you don't believe me. See if he'll be honest with you."

"I will never hate my father as you do. No matter what he did."

"You don't care that he ruined my life?"

"Grow up. You did that all by yourself." Raúl hung his head, and looking down, he couldn't help but contemplate his injured leg. I could tell he was truly hearing me for once. "We're here in the jungle because you asked me, and I wanted to go, not because Papa told you to take me."

"That's true."

"It was a mistake we both made, right?"

"Yes, Benita."

"I think it's sad that you're so lucky and you don't even know it. You have found the thing that you love to do. To farm the land of Paíta."

I thought about how the plantation was a dream that Raúl and Papa could have shared, but it had only driven them apart. "You'll have to find a dream of your own. You shouldn't try to steal Papa's."

"I sometimes dream about us," he said. "That we live together. Do you think it could happen?"

"I'm sorry."

"Listen to me. Someday your father's plantation will be worth all the hard work it took to build it up, worth more than you know. We could farm it together. I know I could make it a success. You would be proud of me again."

"I've told you I'm not interested in Papa's plantation, and what's equally true is I no longer want to be with you." He lay back in the boat, and I realized that I had just hurt his feelings, and not for the first time. "I'm going to look for some food," I said. "You'll stay here?"

"Where could I go without you?"

"I'll be right back."

"That's good," Raúl said, and then he closed his eyes.

I still couldn't figure out why Raúl was so interested in Papa's dried-up plantation. It would take some kind of heavenly intervention before those coconuts appeared.

Yanasa's words echoed in my heart. *Save them and then save yourself.* Did this mean I should work on the farm? Would that be the thing to save them? I didn't know, but I felt certain the proper solution would come to me at some point, and all my thinking about it wouldn't solve anything.

I spotted some wild blueberry bushes and ate several handfuls of the fruit. After filling the front of my shirt with berries for Raúl, I made my way back to where I had left him. I found the canoe filled with rainwater, deep enough to lick at his chin. I woke him, tipped him sideways out of the boat and drained the water. When I put him back in, I lowered him as gently as I could. Then I took the rope in my hands and dragged the boat again.

"And, Benita . . ." He had to struggle to focus on me. "I want you to know . . . I *do* love you."

My voice came out as a grunt. "Please don't talk anymore, Raúl." And then, I spoke silently to my absent friend.

Yanasa, give me strength.

CHAPTER
28

The hard wind blew sheets of rain across the land, and the raindrops pelted my skin as if they meant to get inside me. I was determined to get back no matter what stood in the way. A secret strength rose in me. I'd never experienced anything like it, and I felt I could move trees out of my way if I had to.

It took two days to get to the base of Asiento del Rey. When I stood there and turned my face to look up the huge ridge, I almost wished I'd taken my chances with the reef back at our cove. I left Raúl in the canoe beneath a dry bower of bent branches and set out to investigate the landscape surrounding the mountain, hoping to convince myself that there was a way around it. I tested my machete on the thick jungle, but as he'd warned me, even a team of men would have trouble getting through.

I was swamped almost immediately, and foliage wasn't the only thing pushing me back; there were trees grown up between rocks, vines wrapped around more vines, and it was dark and steaming inside that mass of green and growing plant life. It was hard to breathe, hard to see anything a foot in front of my face. Panic rose in my throat because I understood that the trip around the mountain would take a very long time. Time I wasn't sure Raúl had.

I returned to the place where I'd left him. Weighing my chances as calmly as I could, I told myself that climbing the mountain would be difficult but hopefully not impossible if I found the trail. But better yet, I'd only have to haul him one way, because on the way down, the canoe would naturally descend without any help from me. So only one half of the trip would be hard. The courage to take the mountain suddenly bloomed in me.

I shook his boat. "Raúl. Raúl! You said the trail is marked with a cross?"

He sputtered and woke. "There is a boulder with a cross. Very green. Much moss."

All I could see were boulders, everywhere around us. "Which boulder?"

He sat up with difficulty in the bed of the canoe and pointed in front of him, slightly to the left. "At ten o'clock. Twenty paces."

I counted my steps and wound up touching wet green rock with my nose. I didn't see a cross on the rock in front of me, but I walked around it and spotted the trail itself before I saw the marker. It was a red muddy path that cut diagonally across the lower part of the slope—overgrown and rocky, but still unmistakable. I spotted one of Yanasa's cross marks etched into the rock right beside the place where my hand rested. The mark wasn't recent; moss grew in the crevice of her etching. But it was a little piece of incredibly good news. Perhaps Yanasa made the trail and crossed the mountain. Perhaps I'd see her again!

I tied the rope harness around my waist and set out once

more. The steep mountain fought me, but the trail was well broken in on the bottom part of the slope, and higher up there was plenty of vegetation I could use for support on the way to the top. Every few yards I would shove the boat's hull against a tree trunk or a boulder, to take a moment's rest before the next little bit of the climb. The rope harness was a torture. It left a red and raw burn mark across my stomach. I tried repositioning the rope, but it perpetually slid right back to the exact same place on my body. I ignored it as best as I could.

The ascent took several hours. Raúl slept through the whole thing; it was just as well that he didn't know the danger we were in.

When we made it to the top of Asiento del Rey, I saw how all the rain had transformed the island. In this magical place, where once there had been an open plain and blue flowers bloomed among the rocks, there was now a lake that covered nearly the entire surface of the mountaintop. I released myself from the harness, letting Raúl's canoe float in this body of water, and I followed it in. My feet barely touched bottom as the wind pushed the water sideways at me. The storm was moving into a higher gear. A bolt of lightning exploded above our heads, and everything in sight turned a shade paler for a few seconds. Raúl's skin lit to the color of bone.

"Raúl," I whispered. "Are you awake? Where is the trail that takes us down?"

But I was talking to myself. Raúl was completely unconscious. I pushed his boat ahead, taking it to one side of the lake, where the water flowed over the muddy lip of the mountain. Close to the edge I realized that the water was moving too fast and we might be pulled into the rushing tide. I took the canoe out, beaching it away from the fall point.

I searched the entire rim of the topside lake and didn't find anything that looked like a trail. And there was no cross to point the way either. In several places where the water ran off, it leapt like a mighty river down the vertical face of the mountain, flying free through the air, a wild and uninhibited waterfall coursing into the valley below.

Fear burst like a bubble inside my chest. The descent I had planned to make now seemed impossible, crazy even. I tried to wake Raúl but it was useless. I sat huddled against the rain, rocking and scolding myself on the edge of the cliff for some time. *If only I hadn't brought us up here . . .* But at the same time, I knew that it was pointless to think like this. It wouldn't solve anything.

I made myself stand up. The only way to go was down. I wasn't about to stay on top of the mountain, and I wasn't going to leave Raúl there either. Trail or no trail, I was going down, and so was he. Whether I retreated the way I had come or picked another place to attempt a descent, I would still be steering him down the mountain in the canoe.

I said a deeply heartfelt prayer. I felt odd to be saying these words out loud and by myself, without Yanasa to guide me, so I kept it short. "Please, O Great Ones, help us to find the end of this difficult path." Without even trying to, I pictured Yanasa as I said these words, saw her sitting across from me in the shelter near her kiln, and a feeling like a soft wind crept across my skin. But this time there was no direct answer to my prayer, none that I could hear or sense in any way.

I tossed away our remaining belongings from the canoe, saving only the machete and my diary, which I tucked into place at my waistband. My stomach was so ravaged from the rope that I couldn't bear to wrap it around me again. Using both hands, I dragged the canoe to the edge of the mountain, to the place I thought was the north side according to Raúl's map, but it was hard to be sure with so little sunlight to guide me. I let the canoe perch there; teetering where the top of the butte ended and the cliff began.

"Are you ready, Raúl?"

His silence was my only consent. I tipped the canoe and lowered it carefully, holding on to the V-shaped back of the boat with both hands and digging into the rocky dirt with my heels to slow the boat's descent. Already the muscles of my neck and shoulders pinched with the strain. A howling wind seemed to rise up to spite me.

The mountain was pitched steeply but evenly, and balancing the canoe against large rocks scattered across the slope, I was able to guide it down slowly. But no more than ten steps from the top was a patch of sheer rock face. The canoe kept moving down, and try as hard as I could to control it, I felt it slipping and skidding, pulling me along.

"Oh, no, please," I cried, and tried to stop gravity from taking him away.

The canoe rattled over the rocky ground and broke away, nearly snapping my bony fingers. I did not let it go so much as the boat left me behind. Then the canoe began to pick up speed, and in those first few seconds, I stood simply dazzled, as if I were watching a daring stunt. But then it bounced off a rock, and Raúl was almost knocked out of the hold.

I ran down the mountain then, following as best as I could, tripping and falling and picking myself up again. I ran even when the canoe fell out of sight.

CHAPTER

29

From high up on the mountain, I couldn't see the canoe anymore but I knew where it had gone. I heard when it hit bottom, the unmistakable crash. I went after it as fast as I could. When I finally got to the base of the butte, I was in time to see the canoe being carried away from me in the center of a powerful river. It looked as if Raúl was still cradled in the hold, but I didn't know for sure.

I tried to run after the boat, but downed trees littered the shore, blocking my way, and I was wading through mud that came up to my knees.

"Raúl!" I called after him, though I knew he was getting too far away to hear.

That's when I caught a whiff of a tart fruity scent in the air. Genipa bushes. I'd been in this place before. Suddenly I remembered when Raúl and I had ridden past it on our first day away. But now, instead of an empty gorge, a river raged once more, red and muddy, just as he'd described it to me. I peered through the rain, to the other side of the river and toward home. We were so much closer now.

But I saw something else that gave me hope. On the other side, the riverbank hadn't been damaged by the mountain runoff; it was less muddy, and there was less debris. Without a second thought, I pulled myself through the mud and muck and dove into the river like a fish too long out of water, determined to make the crossing.

The strength of the current was a shock, but I was nearly as strong. My strokes cut the water easily and I was propelled forward. I swam without stopping to rest or see how far I had gone, and just when I started to tire, my hands landed in a pile of underbrush and stones at the river's edge. *I made it!* I dragged myself out and saw that the current had brought me far beyond the mountain. In the distance I could see Raúl's canoe, moving away from me still.

I ran after it, and a meaner rain fell. All I wanted was to catch that boat and pull it to shore. There was nothing holding me back, and the ground beneath my feet flowed like a ribbon of silk blowing away in the wind. I ran on, bolstered by the sensation that I did not run by myself, but was carried on a wave of energy that the jungle provided.

Before too long I was running behind the canoe, and then I was alongside it. I could see that Raúl was still in the hold, and I yelled again, "Raúl! Raúl! WAKE UP!" But he was motionless inside the boat, which sat very low in the water, so I knew it must be sinking. Just ahead of the boat was a jagged embankment jutting into the river, a mass of branches and twigs and rocks, built like a beaver's dam. The canoe was headed right for it.

I yelled over the roar of water, "I'll try to grab you!"

I had to get there before the canoe did, or what might be my only chance to get hold of him would be lost. I rushed toward the embankment, but as soon as I took my first step onto it, branches dropped into the river and sped away into the current. Treading very carefully, I worked my way out to the tip, and I crouched down to receive the canoe, reaching toward the place I thought it would land.

The worn canoe came at me rapidly. It was going to hit hard and I knew I might not be strong enough to withstand the impact. *If he'd only wake up!* Maybe then he'd be able to hold on to me too. "RAÚL! RAÚL!" I yelled. I could see his face clearly now; his eyelids were fluttering. I screamed louder. "HELP ME!"

He heard me that time. He lifted his head and his eyes opened wide. Then he screamed too, with all the strength he could muster.

At first I thought he was frightened to find himself hurtling fast downriver in a boat. But his cry did not go unanswered. From a large tree that leaned out over our heads, there came a powerful, gut-wrenching growl. I knew what animal had made the sound. I looked up and spotted it hovering there, a large and ferocious cat whose focus on us was intense and unwavering, like a beam of light. The animal stood up on its branch and roared once more.

In that instant I forgot what I was supposed to do. The canoe hit, ramming hard against the rickety embankment. It splintered in two, and Raúl was released into the river. But the swift current spun him around to the other side, and he managed to get hold of a loosened branch that wavered in the swirling water, ready to fall off. I carefully stepped over to where he clung for his life, and I crouched down to the very edge of the river and tried to pull him to shore, but the embankment was beginning to break apart. The more I pulled at him, the more the platform under my feet gave way.

"*Dios mio!*" Raúl cried, and the entire flimsy construction shook. I turned to see that the cat had dropped from the tree. More branches peeled off and were washed away in the river as the cat headed straight for us.

"Let me go," he said. "Run!"

"No! Don't give up."

The cat came closer still, moving quickly now. I could tell it was more interested in the weak and thrashing man in the river than it was in me. Instinctively I tried to stop it in the only way I knew how. I held up my hand and yelled as loudly as I could, "*ATI! YANASA! ATI!*" and the cat did halt. We stood there, staring each other down, and in those few seconds I saw a shade of the crone in the cat's fierce face. Then it was gone.

And almost as if calling the name of Yanasa brought her to me, there came another familiar voice from deep in the woods.

"*Faicani ani muran . . . Yarcani huanin uran . . . Iricandi aqui namaen . . .*"

The cat growled at us once more, then turned and scampered away, its tail high in the air, bounding toward the voice.

I dragged Raúl to shore and we slumped together on the beach. The dip in the river must have awoken him. He couldn't move but he was fully conscious now. As we lay there together, I sang along with Yanasa, hoping and waiting for my friend to stand before me. I stole a quick look at Raúl, worried that he would erupt into panic when he saw her once more. But her sweet song seemed to have calmed him; he had melted into a tranquil state, loose-limbed with eyes softly searching for a sign of her, just as mine were.

It was not long before she became visible, moving slowly

through the tall trees, coming toward us, her voice rising to its highest notes. When she stepped away from the protection of the deep green jungle, I saw that the wild cat was prowling at her side, keeping pace obediently at her knee.

Now I knew for certain that Yanasa was not the cat woman Ay Pook, the witch Raúl's superstitions had conjured up. She didn't turn into a cat, and she hadn't attacked him. Turning to Raúl, I said, "Do you see now?"

He nodded, speechless. I think I was as relieved as he was to finally learn the truth.

I stood then and sang to Yanasa as she came closer. I wanted to rush and throw myself into her arms, but there was something different about her. She did not approach me with the same glee she had shown in the past. It was almost as if she barely recognized me, even though we stood looking at each other and singing the same song.

When we were standing face-to-face, we stopped our singing. She hugged me to her with such force, I felt the heat of her soul through my skin. Instantly I knew that Yanasa's powers had touched and changed me and made me like her in all the ways I wanted to be. I was her equal now, and we were honoring that.

"Thank you, Yanasa," I said to her, and she smiled with pure joy.

The cat growled again, but this time the sound was one of contentment, as if the animal were sitting beside a nice warm fire. But when we heard another growl just like it—Yanasa stiffened and the cat stood up with its fur bristling—I realized something was terribly wrong. Another cat had made that sound.

Almost immediately we heard yet another growl, tentative, questioning. It was coming from the jungle.

My friend let go of me, and I could see the fear in her eyes. Yanasa nodded once to Raúl where he lay, and he bowed his head to her. It seemed a gesture of great respect. That amazed me almost as much as anything else I'd witnessed on Paíta. Then Yanasa cast one last loving glance my way before she turned, with the cat following in her footsteps. I could do nothing then except watch the jungle take them back.

I wished with all my heart that I could go with her, but I could not, and I knew it.

We heard the foreign cat in the jungle growl, much closer this time. I reached for the machete at my waist, pulled it out and held it high in the air, my hand shaking. I didn't know why Yanasa was afraid of this cat, but it made me more scared than I had ever been before.

Another growl came to us from the forest, but then it got very quiet, as still as a tomb.

"Do you think it went away?" I whispered to Raúl.

"I think it's scared and waiting to see what we will do," he whispered back.

We heard one final cat call, and it sounded very strange. Then I knew it wasn't a cat at all, but a poor imitation. A cat made from a calabash.

"Show your face," I called out.

There was a tremendous crash in the brush, and five men from the village, leading their horses out of the jungle, surrounded us. We were all shouting at once.

"Where is the cat?" asked one of the men.

"Gone," I told them, then looked at Raúl. He said nothing more about it.

"Were you hunting?" I asked.

"Yes. But for you. Your fathers sent us," said another man.

"My father?" asked Raúl.

"Yes, he knew something bad had happened to you. You were gone too long."

"And my father?" I asked.

"He gave me his horse to ride."

The men surrounded Raúl then and peeled back the dressing to look at his wound. "Did the cat attack you, then?" said a third man, looking around nervously. "We'll have to kill it."

"We were on its trail when it vanished," said the fourth. "That is the way of Ay Pook."

Raúl shook his head. "Don't be afraid. There is no Ay Pook. Isn't that the truth, Benita?"

I smiled at him and gave his shoulders a squeeze, because I knew he was protecting Yanasa.

"We are wasting time," said the fifth man. "We must get Raúl home."

They erupted into a flurry of activity, chopping down some stalks of bamboo and stringing it with their shirts to make a sling that would carry him between two horses.

As they worked, I sat on a rock. I found I was singing Yanasa's song on my own. After a while I could hear her singing it right back to me. It sounded as if we were singing our goodbyes to each other. As I sang, I thought about this last thing Yanasa had just taught me. The song that is hello sounds the same as the one that says goodbye. Arriving and leaving are like the same act. . . . The spirit must travel where it needs to go.

A tracker called, "We're ready now."

I stood from the rock. "So am I."

PART 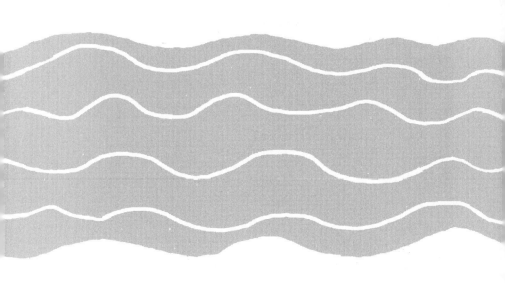8

TAPPING THE SOURCE

CHAPTER
30

The worst of the storm season seemed to have passed over the island. It was still raining, but gently. The last thing Raúl said to me before they lifted him into the sling was, "We should name this river. . . . What do you think?" His voice sounded dreamy, as if he were floating away. He reached for me. "I can't see you, Benita. Are you nodding?"

He was sinking back into a delirious state. I took his hand. "Good idea. What name did you have in mind?"

"El Rio Salvador," he whispered, and then he shut his eyes.

I expected that when they lifted him up it would cause problems with his leg, but Raúl didn't make a sound. They tied him to the sling, wrapping a rope around his waist. And then one of the men turned to me.

"Say goodbye to him now."

I was confused. "Aren't we going all together?"

"No, Raúl must go very quickly. It's for the best."

Raúl's breathing was once again labored and shallow, his chest barely rising with each breath. I whispered to him,

"You'll get better soon. I know you will," although I knew nothing of the sort and I was sure he didn't hear me. Then two of the riders spurred their horses and took him away in a flash, so fast all I saw was stamping hooves and a spray of mud. The jungle felt emptier without him. And it felt strange to know that this part of my life was now over. We'd never be together again. Funny how I'd expected to feel glad when this day came.

I turned to the men who'd remained behind with me. "I don't even know your names."

"I am Tito. And these two are Jorge and Santos."

"I don't know how to thank you. If you hadn't come along when you did . . ."

"No need for thanks, señorita. We are being paid well."

"By my father?"

"Captain Pepito gave us a month's wages to search. None of us thought we would be gone that long, though."

I realized I was disappointed that it wasn't my father who had tried to get me back.

"And Señor Mariah gave me his horse. She's a fine animal."

"She is?" I remembered a rebellious beast, but the tracker was looking at the horse proudly.

"Now we go. I'm sure your father will start worrying more when he finds out what happened to Raúl."

I rode in the saddle behind Tito. It took half a day to make the coast, where the river flowed swiftly from the jungle, surging out to sea. Seeing that river set loose—wild and free—lifted my spirits.

I knew that it would be a lie to tell myself I could be like the river, when I was going back to Subidalta and the troubles I was sure to find there. But Yanasa's words kept me from falling back into despair. I had a mission. *Save them, then save your-*

self. And when that was accomplished, I would have the kind of freedom I'd wanted for so long. It just had to be true.

We arrived at a cliff that looked over a village set on the shores of a half-moon bay. The trackers stopped the horses at the very edge. But it wasn't until I began to see people pouring out of the huts below, calling up to us, that I realized we were home. We were on the hill called Cotochachi, that high place above Subidalta. I'd never climbed it before.

Soon we were surrounded by all the people of the village. I'd had no idea I would be welcomed as one of their own. The women were crying out just as I'd heard Yanasa do when I arrived at her den after having been away. I couldn't make the same noise they did but I let myself be taken into the crowd, and I tried to let them know how grateful I was by swaying to the sound of their voices. All the men were congratulating the trackers.

"Benita!" I turned to see Papa running along the shore, waving his arms frantically, as if we couldn't see him. He climbed to meet us on the hill in seconds. He looked so different; his hair hung to his shoulders and he'd grown a beard. He held my face in his hands and would not let go.

"My precious, precious daughter, I never thought I'd see you again. Four long months! It was a terrible way to learn just how important you are to me. I didn't want to go on living." Papa kissed my cheek. "Are you all right? Can you walk? Your mother and brothers want to see you very badly. They're waiting now, on the farm."

"I'm fine, Papa. Let's go home."

"There's just one thing I must do," he told me. "It won't take a minute."

I thought he was going to thank the people who'd brought me back, but instead he got down on his knees and joined his hands together in prayer. The people crowded around to listen, which made it seem as if they were praying, too. "Praise be to God our Almighty Father. You have answered my prayers . . . returning Benita to us . . . safe, sound and strong. And I will now keep my promise to You. I vow to build a church here on Paíta, a testament of my gratitude, where all can worship Your glory and Your grace, forever and ever. Amen."

A church on Paíta? Where the islanders worshipped their own spirits? It sounded so wrong. Oh, Papa, Papa!

Papa stood, and his eyes were filled with joy. "Let's not keep your mother waiting a moment more." Then he properly thanked my rescuers, and all the people led us down the hill before disappearing into their huts.

Papa and I were silent on the walk home. It was hard to talk, mostly because I wasn't certain he was ready to hear what I had to say. I was no longer the same girl as I was when I'd left home, and that might be more than he could handle. But Papa said, "I'm amazed. I expected to find you barely alive, and instead you're—dare I say it—better than before. So healthy and strong. How *did* you survive out there?"

"Raúl took very good care of us until he was hurt. He built a sturdy hut. We had an incredible garden, and he hunted for deer and wild turkey. He has many talents of this kind. And he was dedicated to making our lives out there as good as he could." As soon as I'd said this, I realized something else about Raúl. "That was his promise—to take care of me in the jungle—and he kept it."

Papa nodded, simply listening. "But I wasn't very happy. And neither was he," I admitted.

"And you weren't safe, either. Because of the cat that attacked Raúl. I can't imagine how terrified you must have been then."

I looked at my father. I should tell him about Yanasa: that she was the real reason I had no fear. But to describe her, or explain what she was doing deep in the jungle, seemed far too complicated. "Let's just say a higher power was looking out for me."

"Amen to that. I am sure that God was keeping you safe, but a day didn't go by that I wasn't crippled with fear that you'd meet your death out there."

"Why didn't you come look for me sooner, then?"

"It was impossible! First, Pepito told us Raúl had taken you away from Paíta. He wouldn't say where. It seemed hopeless. But then more time passed, and I could see Pepito getting worried. One night I found him sitting in his boat at the end of the day, saying the rosary over and over, crying. I knew that he was afraid for Raúl. That something bad must have happened. I thought he knew what it was, but he didn't. It took many weeks to get that information out of him."

"He was very mad at you, wasn't he? I know you two fought before I left."

"That's all over now. In the past. I count him as a good friend. Unlike any I've ever known."

"You do?"

"We had something in common. We'd both lost our children. As it turned out, while Pepito knew that Raúl had taken you up Asiento Del Rey, he also thought you'd be coming back in two months' time. And when Raúl didn't return, he asked me for help. We pooled our resources and sent those hunters out to search."

"I'm sorry, Papa. I didn't mean to frighten you like that."

"I could hardly stand it, and for so long there wasn't anything I could do. So I did the only thing I could. I threw myself into work. Fired your brothers from the plantation when

I realized they hadn't been watering. They didn't cry over that."

"How *is* the plantation?"

"It's doing very well. It would make me so happy to show it to you. Shall we go there now?"

I almost laughed out loud. Papa was still so proud of his ratty old farm. "Sure we can go, if you'd like."

He led us toward the grove. To my great surprise each and every tree was taller than me by a full foot. They stood up like solid soldiers and their leaves waved in the breeze. It looked as if all two hundred were thriving.

"Is it because of all the rain?"

"Yes, that's made a big difference, and Pepito heard that ground-up fish is a terrific fertilizer. We're thinking of going into business together, selling it to farmers."

"I can hardly believe what I'm seeing, Papa!"

"Thank you, Benita. I thought you'd be impressed."

"You're right. It's an amazing sight."

Papa took my hand and we went down the path toward the house. But the sights that awaited me were almost as startling as what I'd just seen. We found Mama sitting in a wooden chair on the porch, and she didn't stand to greet me. She was disheveled, with her hair hanging about her shoulders. She seemed to have deliberately given up taking care of herself.

I knelt next to the chair containing her small pale form, and I said, "I'm sorry you had to worry about me, Mama. But I'm fine, can't you see?"

She turned to look at me but her face was a blank, as though she didn't have the energy to be sad, angry or happy. "Are you married?" Mama asked, her voice shaking.

"No." I patted her hand, and she merely sighed, but it sounded as if she was relieved.

My brothers came out then, and they looked hungry as wolves. But like me, they'd grown a lot. José and Manuel had filled out; their chests and arms swelled with muscles. All three crowded around and gave me a huge hug. Alfonse had tears in his eyes. "We're so glad you're back," Manuel said, and I knew he meant it.

"Can I fix you some food?" Mama asked. "We haven't got much, but I can fry an egg." She got up from her chair, ready to do whatever I needed.

"I hope you don't mind . . . but I am very tired. I'd like to rest now."

"Of course, of course," Papa said.

I walked straight through the house and fell into my bed. But it was almost impossible to stop my mind from racing. So many changes. I shut my eyes and the things I'd just seen flashed behind my darkened eyelids: the farm now healthy and green . . . my brothers not children but young men . . . my mother lost in worry for me . . . Papa's dream come true. And as for my own . . .

I was too tired to think about that. I fell into a deep sleep that lasted nearly three days.

CHAPTER

31

I woke to the sound of men's voices coming from the main room of our house. I had no idea what time or even what day it was when I opened my eyes, but I knew it was no longer morning because there was no warm sunlight pulsing into my room through the open window. I dressed as quickly as I could and went out to see who had come to visit.

Pepito stood when I entered, and held on to my hand, but even though he seemed glad to see me, I could tell he wasn't a happy man. "Thank God you're safe," he said. "That's a blessing, at least."

"How is Raúl?" I asked. "Is he getting better?"

"The boy lost his leg," Pepito said.

"Oh, no!" I cried out. I couldn't help myself. Tears sprung into my eyes.

"I had to take him by railroad to the hospital in Quito. The doctors tried to save it. Then they decided the infection had spread too far, endangering his liver and kidneys. He wasn't going to live if they didn't amputate."

"This is just terrible," Papa said. "So much is my fault."

"And his. He knows that now," said Pepito. "It broke my heart to hear him moaning that he wanted to die rather than live with only one leg. I tried so hard to cheer him, to tell him he had much to look forward to. In the end he claimed he did not want me to suffer and gave permission for the surgery."

"So where is he now?" I asked.

"I left Raúl in the hospital, where they will teach him to walk on one leg and he will get strong again. But the days when he could work on the boat for me are over. I don't know how he'll make a living."

Papa stood up then. "I must do something for Raúl. Tell me, Pepito . . . what sum of money do you think would be a help to your son?"

"My son will not be happy to receive a handout like a handicapped man."

"Papa, I know what would make Raúl happy," I said, trying not to sound too eager. "More than anything he wants to work on the plantation, to grow coconuts."

I could tell that Papa wasn't completely in favor of this idea. "Remember, I told you about the garden he grew for us," I continued. "We survived that way for months. Plants and vegetables thrive under his care."

Papa cleared his throat, and I knew what he had to say was hard for him. "I will do whatever you want, Benita. You know that. You want Raúl here?" I could tell Papa felt bad for Raúl but he still didn't want him for a son-in-law.

"Papa, I'm not asking for myself. The plantation is what Raúl wants. It's the only thing he really cares about."

"I'm sure that's not true," said Pepito.

Papa stared at me, but he seemed to understand he had

nothing to fear when it came to Raúl and me. "Pepito," Papa said, "Raúl will always have work here."

Mama said from the kitchen, "Lunch is ready."

Pepito stood up to leave. "I can't stay, señora. I have much to do."

I could tell he was too upset to eat. As he turned and went toward the door, I saw how the old man's broad back was like Raúl's, but hunched over, worn down by time. It was an image that I could not put out of my mind.

But at least Raúl would have his chance to make the plantation a success.

I only hoped it was what he still wanted . . .

Save them. . . .

because it would put me one step closer . . .

Then save yourself.

At lunch Papa said, "I asked Joam to call a meeting of the village council so I can ask permission to build the church. But I didn't tell him anything more." He turned to me. "I want it to be at the site of our reunion, Benita . . . on top of Cotochachi. Everything is arranged for tomorrow morning."

I had a sinking feeling. I'd almost forgot the church. Papa's newest crazy idea wasn't going away.

"But I don't believe we have enough money to build a church, Josef," Mama said. I could tell she was trying to keep her temper in check.

"The Franciscans have resources for such an endeavor. You remember Brother Pantomon, don't you, Benita? He stayed on to tutor the boys. And he's going to help us with funding. It's his mission to spread the word."

"Well, hallelujah, then," said Mama, and I had to laugh. Her bluntness struck me as especially funny at that moment.

"Papa, do you really think you can convince the people to

let you build a church?" I said. "They have their own religion. Don't you know that?"

"They won't be forced to attend. I'm not about to cause more problems," Papa said. "Please try to trust me, won't you?"

"Why should I trust you, Papa? From our very first day on Paíta, you treated the people badly, like peasants put here to serve you. And I know that you cheated them on the cotton and that's why they kicked you out."

Papa looked so scared right then. "How did you know about the cotton? Did Raúl tell you about that?"

"He tried to tell me, but I know the truth from the look on your face right now. I want all that has gone wrong on Paíta to stop right now. It must start with you."

"Why don't you wait and see what happens, then? Come with me. . . . I want all of you there."

"Of course we'll come, Josef," Mama said.

"I thought only men were allowed to speak before the village council," I said.

"I will speak, but I will speak for my entire family this time, not just for myself," Papa said. "That's why it's important for you to be there."

That was the only good thing to come out of trying to convince him that building a church was a bad idea. At least I would be at the council, to make sure he didn't offend the islanders again.

Early the next day we got ready to face the people. Papa wanted us to look our best, to show that we took their council seriously. He tied his bow tie ten times before he was satisfied. My brothers bathed at the cistern. I don't think they'd been so well scrubbed since the last time they went to church back in Guayaquil.

Mama presented me with the special outfit that she kept

wrapped and protected for me. It was the same one she wore the day we arrived on Paíta, but the white skirts were now yellowed and ragged-looking, despite her efforts to keep them fresh and clean. It was a fancy lady's dress, best suited to a parasol stroll along the boulevard.

"I'm sorry, Mama. That's not the right dress for me."

"You poor girl. There's nothing else for you to wear. I'm so ashamed. You should have a closetful of beautiful dresses." Mama sat on my bed. She looked more in control of herself; her hair was up in a bun again. She was crying a little bit, but not making a big deal about it. I wasn't going to comfort her.

"It's not really so important, Mama, is it?"

She shook her head. "I guess not, but I wish we could have given you a better life. That's all I'm trying to say."

"It's not over yet."

Mama looked up at me, and a tear trickled down her face. "Benita, did you leave with Raúl because you thought it was what I wanted? I have to know whether it's my fault that all this happened. After all, I was the one who encouraged you to marry him."

"Do you remember when you said there was no way to stop me from seeing Raúl if my heart was set on it? Well, that was true, Mama. I certainly didn't do it because you told me to. And I had to learn for myself that I wasn't meant to be with him."

"He was a disappointment to you, then?" Mama asked shyly. "It wasn't what you'd hoped?"

"No. But I can't blame him. We're very different, and he didn't love me to begin with."

"Well, love is something that grows over time. In the beginning, it feels like love, but . . . really it's desire and just a lot of mystery and intrigue about the things you're not supposed to be doing. That's how I remember it."

"I wish you'd told me that four months ago. But I probably wouldn't have listened. I thought love meant being excited by someone. And I did feel that way about Raúl. But only, I think, because I knew so little about him."

She smiled. "We were both very young when we left home, weren't we?" She started crying again and threw her arms around me. "I want you to know how much I missed you! I can't believe I thought it was time for you to leave and get married. I must have been out of my mind."

I wondered if Grandmother Tita was this distraught when my mother left home. She must have been, but she'd expressed it so harshly. Disowning her daughter. Refusing to be her mother anymore. I couldn't help thinking that if Mama was out of her mind, I loved her for it right then.

Mama sighed and dried her eyes with a well-used handkerchief. She picked up the enormous white skirt once more. "Are you going to wear this? You know Papa wants us to look our best."

"There's got to be another choice." I took a look around my room and spotted the bolt of black linen Papa had bought for me, gathering dust on my shelves. I unrolled yards of the fabric, wrapping it around my body like a tunic and leaving my shoulders bare. The bottom hem skimmed my ankles. I tucked in the corner at my breast. My new outfit was very similar to the one Yanasa wore every day of her life. "How do I look?"

"I can't believe it, but it's somehow quite suited to the occasion. Let's go show your father."

We found him dressed and waiting with my brothers on the porch. "She looks like a goddess!" Alfonse said.

"How would you know? You can't see two feet in front of your face," said Manuel.

"I can see just fine."

Papa said, "My goodness! I'm so glad I bought that fabric for you. You look beautiful, my dear."

"Benita is blushing!" José teased.

Brother Pantomon met us on the porch. "Miss Mariah," he said, "I am so happy to meet you once again. For your sake and your father's. He was a man bereft without you. And no amount of consolation I could offer did him any good." He hugged Papa, who relaxed into the embrace. I could see the monk did give my father comfort and solace, because he was a man of God and also because they were friends. It occurred to me that Papa needed this in his life. Maybe a church was a good idea. *To save Papa.*

We all walked down the beach toward the village. My brothers were quiet and solemn, and they kept their hands off each other. Papa and Mama walked arm in arm. When we got close, the villagers fanned out toward us in a stream. I don't think anyone on the island wanted to miss this meeting. Not one person uttered a word, but they parted to let us pass, and Joam brought us to sit by the fire that had been built on the beach, in the same place as when I'd sneaked over there uninvited.

Papa made his case to the people regarding the place of worship he hoped to build. I was so proud of him. Speaking through Joam, he did not tell stories to the people or make promises he couldn't keep. He did not trick them into thinking he wanted one thing when he wanted another. He simply asked for permission to build his church. But they had many questions.

"Where will you build it?"

"Ah! The location we have in mind is atop the hill just beyond the village and overlooking the ocean—the high place called Cotochachi."

"What will you do there?"

Pantomon spoke up. "I can answer that. We will worship the one true God, and his son, the Lord Jesus Christ."

"And what is a church?" asked another member of the council. Listening to how the people spoke, I realized that the crone's language was not much different from theirs. I whispered to Papa and Joam that I might be able to make everyone understand if I could speak to them myself, with the translator's help, of course. Joam conferred with the council, and they allowed me to speak.

I stood up and said, *"Sui a chuna."*

We are a family.

Now I had the full attention of every single person at that meeting. I pointed out my *papajo,* my *mamaja,* and my brothers, the *cuinanos.* Then I asked for Joam's help. "Tell them we want them to be Yanasa. We need them to be our friends."

Joam smiled at me, and whispering in my ear, he gave me the correct words and taught me how to say it for myself, and I did.

All this time the meeting had been so quiet, but then everyone was talking at once. Through Joam they asked me how I learned to speak, and I told them that a spirit of the jungle had taught me. When Joam translated my answer, the entire crowd erupted. I knew I had to be careful not to upset them. "I don't know where that spirit came from. All I know is that it offered comfort to my soul when I was most unhappy."

Most of the members of the council were nodding as they conferred.

"They want to know what else you have learned," said Joam.

But I didn't say another word. I sang for them instead. *"Faicani ani muran . . . Yarcani huanin uran . . . Iricandi aqui namaen . . ."*

I was immediately surrounded by many women of the village, and they sang with me, but when we were done, the men on the council said no to Papa's church. "Cotochachi is a special place for us, too," said Joam. "It is the place in the village closest to the sun. We often go there to give our thanks."

I spoke once more. "The church Papa builds can be for all of us. We will burn candles, and you may burn your fruits and nuts. We will gather on our special days to celebrate our beliefs, and you too may come together and rejoice. Like when the fish are harvested."

Papa stood up. "This is unacceptable, Benita."

"This is their island, Papa. And you will respect what they believe. Or go build your church somewhere else."

Papa's mouth hung open. Finally he said, "I think . . . I understand how important this is to you, Benita. I think I do."

Papa stepped forward again, to ask the people of Paíta to accept each member of the Mariah family as one of their own, and to judge his request as they would for any other person on the island. The members of the council conferred for several minutes, and then Joam told us that the permission was granted. We could build the church I had described for the whole island.

As a group we went to the top of Cotochachi. On the way up Papa's happiness was tempered by Brother Pantomon. "I don't know how the Church will feel about allowing pagan rituals to take place in a house of worship. But don't despair. There may be a way this can work out."

"I will pray for it, Brother," said Papa, and he turned to me.

306

"I know you have a gift for languages, Benita. But how did you learn to speak like that, and to sing such a song?"

"Do you remember what I told you when you asked me how I'd survived in the jungle?"

"Yes, you said a higher power looked after you."

In all the days since I'd left Yanasa, I'd had no real explanation for her presence on the island or in my life. And in a strange way, I felt that if I went back to her cove, I probably wouldn't find her there. Not in the flesh. Maybe it was that she was now a memory, or maybe she was never really something earthbound to begin with. But I realized she was, in essence, my guiding spirit.

I tried to explain this to Papa. "That's what I believe," I said, and looked up at him, hoping so hard that he would be able to understand.

"You will never cease to surprise me," he said, and took me under his arm. "For instance, you have become very good at getting your way when it comes to the islanders."

"It's not so hard as you think. . . . They're good people. You know that by now, don't you, Papa?"

"Yes, yes. Of course. They've saved our lives. More than once."

As soon as we arrived, Papa ran all around, marking out the ground where the building should be. Looking down the beach, I could see all the way to the small blue shack that stood close to the water. We'd never bothered to tear it down—there was always something else that needed to be done. Now I was glad it was there, as a reminder of how far we'd come since our first day on Paíta.

CHAPTER

32

We broke ground for the church shortly after the village council meeting. The Franciscans agreed to pay for the building costs despite our promise to the islanders that they could use the church to worship as they wished. "My superiors are confident that once we expose them to the truth of Christ, the islanders will all want to be enfolded in his love," Pantomon said. But they decided it was a good idea to send a high-ranking representative to properly bless the building when it was done.

We started digging the hole for the foundation, working in stages, first breaking the ground with pickaxes. While Papa and Pantomon shoveled out the loose soil, my brothers and I took it away in buckets. It was hard labor, but we saw the progress we made every day, digging that deep hole, and it felt good. The fertile, wet earth beneath our feet seemed so fresh and alive, and in fact, the earth seemed to get wetter the deeper we dug. Then one day Papa stuck his blade into the ground, and a small pool began to form.

He grabbed Pantomon by the shoulders and shook him. "I believe it's a miracle," he said.

Pantomon stammered, "I know . . . I know it is."

Manuel said, "Why is everyone so happy?"

"A spring!" Papa said.

As it turned out, the spring was a robust and healthy source of water, and the fall from the hilltop to our farm meant that the water would pour down, just as it had on Asiento del Rey. Tapping the source, we'd have enough water to divert toward the cotton fields, and also a new supply for the village, where the islanders could wash clothes and gather water for cooking. Papa offered to build it for them in exchange for their promise to gather all the tin in Subidalta, which we needed to make the pipes that would conduct the water; the church funds were not enough to build a water system. Although it meant replacing their tin roofs with thatch, they agreed to supply Papa. Some even agreed to help dig trenches for the pipe.

No one was happier than Papa with this turn of events, and we all shared in his joy—my family, Pantomon and all of the islanders—everyone except for Raúl.

News of his return had reached me several days before the discovery of the spring. I would linger close to his hut hoping he might show his face, but he never did. I debated with myself: should I visit him or not? Would my presence make him feel better or worse? I didn't know what was best, so I did nothing.

After the discovery of the spring, Papa came to me. "I figured out how Raúl can contribute to the farm right away! But are you ready to see him again?"

"He needs our help," I said, and the following day we paid Raúl a visit.

We knocked and called out, but there was no answer. The

intense stillness inside his hut was a clue that he was hiding there.

"We're coming in," Papa said. As my eyes slowly adjusted to the dimness, I saw Raúl lying awake on his cot. He was turned away from us, facing the wall. A blanket covered his body.

"How are you feeling, Raúl?" Papa asked.

"Tired."

Papa immediately launched into the story of the new spring and explained that the reason for our visit was to offer him a job.

"I can't get around," Raúl said. "I can hardly move."

"That's why this would be perfect for you," Papa said. "Because you can stand in one place working over a fire to make the pipes for the new water system."

"Yes, I see," was all Raúl would say.

"It's a very important job," I said, "because if there are any leaks, it'll be impossible to repair without tearing up the whole thing to find the problem."

"Are you interested? Will you work with us on this project, Raúl?" Papa asked.

Raúl took his time answering. "You are only here because my father demanded it," he said finally.

"There are many reasons why I came," Papa said. "Your father, my daughter. My conscience. If I had treated you more fairly, none of this would have happened."

Raúl simply nodded. "I can only blame myself."

"Yes, that is what I do," Papa said. "I blame myself."

Raúl looked Papa in the eye for the first time since we'd entered his hut. "I cannot do this. I cannot show my face. Not as your worker. None of the people would respect me anymore. I told everyone I would be your son-in-law, married to your daughter when I returned. Do you know what they said to me when I told them that? They thought I was turning my back on them. The whole village. That I rejected them and that I wanted to be like you, like the Mariahs. Now they all hate me."

"I have not heard anyone utter a single bad word about you, Raúl," I said.

"They would not say it to you, Benita, but I know well enough how they think. To each other they say I lost my leg because I was greedy. I don't have to hear this to know they say it. I cannot escape their gossip. I can only hope to outlive it."

It was the first time Raúl had spoken to me directly. I thought about how the people had kept quiet about him; it dawned on me that this was a bad sign.

"Perhaps Papa can call you his partner. Would that make you happy?"

Raúl pretended to think about it. "That would be better. Yes."

Papa looked at me, stunned. "What do you think, Papa? A partner means he gets a percentage of the coconut profits. I think ten percent is fair, right? Along with a small working wage."

"Benita . . . ," Papa said.

"That's nothing! Ten percent." Raúl was pouting again.

"It's a start, Raúl," I said. "You told me you wanted to show my father what you could do on the plantation. Here's your chance."

A bare wisp of a smile crossed his face. "If you make me your partner, I'll work harder than anyone you've ever seen."

"He will, Papa! He will."

Papa stood to leave. He was shaking his head, yet he managed to say, "I'm sure you'll do a very good job. You can start next week. All right?"

Raúl called out, "Josef? How do you know I'm not so angry at you that I wouldn't wreck the pipes just to get even?"

"Benita told me you care too much about the farm to do such a thing," Papa said. "And I trust in that." And we left him alone, shutting the door behind us.

After that meeting, I just sat in my room. I felt proud to have survived our ordeal, but ashamed for my part in what had happened to Raúl. I felt sorry for him, but I was still mad at him for lying to me. And though I hated to admit it, it did hurt to know he never loved me. But most of all, I was relieved that I wasn't his wife, because I'd never wanted to marry him either. And that's when it hit me. The truth was, I was no better than he was, for I had lied to him too. I realized that maybe the best thing I could do for him was admit that, and then maybe together we could find a way to forgive each other.

Over the next few days, I had much time to myself, and I was drawn to do certain things that I hadn't even known I missed while I was away. I visited the altar and lit a candle there, and swam in the ocean in front of our house just to show that shark I was no longer scared. But the thing that I had loved to do most—sit alone in my room thumbing through my encyclopedias—wasn't as compelling as it used to be. I knew my books were there for me, and that was comforting, but they no longer seemed like the whole world.

Instead I went to the village every day, and often I would be invited into someone's hut for a visit. Usually not much was said between us. I would sit on the mud floor and watch a woman cooking, a mother feeding her baby or a man smoking his pipe. Sometimes one of the people would pat me on the back. If food was already prepared, I would generously be offered some.

I couldn't help thinking of the day I'd arrived on Paíta, when I'd got my first glimpse of how the people lived and how unkempt their lives seemed to me. Looking about now, I noticed there wasn't much difference. The huts were a bit messy, fire smoke filled the rooms, foodstuffs lay about. They looked just like the hut I had shared with Raúl.

Now that I was welcome inside, everything seemed exactly as it ought to be. And I wouldn't wish to change a single thing.

The building of the water system began a few days after Papa hired Raúl; things were very tense to start. The foundry had been stationed behind Raúl's hut so that the people wouldn't see him hobbling around on one leg. The smithy consisted of a fire pit for heating the tin sheets, and basins of seawater for cooling them after they'd been shaped around rods. As soon as Raúl had a pipe or a section ready, we put it into the ground. Often we had to wait for him to finish a piece, for it took longer to make the pipe than it did to place it. Raúl worked steadily, struggling not to fall behind in his production, but he wouldn't speak to any of us. We didn't try to draw him out of his shell.

Nearly a month later all the pipe trenches were dug and lined properly in Paíta clay. Raúl was going to need assistance finishing up the work on the pipes, or else everything would be held up.

We went as a family to tell him that pipe-making would have to become everyone's job for the next few weeks. It was the first time he and I had stood side by side since before his accident. I was the last of my family to go into his yard. The minute Raúl saw me, he hung his head and pretended I wasn't there. He stood morosely listening to what Papa had to say. He looked older, and thicker around the middle, and he had a defeated slump to his shoulders. My eyes traveled down to the lower half of his body. I couldn't help seeing what was missing, and I stopped looking at him then.

But within a few days of working around the same fire, we began to seem like one big clan, and slowly I watched Raúl change. He teased my brothers again, he was patient with the metal in his hands and he managed to look at my father without an angry glare.

I decided it was time to end our silly silence. One day, at the end of work, I spoke to him from across the fiery pit. "Raúl. I want a word with you. Alone."

Raúl looked bewildered. "Yes. That would be good."

I walked to the beach and turned to see him following me as fast as he could, using his crutch. I decided not to help him, but if he had trouble sitting down in the sand, I would give him a hand. He dropped heavily beside me and waited for me to begin.

Even though I knew what I wanted to say to him, I was having trouble finding my voice now that he was beside me. The silence that followed wasn't simply awkward. It was something far worse.

"You have no idea how sorry I am for the way things have turned out," I said.

"Yes? How have they turned out?"

I wasn't sure what he meant. "Your leg . . . ," I said.

"No, that's not my question. I'm asking if you think you know how everything will end."

"Well, no. I feel that things are just beginning. In a way."

"The beginning of what?"

"My life."

"Is there a place for me in it?"

I took a deep breath. "I have to be honest with you, Raúl. You weren't the only one who had secret motives for wanting to run away into the jungle. I never told you why I left with you. The truth is . . . I was just as mad at Papa as you were, and I wanted to get away from him."

"So . . . you didn't want to go away with me?"

"That's not what I'm saying. I wanted to be with you, but I never wanted to marry you. I thought maybe I would come to want that, but then I realized I didn't love you, either. I thought I did, but now I see I didn't understand what that really meant."

"Is this the thing you had to tell me? It seems we have nothing left to say."

"That's not true." I reached out to touch his arm. "I do have something important to tell you, if you'll only listen. Please try."

Raúl didn't answer.

"I'm not sorry we went away together. I wouldn't know myself as I do if I hadn't gone away with you. For that alone I will be grateful to you forever."

He waved me off, but I knew him well enough to know that he wanted me to go on praising him.

"And you reunited me with my father. If I hadn't left with you, he would never have come to accept me as he does now."

Raúl shrugged. "Is this why you made your father help me? He would not have offered me a job if you hadn't convinced him. I am sure of that."

"Yes, I did convince him. But do you know why? Because of something you taught me."

"And what was that?"

"On the night you proposed, you told me what love is. You said it means taking care of someone. Do you remember?"

"I do. I believe that still."

"That's why I helped you with Papa. That's why I want to make sure that you're okay."

It took Raúl a moment to understand what I was saying to him.

"I didn't love you on the night you proposed . . . but I do now."

Oh, the hope that I saw in his eyes right then . . . I saw the thing reflected there that he wanted most of all now. It was me.

"I mean . . . I care about you, Raúl. You *are* in my heart," I said. "But I am not going to stay on Paíta. And we are not going to be married. I hope you can forgive me. It wasn't meant to be."

Raúl was quiet, as was his way, but he nodded solemnly and I could see that he wasn't angry. I reached out to hug him then, and he let me. It was like the embrace of a brother and sister. It made me feel warm and peaceful and nothing more.

"There's one thing I need to ask," I said. "A favor."

"What is it?"

"The day we were rescued, you told the men that there was no such thing as Ay Pook. But you and I know there is an old, old woman here who no one else has seen. And she's very special to me."

Raúl nodded.

"I need you to promise me that you will protect her. If she ever comes to the village, or if anyone travels to the other side of the mountain and finds her there . . . she should not be harmed."

"What makes you think she'll come this way?"

"Because I believe she made the trail we took on the mountain."

"No. That trail has always been there. My mother told me about it, and she learned of it from her grandmother. . . ."

"But do you know who made it? That trail is marked with a cross—it's the old woman's mark."

"I don't know who cut that slope. That's true. But do you think she's been here longer than my own great-grandmother?"

"I think she's been here a very long time."

We both sat there pondering the mystery of Yanasa. After a few minutes he said, "She will always have my protection. You can be sure of that. Let it be my way of thanking you for arranging for me to become your father's partner."

"You're not frightened of her anymore, are you?"

"No. I believe what you believe. That she is to be honored, not feared."

I sat there for a moment. Who'd have thought Raúl and I would ever have something in common? But it really wasn't so surprising after all we'd been through together. Still, I never could have imagined that the thing to connect us would be a respect for Yanasa.

I stood up and held out my hand to him. He used me for balance, hoisting himself up to stand steadily on his one leg.

"Thanks, Little Girl," he said, in that same way he had the day I'd brought him the eggs.

I walked away from him, turning back only once. Raúl hadn't moved; he was watching me go. "See you tomorrow," he said, and I waved goodbye. He went into his hut and I went home. Papa was waiting for me on the porch.

"Is Raúl all right?"

"He will be," I said. "Thank you, Papa."

CHAPTER

33

My family didn't have a moment's rest in the months following my return. There was so much important work to do. Not only did we finish building the water system, but there was also the raising of the church. We then helped harvest the cotton crop, and the people let Papa take it to market, and once again we had money in our pockets—not as much as before, when Papa was keeping the lion's share, but more than enough to live comfortably.

Each of these events passed like milestones in the lives of everyone on Paíta and was accompanied by celebration and much joy. The first time my mother was able to turn a knob on her kitchen sink to wash a head of cabbage, she dropped it on the floor and cried. Papa made the dinner that night and would not let her help.

I thought we'd reached the end of our bad luck once and for all. But despite things having turned around for the better, our island life came to an end only a year later. Though the coconut farm had been restored and the trees had grown tall and full, no fruit came, and we realized we'd been hoping very hard for something that was not to be. Then Mama came down with a cough that wouldn't go away. Papa told her to go back to Guayaquil to recuperate.

To his surprise she said, "I want to stay with you."

But Papa wouldn't allow it. "Think of Benita. She and Pantomon have made such progress, and she'll soon be old enough to go to college," he said. "But she's still too young to live on her own in the city. When you are well and she begins her studies at the university in Quito, you can return."

As soon as Mama and I started making preparations to depart, my brothers admitted they wanted to go back as well. It all made sense. José was now almost a young man and ready to make his own way in the world, and Manuel was not far behind. Neither of them wanted to be coconut farmers. And Alfonse would be lost without his mother's love and attention.

Papa was taken by surprise. He hadn't expected to let all of us go at once. But he looked at us, his family, standing before him, asking for his understanding.

"We want you to come too," I told him. "Let Raúl run the farm. He can supervise now." I knew it was pointless to ask. I could see that Papa had no intention of leaving.

"I can't go now when the coconuts are finally going to come. Just one more year," he said. "Then I will come back to Guayaquil. I promise."

The day we departed, everyone tried to maintain the optimistic spirit that had been built with our hard work, but the prospect of leaving Papa behind tore at our hearts, and we moved around the house slowly, gathering our things together as if we were packing for hell. But Papa stayed upbeat as he helped. Before anyone knew what was happening, we were standing on the shore surrounded by islanders whose sad faces mirrored our own. Our possessions were loaded in Pepito's boat and it was time to say goodbye. No one managed to say those heartbreaking words. Instead we said, "See you soon," and "When will you come to visit?" and "You must write every week," and "We love you."

When we were on the water, I turned around a final time to see Papa standing on the shore with Pantomon. Raúl was leaning on my father's shoulder. All three of them waved. I waved back and felt that pain that happens at sad endings. A lump in the throat that could not be swallowed. I turned to face the mainland of Ecuador, still too distant to be seen.

The only good thing about leaving was that Papa and I kept up a steady correspondence. Pepito would bring me a letter from my father every week, and on those pages I got to know him in a way I never had, as if he felt freer to share his innermost thoughts now that I was grown up. He told me that the day he watched us all sail away, he experienced a great sense of relief. "They will be happy," he said to himself, "and so will I." Over the following months his life went exactly as he expected and was exactly how he wanted it to be. "The trees are growing fuller. Every night I eat dinner with Brother Pantomon and Pepito for company. Raúl has proven himself to be a dependable, hardworking partner. This life is peaceful."

I wrote about how it wasn't easy to adjust to life in the city. The noises kept Mama up at night. In the heat of the day, I often wished I could go for a swim, but the river was too dirty. I also had to wear a lot more clothing than I was used to. But

I was happy to resume my studies at high school, and I excelled at French thanks to Pantomon, who'd taught me well.

I told him that everyone in my class seemed like gangly youngsters who were going on dates for the first time. "Soon I'll be seventeen," I wrote. "And though it was not quite three years that we were away on Paíta, so much time seems to have flown away from me like something that got lost."

The next time Papa wrote, he sent his letter inside a package, and when I opened it, I found his gold-toned wristwatch and a note that said, "May you never lose time again. Love, Your Adoring Papa."

He came to visit us in Guayaquil at the tiny apartment we had managed to rent in the old section of the city. He was there to bring the cotton harvest to market, which would provide us with money to cover our rent for a couple of months. We had a small tea party to celebrate his visit. The Herreras came. And Olga was there too, with her husband, a struggling medical student. She hung on his every word and I could tell she was madly in love. I was thrilled for her. Her parents made some weak excuse and stayed away. Mama and Papa didn't seem to care one bit.

But Papa surprised us by returning to Paíta after only a week.

"The changes I see in all of you are remarkable," he wrote to me later. "Almost overwhelming to see how the boys are now young men . . . the way Alfonse helps Mama to her seat at the table and quietly listens to the conversation. And both José and Manuel speak in such stern voices and behave with utter seriousness. . . . I can barely remember how rowdy they were as children. . . ."

This made me laugh. My oldest brothers had quit school early. At sixteen, José had a good job working for an oil company setting up operations in South America, and Manuel,

who would soon turn fifteen, was an apprentice in construction. They were helping to support us with decent wages, as
Mama had always hoped they would.

Still, my father was concerned about her. "I'm happy to see
that Pilar is very much the lady of the house again . . . worrying if the boys use the wrong fork and if the tea is too cold. But
she seems more nervous and weaker than when she left Paíta.
What does the doctor say?" I told Papa there was nothing to
be done for Mama. She was a fragile lady who needed to be
treated with care. Nothing could change that fact about her.

Regarding me he wrote, "You amaze me more than I can say.
I have no doubt that you will attain whatever you set your
heart on. . . . Always dream big, my girl. Just don't let it ruin
the life you are living." The first time he'd said that to me, I'd
thought it was the most awful thing I'd ever heard. It sounded
like giving up. Now I understood that it meant he only
wanted me to be happy.

Exactly nine months to the day that we left the island of
Paíta, Pepito delivered a letter to my family, and he told me to
sit down to read it. He refused to say anything more, except
that I should open the letter. It was dated the morning of the
day before. I didn't recognize the handwriting, so I read the
signature first and then knew it to be from Brother Pantomon.

He had written to tell me that Papa had awoken in his bed
after a long night's sleep and said he felt his body was very
heavy, as if he were weighted down, and he had asked not to
be disturbed while he slept a bit more that morning. But by
afternoon there was still no sign of Papa. In the early evening
Pantomon went to bring him some dinner. Papa was lying
propped against some pillows. He was staring out the window
and did not turn to face Pantomon, who stood in the doorway waiting to put down the tray. The friar went closer to the

bed and saw that Papa's eyes were open and as still as glass, and touching Papa's arm, he found it stone-cold. That was when a tower of ash fell from the cigarette clamped between my father's fingers, and Pantomon knew that Papa was dead. His passage out of this world had been so smooth it did not even disturb the ashes of the cigarette he did not get to smoke.

I looked up at Pepito to see that there were tears in his eyes. And I could barely swallow my own as I read the letter to my family.

A type of numbness took us over then, as we made arrangements. José returned with Pepito to retrieve Papa's body. I went with my mother to purchase a casket. Manuel arranged for an autopsy, which showed that a heart attack was the cause of Papa's death. The following week we returned to Paíta with my father in his coffin. He was to be buried on the hilltop beside the church. His was the only grave. Eventually there would be more, but no one from the family would join him there. I wore a dress made of the same black linen that Papa had purchased for me. I'd had this dress made a few months earlier and was saving it for a special occasion, but I never expected that event would be his funeral.

Despite all my sorrow, I was amazed by what a beautiful service we had. All the islanders came bearing burning torches, and they sang the song I asked for, the one I'd learned from Yanasa and knew by heart, though I didn't sing. Then Pantomon gave a proper sermon, and Pepito made a beautiful speech asking that Papa not be mourned, but that his life be regarded with awe for all he had accomplished despite the hardships he'd endured in the world and overcome within his own heart. My family found some comfort in these words and knew that Pepito would miss Papa as much as any of us.

We all threw a handful of red Paíta earth onto my father's casket. The clumps of soil landed against the closed wooden lid with dull thuds. My father's grave marker had not been prepared, which upset my mother greatly. Raúl began to carve one that day and promised to stake it at the head of the plot until a properly cut stone arrived.

When everyone went down to the village, I stood alone on the hillside staring at the horizon. Where the sky met the ocean, I saw Papa's face hovering like a wisp of smoke my mind had made real. "Father," I called to him, but he did not answer. When I reached out to touch him, the image disappeared, and I saw that my palms were stained red from the earth I'd thrown upon his grave.

Pepito took us back to Guayaquil one last time. I'd never imagined that we would be leaving my father on Paíta forever. I cried all that night, and when I woke in the morning, I was still crying. There was nothing I could do to stop. I couldn't get out of bed to go to school, I fell behind on my work and the envelope containing the application I had to fill out for the university in Quito sat on top of my desk unopened.

One day I locked myself in the bathroom, and I stared at my reflection in the mirror that hung over the sink. I simply stood there and watched my tears fall. After a while the watery image of me wavered in the glass like a mirage, and my image disappeared before my eyes. In that moment I was reminded of the day I'd sat down across from Yanasa in the kiln hut, and we'd gazed upon each other until my vision blurred and she turned into me. Now, looking in the mirror, I saw my image wash away, and I became Yanasa. The gray hair and the kind, wise face appeared before me in the bathroom glass.

"Please help me," I said.

"You must help yourself."

"I don't know what to do!"

"What have you always done?"

"I don't know! I don't know."

There was silence for a long time, and then, "Did you not once say . . . *Where do you want to go?*" the Yanasa face asked in a soft voice.

All of a sudden my eyes were clear and the tears were gone. I went into my bedroom and walked over to the shelves where I kept my encyclopedias. I stood before these old books and let my fingers run over the spines—A-C, D-F, all the way to the end of the alphabet and back—but this time I knew which book I would pick. My finger traveled to the letter *P*, and I opened that book to the page that was all about Paris. I knew it so well.

"I want to go to Paris," I said alone in my room, and I knew it was true. That was what I wanted to do with my life. I wanted to leave Ecuador and go to a university in Paris. I remembered my father's written words to me: *Always dream big, my girl.*

"I will, Papa. Just watch me."

I applied and was accepted to the Sorbonne in Paris. I would be the first person in the Mariah family to attend college. Mama sold her family's land on Paíta to Raúl. This cash, and a government scholarship, would pay for my schooling.

I left home in August of that year.

The first week away was the hardest time of all, as everyone I met wanted to know, "Where do you come from, Benita Mariah?"

I always answered in their language. *"Je viens de Paíta. C'est une île dans le pays d'Ecuador."*

I come from Paíta. It's an island in the country of Ecuador.

The young women, all of them French, who lived on my floor in the dormitory on the Rue Des Ecoles reminded me of butterflies, they were so delicate in their manner of asking about me, fluttering around in pairs. I could tell from the way that each and every one of them seemed to take me in—with a quick glance from head to toe and back again—that they thought I was strange. It wasn't the first time I was new to a place—and I knew how suspicious the natives could be.

But there were always more questions. So I tried to answer as best I could. When they'd ask me what Paíta looked like, I would describe an amazing landscape covered by a deep green jungle with fantastically strange plant life. I'd tell them about the red palms on a mountain that changed with the weather. When they asked me what I liked most about the island, I told them about a race of people whose beliefs were primitive but whose hearts showed me how to live. When they asked me whether I was born on the island, I always said yes, because in a very meaningful way, I *was* born on Paíta.

The funny thing was, the more I told them, the more they were drawn to me. Like the crone with her crickets, I played my tune and they came closer. They listened to my story, pulled it from me with all their might, until they were no longer strangers but new friends. Dominique and Paola, Renata and Belle. We formed our own tribe and now we share the same language, too. The first word I taught them was Yanasa.

But my oldest and dearest friend is with me still. Whenever my life becomes difficult and I feel I can't bear what is happening to me, Yanasa comes up from some dark depth, to counsel and direct me and give me the strength I need. I don't know whether she is real, or whether she is some foreign part of my own soul that I know very little about. I am only glad that I have her in me and that I can understand what she has to say.

Even now, when I think about my father, the tears can start without warning. But I don't hold back. For me, the salt that I taste in my tears is a welcome reminder of the life I once had on the island, and I let them come, bringing every lingering and cherished memory back to me.

A(KNOWLEDGMENTS

I would like to express my gratitude to the Society of Children's Book Writers and Illustrators for providing me with a grant while this was a work in progress—their early vote of confidence kept me going until the end.

To my editor, Wendy Lamb, *muchas gracias* for traveling with me to this faraway place. The same goes to editorial assistant Alison Root, whose enthusiasm gave this book a home. And I owe much gratitude to diligent copy editor Jennifer Black and designer extraordinaire Marci Senders, as your contributions were the perfect polish.

I am endlessly grateful to my agent, Dan Mandel, whose faith was sometimes the only faith I had.

I'm also indebted to my first editor, Maurine Tobin, and Bob Nixon for travel assistance. To the readers the friends the talented Bethany Lyttle, Alix Pearlstein, Shoshana Perry—I hope you know your support, encouragement and wisdom have been the greatest help of all.

And JMT, no book is possible without you.